Treasu

As we drew nearer, I saw that Mr. Brown had spoken the truth. Jules Carron's house was a desolate log structure set down in a virtual wilderness. The outbuildings were a collection of ruins, and the entire scene was reminiscent of a settlement lost in time.

World's End might be a more appropriate name for the place. Had Jules Carron's life ended within its walls? I wasn't so fanciful as to think that the house was haunted, but I sensed something unhappy about Trail's End. It hovered in the very air. I could almost believe that a shadowy presence beckoned to me.

What an absurd notion! Perhaps I would discover the nature of Jules Carron's connection with my mother here, but surely nothing more.

"I hope the key still works," I said.

What They Are Saying About

Treasure At Trail's End

Pepper this with secondary characters that will both send shivers down your spine and delight you, add a dollop of jealousy, rivalry, deception, hidden dangers, and a hunt for the treasure reputed to be hidden at Trail's End, and you have a novel that is impossible to put down. Who will Mara choose? Who can she trust? I'll never tell. That's as far as I dare go without spoiling the edge-of-your-seat ending that I promised you to this wonderful read. *Treasure At Trail's End* delivers--a treasure, indeed, from an author who has perfected the art of weaving mystery and romance into an unforgettable tapestry that will stay with you long after you close the cover.

--Dawn Thompson
Drake's Lair
The Ravencliff Bride
The Waterlord
The Falcon's Bride
Blood Moon
www.dawnthompson.com

Ms. Bodoin weaves a delightful story that keeps you entertained and on the edge of your seat until the last page. I could not put the book down until the dramatic conclusion. This book is definitely a keeper. An engaging story that keeps you guessing until the end. Delightfully intriguing in every sense of the word.

--Cherokee
Coffee Time Romance
http://www.coffeetimeromance.com

Other Works From The Pen Of

Dorothy Bodoin

Winter's Tale

On her first winter in Foxglove Corners, Jennet Greenway battles dognappers, investigates the murder of the town's beloved veterinarian, and tries to outwit a dangerous enemy.

A Shortcut through the Shadows

Jennet Greenway's search for the missing owner of her rescue collie, Winter, sets her on a collision course with an unknown killer.

Cry for the Fox

In Foxglove Corners, the fox runs from the hunters, the animal activists target the Hunt Club, and a killer stalks human prey on the fox trail.

Wings

Treasure At Trail's End

by

Dorothy Bodoin

A Wings ePress, Inc.

Gothic Romance Novel

Wings ePress, Inc.

Edited by: Lorraine Stephens
Copy Edited by: Leslie Hodges
Senior Editor: Lorraine Stephens
Executive Editor: Lorraine Stephens
Cover Artist: Christine Poe

Wings ePress Books
http://www.wings-press.com

ISBN 1-59088-601-1

Published In the United States Of America

November 2005

Wings ePress Inc.
403 Wallace Court
Richmond, KY 40476-0038

Dedication

To the memory of my mother,

Helen Bodoin,

my first reader.

One

It is the greatest irony of my life that on a dreary April afternoon, when my future seemed as uncertain as the return of spring, I became an heiress. The legacy, originally intended for my late mother, had never been claimed, nor even mentioned in my family.

The proof of my inheritance, a brittle old letter, had been lying in my father's roll top desk for ten years. Although he made no attempt to conceal it, not once did he ever speak to me of the Colorado Territory, Trail's End, or my mother's mysterious benefactor, Jules Carron.

If I hadn't been looking for the deed to my house that I was about to sell, I would never have known about Jules Carron's gift, and my prospects would have been as dull as my worst imaginings. Then I found the letter, and my future was suddenly filled with bright possibilities.

Jules Carron had willed the property, a ranch in the Colorado Territory known as Trail's End, to my mother in 1866, the year of his death. I assumed that she was in some way connected with him, but the nature of the relationship and her reason for secrecy eluded me.

After my mother's death from influenza in that same year, my father and I had lived alone until his sudden passing last winter. In the long, lonely months that followed, I'd grown accustomed to having no family. That hadn't changed, but now I was also a woman of property.

The pride of our small northeastern Michigan town was the new railway station. From my bedroom on the second floor, I could view trains departing for far places. Often I longed to be going somewhere, anywhere, but I never did.

For a moment, standing in my father's study, I remembered our family legend, my Aunt Marjorie, who had traveled westward to the gold fields. We didn't know what had happened to her, or even if she was still alive. Perhaps, thanks to the largess of Jules Carron, whoever he was, I would also have an adventure. Maybe my aunt and I would meet in some far-flung frontier town.

Until my discovery, I had been contemplating several prospects, each one less appealing than the other. My savings were dwindling at an alarming rate, and I was on the verge of desperation. The most suitable of the positions I was considering was that of companion to an elderly widow who lived in a fine residential area of Detroit, but that wasn't what I wanted to do.

So the ten-year-old letter was literally a godsend. Still, I was cautious by nature, and even with the proof in my hand, I couldn't believe in my good fortune. I carried it to the parlor window, where a few beams of weak sunshine filtered in through thick pine branches, and read the momentous sentences again.

They were brief and clear, written on fine stationery, to Mrs. Adam Marsden by Mr. Joshua Johnston of Silver Springs in the Colorado Territory. After briefly describing the ranch and referring to other property, Mr. Johnston asked her to contact him and advise him of her intentions.

Since the letter had been written in the year of my mother's death, I had no way of knowing whether she had received it. It was now 1876, and much could have happened in the intervening years. Perhaps the inheritance was no longer valid. I had to find out, and fortunately, I knew someone who could make the necessary inquiries for me.

Mr. Douglas Cameron, the father of my good friend, Eliza, owned the Pineville Lumber Company and much of the surrounding land. He had always treated me as another daughter, and I knew he had many friends throughout the United States and the Territories.

That same day I took him into my confidence and showed him the letter. As I hoped would be the case, he knew a lawyer in Denver, Mr. John Barclay. They had served together in the War and were still in contact with each other. He promised to have my western inheritance investigated.

Eliza was in Ohio at the time. She was engaged to a country doctor whose practice was in that state, and the wedding was being planned for August.

The practical aspect of my inheritance handed over to the capable Mr. Cameron, I went home and settled down to wait for the verdict from the Colorado Territory and to ponder the identity of Jules Carron.

Who was this man with the melodious French sounding name? At first, I assumed he was a relative, but neither of my parents had family still living, except perhaps for Aunt Marjorie, and she had gone with the gold seekers into oblivion. He couldn't have been a family member then.

Still, I searched through my mother's Bible and confirmed that they were all accounted for, dead, the ancestors I had never known. There wasn't a French name among them. Jules Carron must have been a friend, one my mother never mentioned. In addition to property, I had inherited a mystery.

~ * ~

The seasons changed. Spring became June, and still Mr. Barclay's letter didn't arrive. Anxious and at the same time hopeful, I turned down the companion position in Detroit. Those endless days were a time of waiting and dreaming.

Then one cool evening in June I was sitting in front of the fire with my mother's favorite shawl around my shoulders and a pitcher of hot chocolate on the table before me. It seemed as if I could see a hundred different and glorious new worlds for myself in the leaping flames, and all of them were possible now that I was an heiress and, like my Aunt Marjorie, about to set out on a grand adventure.

A sudden pounding on the door interrupted my reverie and brought me back to the present.

My visitor was Mr. Cameron. Not since my father's death had he come to my house, even with Eliza. He never left his comfortable library in the evening where his brandy, books, and memories were sufficient company. I could think of only one reason for his presence here tonight.

Trying to appear calm, I said, "Good evening, Mr. Cameron. I've been waiting for you."

"Yes, Mara, I can believe you have."

He was tall, bearded, and blustery, and although nearing seventy, still an attractive man. In his youth he had been a logger and then, during the War, an officer in the Union army. Today he was Pineville's richest and most influential citizen.

He sat down beside me, and all thoughts of my aunt evaporated.

"Did you receive an answer from Mr. Barclay?" I asked.

"Yes, today, and the news is good."

There was a twinkle in his eye that was not often present since the defection of his Southern wife. She had gone home to Louisiana with her baby daughter, Camilla, for a visit just before the firing on Fort Sumter and been trapped behind the Mason-Dixon Line. After the War, she had remained in the South, where she died soon after, leaving one of her cousins to bring her child back home.

In a great booming voice, he announced, "You have inherited a silver mine, my dear." He leaned back in the chair, thoroughly at ease, and told me the details.

"The ranch, Trail's End, has been deserted for several years, but your claim to it is clear and undisputed. It's a valuable property. You're more of an heiress than we suspected, with ten thousand dollars in a Denver bank and a genuine silver mine."

In that moment I had only one thought. Now I had enough money, even without the ranch, to continue to live in my own house and avert the grim fate of companion to an elderly and needy woman. The deed to my house could remain misplaced forever.

Mr. Cameron was saying, "When your ranch is sold, you'll have enough money to do whatever you wish. Barclay thinks you'll receive a good price for the land. There are several ranchers in the area wanting to expand. As for the mine..."

"Sold?" It was as if I had heard the one word only.

I brought another cup from the kitchen and, lifting the pitcher, carefully poured the still-warm chocolate. I suspected that my guest would have preferred the drink laced with brandy, but this would have to suffice.

He accepted the cup, lifted it to his mouth, and in one swallow, drank half of the contents.

"Thank you, my dear. It's very thoughtful of you. The mine is rumored to be worthless, although I understand that at one time, rich strikes were made in the area. Barclay can advise you."

I still stared into the fire as if the road to my future lay in the flames. I could almost see a livable house at Trail's End and a man who would belong to me, waiting for me in front of a similar fire.

"I don't think I want to sell the ranch," I said.

My announcement came as a surprise to both of us. A minute ago, I hadn't intended to say this at all.

Mr. Cameron nearly spilled hot chocolate on himself. "Why, what else would you do with it, Mara?"

Instead of answering directly, I asked a question of my own. "You knew my parents for years, Mr. Cameron. Did you ever hear of Jules Carron?"

"No, but then I don't know everything. He left his property to your mother. Now it belongs to you. That's what's important."

"You're right, but I can't help but be curious. I've been wondering why an unknown man would make my mother his heiress. There's only one possible answer. He knew her."

"Of course, he must have. Did you search the rest of your father's desk?"

"Yes, I looked everywhere. There was nothing, only the one letter. At times we could have used the extra money. I can't understand why Father wouldn't have inquired about the inheritance."

Mr. Cameron looked down into his empty cup. "Is there any chance he didn't know about it?"

"I've thought about that. I don't see how it's possible. I found the letter in his desk, after all. He may have planned to tell me and waited too long. My mother might have told me, but she was so sick and withdrawn before she died, and I was very young then. Now there's nobody left to ask."

I reached for the pitcher and found it empty. Mr. Cameron broke the brief silence. "If you don't plan to sell the ranch, what will you do?"

I knew what I was going to say even before the words were formed. An alien spirit must have taken possession of me this evening. "I'm going to go to Silver Springs and claim my inheritance. Perhaps I'll find the answer there. I want to know who Jules Carron was and why he left his ranch to my mother."

Quickly and firmly, he said, "But you can't do that."

"Why not?"

"You're too young to undertake a long journey alone." His expression was stern, his voice commanding. He might have been addressing one of his recruits.

"I'm twenty-one," I said. "That's only two months younger than Eliza, and she travels to Ohio frequently."

"That's different, Mara. Eliza is engaged to Doctor Lexington, and she stays with his mother. Besides, Ohio isn't a wild frontier."

I set my empty cup on the table and tried to conceal my amusement. No matter how many arguments Mr. Cameron threw down in my path, we both knew no one could order me to sit by the fire and spin in Pineville when I wanted to go West. Still, I allowed him to talk. His objections only made the trip seem more exciting.

"You'll be leaving the United States of America for an Indian-infested territory full of rough men where a lady such as yourself would be devoured; and I believe this Silver Springs is a glorified mining camp. You have a fine, comfortable house in Pineville. Eventually you'll probably find a husband. It's what your poor dead parents would have wanted."

"Now that's unfair, sir," I said. "They're not here, and I can live alone as easily in the Colorado Territory as here. I'm responsible for my own future, and my chances of finding a husband in this tiny town are practically non-existent. I appreciate all you've done to help me, but I've decided, and

I'm not afraid, neither of these rough men you talk about nor of Indians."

That last wasn't strictly true. I didn't know much about the Territorial natives, only what I read in the occasional dime novel that came my way, but I knew I wanted to do this in spite of any possible danger.

"If I have ten thousand dollars in that bank in Denver, I can afford a train ticket," I said. "But how do I withdraw the money?"

Acknowledging defeat, Mr. Cameron stood up and lifted my chin with a gentle hand, a gesture that reminded me of my father.

"It might do you good at that, Mara. You're pale, not like my girls. Perhaps a change of scenery will make your cheeks glow again, but you must let me make all the arrangements and advance you the money. You can repay me later. Anytime."

He was speaking as if the idea had been his own. I didn't want to accept his financial help. I was certain I could manage to move myself from Pineville to Colorado Territory with the last of my own funds. Once there, I would have the inheritance.

"Please," I began, although I sensed that I was about to lose this battle.

"No, Mara. For your father's sake, you must allow me to do this. He would have done as much for Eliza or Camilla. I'll buy the ticket and wire Barclay to make reservations for you in a good hotel in Denver. You can visit Silver Springs, see your ranch, and arrange for him to sell your western property, if that's what you want to do. Then you can come home."

"Or I can stay there."

He continued talking as if he hadn't heard me. "Whatever you do, don't talk to strangers on the train. If you keep to yourself, you should be safe. I think the Indians are subdued in the Territory at the moment. That's one danger you won't have to worry about."

"I'm sure I'll be all right," I said. "Now goodnight, Mr. Cameron, and thank you again. I know it's late, but I'm going to start getting ready for my trip."

~ * ~

After that night, time raced ahead at a dizzying pace. Now that I had made my decision, I wanted to leave at once. The excitement of traveling by rail all the way to the Colorado Territory, seeing Trail's End, and solving the mystery of Jules Carron was invigorating. As I set about preparing for my departure, occasionally I glanced in the mirror. I thought I could already see the beginning of a glow.

Mr. Cameron took care of the arrangements. All I needed to do was pack and write to Mr. Johnston, informing him of my travel plans and intent. No doubt, as Jules Carron's lawyer, he would have known him well. When we met in Silver Springs, I could ask him a few discreet questions about his deceased client.

I also penned a short note to Eliza, who wouldn't return to Pineville before late summer, and wished her happiness in her marriage. I was reasonably certain I wouldn't be coming back to Michigan, and, strangely, I wasn't unhappy about that. My loved ones were gone from this place, and I could take my memories with me.

That night, after a hasty supper, I gathered together the most serviceable and attractive of my garments, which proved to be a formidable task. My wardrobe was in sad shape, suitable for living alone in Pineville, but not for railway travel.

I had two fine dresses, both of them silk, one light green and the other black. I hadn't cared about being fashionably clothed since my father's death and had worn primarily dark colors. Now I had no time to sew a new wardrobe.

These went into my small trunk, along with the best of my under attire, and I set aside a plain, heavy dress of dark brown to wear on the train. Although it was summer in Michigan, Mr. Cameron said that a mountain state would be cold.

As jewelry, I would take my pendant watch and my mother's pearls. They were now mine, but I had never worn them, nor even moved them into my own room.

After my father's death, I had closed the door to his bedroom. Now, I paused at the head of the staircase, reluctant to enter the room in which both my mother and father had died. I closed my hand on the knob, turned it slowly, and pushed the door open. The warmth of the June morning followed me inside.

This was the largest and most pleasant room in the house with a view of the garden. Faded floral wallpaper covered the walls, and the furniture was oak and massive. Bright and soft touches were everywhere, constant reminders of my mother.

As I stepped over the threshold, I breathed in the scent of roses. Although I had neglected the bushes, still the flowers bloomed profusely in red and pink colors. My mother had perfected the art of drying their petals and preserving them in jars, using her own recipe.

One of the delicate glass vessels was still on the dresser, amidst miniature family portraits. That must be the source of the sweet rose fragrance in the musty room.

I knew that my mother's jewelry box was in the top drawer of her dresser. Feeling only a faraway sense of loss, I opened the case to take out the pearls she had always said were to be mine one day.

It was there that I found the ring. Wrapped in a small square of white material, it had been pushed to the back of the case. Now, freed to the light, its brilliant green and white fire blazed at me.

The ring was exquisite with a gold setting in the shape of a bouquet on which dozens of small diamonds clustered and sparkled around an emerald of immense size. I could never remember seeing it on my mother's finger.

Two strange things happened then. A coolness drifted through the room. Like a draft from another world, it cut through the warm air. Through the years, I remembered the sound of my mother's voice.

"This pearl necklace is my only possession of value, Mara. One day it will be yours."

At the same time, an image began to form in my mind. While the emerald winked its green fire at me from my palm, a memory from the distant past replayed itself in fuzzy hues.

A woman in gray sat at the window reading a letter. Slowly, with a sigh, she folded it. I could feel the heartbreak pulsating through the years. Her emotions were mine, and they were connected with the ring.

Was I remembering or imagining my mother reading Mr. Johnston's letter? But why was I assuming the letter had come from him? Perhaps Jules Carron had sent it.

My mother often said I was overly imaginative. It seemed she was correct.

She had never spoken of the magnificent emerald, but somehow I knew that Jules Carron had given it to her and she had kept it hidden. Why? I now had one more question without an answer.

I slipped the ring on my betrothal finger and wasn't in the least surprised to see that it was a perfect fit. The emerald matched the green glints in my eyes that were like hers. That was why he had chosen this particular stone.

I knew I would never wear this ring. Carefully, as if handling a precious relic, I returned it to the back of the jewelry box. With the pearls in my hand, I closed the dresser drawer.

"Jules Carron," I said, "I will find out who you are."

The room was silent and June-warm again. As I closed the door, it seemed to me that the scent of roses grew stronger. It followed me wherever in the house I went until the end of the day.

~ * ~

Before sunrise the next morning, I locked the house and walked to the train station with Mr. Cameron and Eliza's sixteen-year-old sister, Camilla. Both father and daughter were energetic for the early hour and as excited as if they were going to accompany me on my Western adventure.

"Remember everything I told you, Mara, especially about the strangers," Mr. Cameron said. "I'll watch your house until you come home."

"Don't stay away too long," Camilla added. "You have to be home in time for Eliza's wedding."

Camilla was becoming more like Eliza every day, just as blonde, almost as pretty.

"Tell Eliza I'll write as soon as I reach Silver Springs," I said. "Mr. Cameron, thank you again for helping me. I couldn't have done this alone."

"Of course you could, my dear. I'm not sure I've done you a kindness, but it's what you wanted. Maybe it'll be for the best."

While I tried to find a response to this less than enthusiastic farewell, I savored my last look at the little town of Pineville. I couldn't see my house in its entirety from the train station because of the trees, but my bedroom window, through which I'd watched hundreds of departures and arrivals, was visible.

In a minute, if I didn't take care, I'd be getting sentimental; in five, I'd be in tears.

It seemed that I was to be the only traveler to Detroit this morning. We waited for the train together, Camilla chattering about outlaws and Indians. At her side, Mr. Cameron was quiet.

"Please write to me too, Mara," Camilla said. "I want to know everything that happens to you. Some day I'll go out West, too."

Mr. Cameron reached for his daughter's hand. "That won't be for many years, Camilla."

I promised to do as Camilla asked. Then someone was helping me with my trunk, and I was inside one of the cars, watching through the window, as Mr. Cameron and Camilla waved to me. This really was goodbye.

As we left Pineville behind on the first part of my journey, I felt the sadness drift away from me. All of my feelings were focused on the future. I could hardly wait to begin my new life.

Two

The Pullman Palace Car that was taking us to the Colorado Territory was an improvement over Aunt Marjorie's covered wagon. We could walk on richly patterned Oriental carpets, sit on luxuriously upholstered seats, and eat and sleep on the train, while we headed in the same direction my aunt had taken almost thirty years ago.

My initial exuberance at riding on one of the great iron horses I had so long admired remained with me. As I was sitting next to the window, I gave all of my attention to the passing countryside. Although Mr. Cameron had assured me that the scenery I would observe on the way West was spectacular, in my opinion, the view so far was rather plain.

As darkness fell, a conductor passed through the cars, setting the kerosene lamps above us alight, and for the first time I became aware of the gentleman sitting across from me. I can't imagine how I could have failed to notice him earlier, for without a doubt, he was the most strikingly handsome man I'd ever seen in illustration or life, the absolute embodiment of male beauty. Black-haired and clean-shaven, he had a dark tan that hinted at years lived out of doors, and his eyes were the clear blue color of a Michigan lake.

His fashionable attire and elegant bearing proclaimed that he was a man who would be as much at home in a parlor as a mining camp. Suddenly it occurred to me that I was arriving at these conclusions with inadvisable haste and also that I was staring at him. Unfortunately, he noticed.

"You look exhausted, ma'am," he said. "You must not be used to traveling by railroad."

Not wanting to admit that this was my first journey of any kind, I said, "I am tired, a little, and the scenery is so monotonous."

"Ah, yes, to be sure. In this part of the country, that's true. But only wait. In a day or two, you'll see a great change."

His eyes had a bright, secret sparkle, and as he spoke, I detected the trace of an unfamiliar accent.

From a faraway place, I heard a familiar voice warning me not to talk to strangers on the train, but I ignored it. My weariness slipped away unnoticed, and I smiled at him.

"I'm looking forward to seeing the mountains."

"The Rockies are an impressive sight, especially if one is viewing them for the first time. Allow me to introduce myself. I am Nicholas Breckinridge."

His smooth and friendly voice inspired instant confidence, and the light in his eyes intrigued me.

"My name is Mara Marsden. Are you traveling far?"

"To the end of the line, Miss Marsden. Tell me, where are you going?"

"I have a ranch in the Colorado Territory near Silver Springs. It's called Trail's End."

In the brief pause that followed, I began to feel uncomfortable. Should I have been so quick to reveal my destination? Perhaps I shouldn't be talking to this fascinating man about anything beyond the scenery.

"There are several prosperous ranches in the Territory, Miss Marsden," he said. "Is Trail's End one of them?"

I slipped deftly past his question. "Have you ever visited Silver Springs, Mr. Breckinridge?"

Although I didn't want to give anything of myself away, I was curious about his background. He might be the owner of a mine, a rancher, or a banker. I sensed that he must be a person of importance, like Mr. Cameron.

"I have," he said. "Several years ago. Surely you don't run the ranch yourself? Is there a father or brother in your life? A husband?"

He was leading me away from the direction I had chosen; I wasn't going to let that happen. "I'm the sole owner of the property." Remembering how he had described his destination, I added, "Where exactly is the end of the line, Mr. Breckinridge?"

His voice grew grave, and the sparkle disappeared from his eyes.

"I'm also bound for the Colorado Territory. My sister has been unwell for a long time. A friend of mine, a doctor, moved to Denver a few years ago to practice medicine, and he writes glowing descriptions of the area and climate. He and our own physician think my sister's health may improve if she moves away from Boston's harsh winters. Eventually I'm going to settle her into a new home."

He lapsed into silence. I, who knew the grief of seeing loved ones fail and pass away, felt a kinship with this man. He didn't say anything more about his sister, but I found myself conjuring a feminine version of Nicholas Breckinridge, black-haired and blue-eyed, but fair. She would be languishing on a chaise lounge while she waited for her brother to take her to a place where she could regain her health.

I was now in a mood for conversation, but since Mr. Breckinridge seemed disinclined to talk, I fell to studying the other two occupants of the compartment instead.

Beside me sat a middle-aged woman whose face was hidden behind a veil. She was plainly but tastefully dressed in black. Her only ornament was the diamond ring sparkling on her finger, and she seemed to have a haughty air. Now that Mr. Breckinridge had fallen silent, she was staring out into the aisle where there was no activity at the moment.

The other, a young woman close to my own age, was sitting next to Mr. Breckinridge, slowly turning the pages of a worn leather-bound book and occasionally looking up, but paying no attention to her surroundings or to us, her traveling companions.

As black-haired as Mr. Breckinridge, she was wearing an elaborately trimmed bonnet and a dress of lavender, a splendid creation but one hardly suitable for a dusty train journey. She reminded me of an illustration on the cover of *Harper's Bazar* come to life, but overly done, rather gaudy.

They looked like brother and sister, Nicholas Breckinridge and the girl sitting beside him, but with appearance, the similarity between the two ended. Nicholas had the clothing and bearing of a true gentleman, while the girl's fancy costume and coloring gave her a vaguely wanton air. Then she looked up and smiled at me. I revised my initial impression, along with my reservations.

In a clear, melodious voice, she said, "Train travel can be so tedious. It was only exhilarating in the beginning. Now I would like to take a walk in the fresh air."

"I agree," I said. "I wish I'd thought to bring a book along. What are you reading?"

"This is *The Tempest*. It's kept me in another world all this time. Have you read it?"

"I'm sure I haven't."

"It's a play by Mr. William Shakespeare. I'm attempting to memorize the part of Miranda."

I couldn't have been more astonished. "But why? Are you an actress?"

The woman in black said, "Actress? I wouldn't think so."

Her comment was softly uttered, but we heard it clearly, and the unkind tone was unmistakable. I felt the force of the affront as if it had been intended for me, and I took a stand. Whoever or whatever the girl was, she had a friendly smile and manner. As for the older woman, she was undoubtedly a snob.

The girl ignored the remark and closed her book, apparently so familiar with the work that she didn't need to mark the page. As she looked at me, I noticed that, like Mr. Breckinridge, she had sparkling blue eyes. They reminded me of jewels.

"My name is Viola Courtenay of England and New York," she said so formally that I could almost see the curtain rise. As she continued to speak, however, a naturalness and warmth came into her voice.

"I heard you tell the gentleman that your name is Mara," she said. "You won't have heard of me yet, but someday you will. You may have seen my father on stage. He's Richard Courtenay."

When I was slow to react to her statement, her expression changed quickly.

"Oh, dear. You don't care for the theatre."

"Well..."

I didn't want to admit that I'd never seen a play but didn't know how to avoid doing so. "There aren't any theatres where I live."

"None at all? How strange."

"It's a very small town. Perhaps I'll have an opportunity to see one in the future. You must lead a fascinating life."

"I do, but it's difficult at times. I knew what to expect because I come from a theatrical family. My father named me for a character in a play. He always intended for me to go on stage."

She opened her book to the first page, turned it around, and handed it to me. The inscription was faded and barely legible:

'To Viola, my dear daughter, on this day, for her sixteenth birthday, from Father.'

I was trying to find something appropriate to say when Nicholas remarked, "I saw Richard Courtenay in London several years ago. He was a magnificent Richard the Third. If you have a fraction of his talent, Miss Courtenay, you'll have a successful career. Certainly you favor him. Now that I know the relationship, the resemblance is remarkable."

She glanced quickly at him and looked away. "Thank you."

"Are you going out West to act in a play?" I asked.

Viola hugged her book to her breast, as it were a treasured sentient object. I sensed that I wasn't the only one waiting for her answer.

She said, "I hope to work at my profession in Denver. My brother is there now with his company. He's invited me to join him."

"Perhaps we'll see you on stage then," Nicholas said, and with ease, proceeded to draw the lady in black into the conversation. She introduced herself as Mrs. Adelaide Haskins. To my amazement, she was willing to be included and warmed considerably to Nicholas' charm. She even bestowed a smile on Viola.

"What a great coincidence!" she said. "I'm going to Denver, too. My home is there."

I had been thinking myself a lone traveler to the Colorado Territory. Now we were four with a common destination.

Mrs. Haskins was not so formidable as I'd first thought. She had lived an interesting life. With a little encouragement, she talked incessantly. We listened, spellbound, as she told us about herself.

"I've been visiting my married daughter in Boston. Except for her family, I'm alone now. Both of my husbands were officers, and I lost them in Indian warfare, at different times, of course."

"You've had two husbands?" Viola asked. "Imagine that."

"I lived for a time at Fort Laramie in the Wyoming Territory. Someday I may remarry. I miss living at a military fort."

As she described the active social life and the challenge of making a home for her officer husband and his successor, I marveled that I had previously thought her haughty. She was friendlier than some of my female neighbors back in Pineville.

"Women are very much in demand on the frontier," she said. "They're almost as precious as gold or silver. Well, maybe not quite. No woman remains unmarried in the West for long. Both of you girls are so pretty that you'll be brides by the end of the summer. Mark my words."

Viola smiled and said nothing. Of course, being a young and beautiful actress in New York, she must have had many opportunities to wed. For myself, there wasn't a single bachelor in Pineville within forty years of my age.

Quickly I said, "I'm not looking for a husband, Mrs. Haskins. I have a home waiting for me and a ranch to manage."

"Wait until you arrive, Miss Marsden. You'll see what I mean."

We talked then about the exciting history of the Territory. Nicholas and Mrs. Haskins exchanged tales of silver and gold strikes since 1859. Before long, however, Mrs. Haskins, or Mrs. Hatchet, as I privately re-christened her, launched herself on what appeared to be her favorite subject: The savage Indians. She referred to them as hostiles.

"It's fortunate there won't be any trouble this summer. During the War, my husband's regiment was recalled to fight for the Union. He sent me to stay with his sister. She and her husband had a small homestead not too far from Denver. I lived with them while I waited for my husband to come home."

Her voice broke, and she fumbled in her reticule for a handkerchief. Nicholas provided his own and touched her hand gently.

"Eighteen-sixty-six was a bad year." Mrs. Haskins appeared to have left the compartment of the train speeding west for a barren plain, where all was desolation and despair. Her voice took on a vicious tone. "So many houses were burned and people slaughtered. Those savages! I saw my own sister-in-law scalped."

If her intent was to frighten Viola and me, she succeeded admirably. We were all silent, trying to absorb this outrage.

Nicholas asked, "How did you manage to escape a similar fate?"

"I was very quiet. I hid in an old armoire Elizabeth had brought out from the East, and they didn't find me. They didn't even look there. But Elizabeth was in the field. They killed her baby, too." After a pause, she added, "Of course they didn't always dispatch the women."

"I think you're frightening the other ladies," Nicholas said. "If they're to be kidnapped, it won't be by Indians."

I knew he was making a gallant attempt to dispel the aura of terror created by Mrs. Haskins' revelations. He was only partially successful.

"There's no danger of Indian attack," he said. "The Cheyenne are gone. The Ute are safely on the reservations. The Army has the problem under control."

I tried to banish the gruesome images that were taking shape in my mind. Here on the shadowy train, rushing toward a place where unspeakable things had once occurred and seeing the pain in Mrs. Haskins' face, I was afraid.

"Did they really scalp your sister-in-law?" I asked.

Unmindful of the warning note in Nicholas' voice, Mrs. Haskins continued. "It's true, and there were worse atrocities. I remember once, when I was a girl in forty-nine, the Indians captured a white man and skinned him alive."

Viola uttered a faint cry, and I felt an unfamiliar faintness come over me. I wanted to run from the compartment all the way back to the cool safety of my Michigan woods, but I forced myself to remain seated. I couldn't believe such atrocities had ever happened in America and yet, according to Mrs. Haskins, an eyewitness of such events, they had.

As she regaled us with her horror stories, unwanted images began to dance through my mind. I was seeing the white man burned alive, the woman stolen away to a fate worse than any death, and now the man tied to a stake while the knife was thrust into his chest and the skin separated from his body.

Fire, screaming, and blood took on a life of their own and demanded my attention. As hard as I tried, I couldn't send the pictures away. They assailed my mind like so many well-aimed arrows. I stood up too quickly and fell back into the seat.

In an even voice that held a hint of barely suppressed anger, Nicholas said, "Mrs. Haskins! There's no need to speak of such horrors."

I rose again, managed to stay upright this time, and rushed out into the aisle. At the end of the car, I found an open window and breathed in the cold night air. Gradually the nausea that had seized me receded.

Out there in the darkness was an unknown new land I couldn't see, and it terrified me. But going west had been my choice. It still was. I had to be able to deal with whatever I might find there.

I was vaguely aware of Nicholas standing near me with Viola behind him. Her blue eyes were filled with sympathy, but they held none of the fear that had enveloped me.

Then Nicholas had his arms around me. "She exaggerates, Miss Marsden, and dwells on isolated incidents that happened a long time ago. You'll find the West a place of civility and wonder. I promise."

Comforted and reassured, I regretted my cowardly flight. "If you can believe it, my aunt was a genuine forty-niner. I'm going to try to remember that."

Viola moved closer to me and lowered her voice. "That Mrs. Haskins is a horrid old witch. Back in England, she'd be burned at the stake."

"They don't burn people anymore, Miss Courtenay," Nicholas said. "I don't believe they have witches either."

"I'm all right now, and I'm sorry for making such a fuss," I said.

I also regretted mentioning Aunt Marjorie. For years I had been dreaming about her great Western adventure. Maybe it had ended in fire or some other tragedy of the worse-than-death kind. That wasn't the way I wanted to remember her.

As we made our way back to the compartment, I realized that before I'd left Pineville, I should have read something substantial about the West, instead of embarking on my journey so blithely uninformed. Thoughts of home reminded me of removing the skin from a chicken and making soup in the big kettle at home. Never again, I vowed.

"Are you fully recovered now, Miss Marsden?" Nicholas asked.

I pushed the chicken out of my mind. "Completely. Such things couldn't happen today, could they?"

"No, not where we're going. Forget Mrs. Haskins' tales. Your skin and pretty hair are much too nice to end up as Indian trophies."

I felt my face grow warm at this unexpected compliment. Viola took my arm and led me back into the compartment, and Nicholas followed us. Mrs. Haskins looked so contrite that I felt compelled to apologize to her as well, for my emotional reaction to her stories.

It was now late, and I was more than ready to rest. In the morning I would be able to view the passing countryside again, and the frightening images would only be a memory.

~ * ~

Mr. Cameron had arranged for me to be provided with a sleeping car. When I lay down, however, I discovered that I couldn't rest comfortably in a moving bed, especially after Mrs. Haskins' harrowing stories. As it happened, I spent many restless hours before exhaustion finally overcame me. Then in my dreams, I was always in motion.

The day was a time for relaxation and camaraderie. We four ate our meals in the dining car, shared stories from our past lives, and speculated about what the West had in store for us. Meanwhile the scenery changed from monotonous to breathtaking.

All this time, the distance between my former home and the vast territory, where I hoped to find my future, grew smaller, and my relationship with one of my companions subtly changed.

By the end of the third day of the journey, I was amazed to realize that I was fairly enamored of Nicholas. Of course, he was the first attractive man to come my way; but even if there had been many, he was truly marvelous and so very handsome that he scarcely seemed real.

At home, in the company of Eliza Cameron, the uncontested beauty of Pineville, I felt that my own looks suffered in comparison. Now, here was the wondrous Nicholas sitting beside a beautiful actress, and I was the one he singled out for attention.

After the incident with Mrs. Haskins' stories, we talked to each other for hours and fell into a close friendship that is perhaps only possible in the intimate, enclosed world of a westward-bound train.

Nicholas had vivid memories of the Colorado Territory and spoke enthusiastically about his previous visits. He was especially interested in ranching. He asked me several questions about Trail's End and how I, a young female, happened to own a ranch in my own right. Gradually I found myself telling him more than I intended. Still I kept some of the details back.

I said that the ranch had been willed to my mother, who had passed on, and a family illness had kept me in Michigan until this summer. Now I was free to travel, and the time had come to claim my inheritance.

"In all these years has no one lived at Trail's End?" he asked.

I murmured something about a foreman, and Nicholas spoke again about his hope of seeing his sister happily settled in her new home. His friend had been searching for a suitable house for her. He thought he'd found the perfect one.

Hoping I wasn't being too curious, I asked, "Will she live there alone?"

"I'll stay with her for a while. I've been traveling too long, Miss Marsden. Only last winter I returned from Europe. Lately I've visited the Centennial Exhibition in Philadelphia. Now I'm heading out West again. I don't worry about my sister being unattended. I have reason to believe that she and my friend will eventually marry."

With each conversation, I felt myself growing closer to Nicholas, and also to Viola. I wished the train journey would go on forever, but that was impossible. Late one afternoon, we arrived in Denver.

It's over now, I thought. *We'll go our separate ways, and I'll never see him again.*

The end of the journey was unusual, however, in that neither Nicholas nor Viola was inclined to say the final farewell. Mrs. Haskins quickly left with a party of friends, wishing us all well, saying she hoped we'd meet again. After she left, Nicholas, Viola, and I stayed together for a while longer, making plans.

Viola was going immediately to her brother's boarding house. "As soon as I can, I'll travel to Silver Springs and surprise you at Trail's End," she said. "Maybe someday soon you can come back to Denver with me and see me perform on stage."

"That would be wonderful. I'll look forward to it. For now, goodbye and good luck, Viola."

I looked forward to continuing our friendship and hoped she meant what she said. I suspected that Viola's life was very different from my own—the one I was going to make for myself, that is.

As Viola hurried down the street, I turned to Nicholas. He had offered to escort me to the Last Nugget Hotel, an establishment recommended by Mr. Barclay, where I should have a reservation.

"I plan to stay in Denver for two weeks, Miss Marsden, and I'll visit you in Silver Springs, too, if I may. When I do, I intend to call you Mara. I'm eager to see this ranch of yours and you turned into a cowgirl."

"I don't think that will happen any time soon, but I'll look forward to your visit," I said.

It would soon be dark, and I was a little disappointed because Denver was my first real frontier town, and I was eager to explore it, but I was very tired. I knew that I wouldn't want to linger in the morning, for I had farther still to go. Like Nicholas, I wanted to see my ranch.

"I'm glad the tracks continue to Silver Springs," I said. "I was afraid I'd have to travel the rest of the way by horseback or buckboard."

"You're going to be very happy in the West," Nicholas said. "You must return to Denver soon. I'll take you to visit my sister, and we'll have a grand tour of the sights."

He turned my trunk over to a freckled young man who scarcely looked strong enough to lift a piece of luggage, and yet he carried it with ease. As we followed him, walking slowly toward the hotel, Nicholas said, "I'd be honored if you'd have dinner with me tonight. The food at the Nugget is very good."

I would have liked nothing better. I was beginning to feel intimidated by the bustling frontier city. Walking into the dining room of the hotel, escorted by Nicholas, would send my confidence soaring. I was exhausted and disheveled, however, and since Nicholas had promised to visit me soon, I could forego the pleasure and security of his company on my first night in Denver.

Also, I wasn't hungry. All I wanted was a basin of fresh water and a bed with a feather mattress. They might be creature comforts, but the Marsden blood had thinned considerably since the days of Aunt Marjorie.

So when Nicholas left me at the desk of the Last Nugget, I was not bereft but satisfied with my journey's end and ready for a good night's sleep in a bed that didn't move. Unfortunately, that wasn't to be my fate.

Alone in a room that was exceptionally comfortable, almost luxurious, for the frontier, I washed quickly, slipped on my nightgown, and lay down on the bed. Almost before I pulled the cover over myself, I was asleep.

At once the drums began, and my dream captured me. I moved through space, leaving the train and cowering in the hotel room that had turned into a prairie. An Indian brave was stalking me, brandishing a knife that bore a resemblance to the one I had used often in my own kitchen, and I was afraid.

Abruptly he vanished, but now I was tied to a stake. I knew what was going to happen before I felt the touch of the knife, and I screamed. There on the floor I could see the long strands of my own dark hair.

There was a pain in my head, and a primitive fear held me in a tight and unrelenting grip, even after I awoke and knew I was looking at shadows on the floor.

You were dreaming, I told myself. *None of it was real, except for the headache, and that'll go away.*

Still, I touched my hair and ran my hands up and down my arms for warmth and reassurance. My skin was still there.

Three

The next day I had my first glimpse of Silver Springs from the window of another train. In spite of Nicholas' descriptions of Western culture and civility, I had been expecting a ramshackle mining camp built on a sea of mud. I was therefore surprised to find a real town basking in sunlight that turned everything in my view to gold, or so I fancied.

Certainly the brightness was powerful enough to drive last night's terrors out of my mind. The sky appeared to be bluer in this land, and I could see snow-topped mountains.

I followed the other passengers out of the car to the steps that led down to the ground. Everyone was in a hurry to disembark, and most of my fellow travelers had friends or family waiting to greet them. I stood still for a moment, taking a longer look at the town to which I had come.

Along the main street, people were hurrying, strolling, or simply lounging and enjoying the morning. Everywhere I looked, I saw horses. Some carried riders, and others were tethered to posts outside the stores. Soon I would have a mount of my own, when I was settled in on my ranch.

"Welcome to Silver Springs, ma'am."

I looked down and saw a courtly, gray-bearded gentleman smiling up at me. He held out his hand to help me alight from the train. I accepted it gratefully and stepped down to the ground, where I instantly became a part of the scene.

Silver Springs might have begun its life as a mining camp, but gold and silver wealth had transformed it into a vibrant frontier metropolis as bright as a freshly minted coin.

I would be new here, too. Nobody in this town was acquainted with me. Therefore, I could be anyone at all, with a past as glamorous as I could envision or invent. But I mustn't forget. My focus was on the future; my background was irrelevant.

I thanked the elderly gentleman and surveyed my surroundings more closely, as I waited for someone to offer to transport my belongings to my temporary home.

The buildings on the street appeared to be of fairly recent construction. The most imposing structure was set apart from its neighbors and lavishly decorated with ornamental wooden scrollwork. A sign proclaimed it The Silver Palace Hotel. That was my destination.

Finally I found a porter to carry my trunk, but I soon realized that he wasn't a railroad employee. On the short walk to the hotel, he told me that he worked at the McKay ranch.

"If y'all want an escort to see the sights of Silver Springs, I'm available, ma'am," he said with a friendly smile. "I'm Mike."

His offer confirmed Mrs. Haskins' talk about the scarcity of unattached women in Silver Springs. I might have been visiting royalty, but I had sense enough to proceed with the greatest of caution. In truth, I retreated with what I hoped was grace and gentility.

"Thank you for your help with my trunk, Mike, but I think I can manage now," I said.

"I'm in town most nights. Sometimes at the Palace. Hope you enjoy your stay, ma'am."

"I know I will."

As we approached the Silver Palace Hotel, I noticed two men sitting on the porch. One of them, older than the other, was dressed in a tattered Confederate uniform, which I thought was strange. It was the younger man who caught my attention, though, because he was staring at me in a bemused fashion.

A Stetson hat rested casually over his light brown hair in which I could discern a sprinkling of silver. As I came closer, I saw that his face was dark and weathered. Tiny lines crinkled about his eyes that were a curious blend of gray and blue.

He wore a camel vest over a blue shirt and the requisite gun belt. Although he looked like many of the other townsmen, a subtle difference set him apart. It was a quality I couldn't identify.

As I ascended the stairs with my escort, he appraised me frankly with those blue-gray eyes. Unnerved and annoyed with myself because of it, I looked away.

Inside the hotel, Mike introduced me to a small red-bearded man he called Andy.

"Take care of this lady, Andy," he said, as he set my trunk down at my feet. "She just came to town, and we want to treat her right."

Andy set aside the biscuit he had been feeding to the ginger-colored cat that sat next to the register book. If the Silver Palace had an impressive exterior, on the inside it was welcoming and homey, with several comfortable chairs and paintings on the walls, primarily of mountain scenery.

"Thank you again for your help, Mike." I reached into my reticule for a coin. "This is for you."

"No, ma'am," he said quickly. "It's my pleasure helping you."

He tipped his hat, smiled, and walked away. In spite of my gratitude for his aid, I felt relieved. Thus far I'd had only the smallest taste of independence, and I wanted much more. Of course, I could never have carried the heavy trunk myself.

Andy had assumed a professional innkeeper's air. He smiled broadly.

"Would it be possible for me to have a room for two or three nights?" I asked. "Beyond that, my plans are indefinite."

"Sure thing," he said. "One nice room coming up. So you never been to Silver Springs before? Are you visiting friends? No, you'd be stayin' with them if you was. As for myself, I been here since fifty-nine, lookin' for silver. Never found it yet."

"Perhaps you will," I said. "It's never too late."

He looked as pleased as if I'd just paid him the greatest of compliments.

"That's what I say, ma'am, but they don't believe me. I'm goin' to try again, one last time, strike out on my own. I always knew I'd be lucky. Just hasn't happened yet."

I listened patiently, signed my name in the register, and looked with longing at my trunk. I wanted to unpack and explore the streets of Silver Springs. I had so much to do that I scarcely knew where to begin.

"Do you know where I can find the law office of Mr. Joshua Johnston?" I asked.

"You want to see old Joshua, ma'am? You're too late. He died in sixty-six during the smallpox epidemic."

So I'd written a letter to a man who had been dead for ten years. I wished I'd asked Mr. Cameron to investigate Mr. Johnston, as well as my inheritance. It was unfortunate that the one man who might have given me information about Jules Carron had died in the same year as my mother and Jules himself.

Was this too much of a coincidence? I thought about it and then reconsidered. Death is never a stranger, no matter where one lives. I didn't need to look for additional mysteries.

Still, I had to see a lawyer in Silver Springs to be certain that my claim to the inheritance was valid. Also I needed someone to tell me how to find Trail's End.

"Isn't anyone else in town practicing law?" I asked.

Andy nodded, gave the cat the last piece of biscuit, and shooed her off the desk. "You'll want to see Mister Jeremiah Brown. He took over for Old Joshua. Jeremiah's a young fellow, but he's good."

"Where can I find him?"

"Nowhere today, Miss Marsden, unless you want to ride back to Denver. He won't be home till tomorrow."

A delay at this point was practically more than I could bear, but I told myself to be patient. I could tour Silver Springs today. After ten years, one day wouldn't make that much of a difference.

Before I went up to my room, I said, "I can see Mr. Brown tomorrow then?"

"Sure thing, ma'am, if he's back."

He would be, I felt certain. Tomorrow was going to be the real beginning of my new life in the West. I was ready to start living it.

~ * ~

My room was not so grandly furnished as the one in the Last Nugget, but it was comfortable enough. I sat down on a chair beside the window and began thinking and planning.

I had confidence that my new home would be welcoming and that I'd soon solve the mystery of Jules Carron and reunite with my new friends, Nicholas and Viola. Now I realized that I wanted more. It was important for me to belong to this land of silver and gold.

I wove an elaborate fantasy of climbing mountains, exploring mines, and learning the names of western trees and wildflowers. Securely established on my ranch, I would become one of the people from diverse backgrounds who had journeyed West in the last two decades to build a fine new city.

The hard days of the Territory were gone, a part of history. I had arrived at exactly the right time. I made an entry in my imaginary journal:

I, Mara Marsden, came West in 1876, the Centennial Year. What follows are my adventures.

Tomorrow I would buy paper and begin a real journal in which to record my impressions of the West and what happened to me. Every day I would write in it, and when I was old, I'd reread the entries and remember how it was when the West was new for me.

With these pleasant thoughts wandering through my mind, I fell asleep. When I woke up, after what seemed like only a ten or fifteen minute nap, long shadows were moving across the floor.

Could I possibly have slept the day away?

I consulted my watch. It was now six o'clock in the evening. The day I had set aside for exploration was gone. I must have been more tired than I'd thought, but my rest had been peaceful. Perhaps my dream Indian had vanished.

Peering into the small mirror, I found not the glow I desired but my usual fair complexion. I wished I'd asked Viola's advice about lip color. A light application of face paint would be part of my new life in the West, but tonight I had to be satisfied with washing in cold water and brushing my hair.

I was now thoroughly awake and ravenous. Except for a hurried breakfast before leaving Denver, I hadn't had any food all day. I would have to dine in the hotel alone, a prospect I found daunting, but if I was going to eat, that was what I'd have to do. Besides, didn't I want to be an independent woman, and wasn't I hungrier than I had been since leaving Michigan?

I lifted my black dress out of the trunk, slipped it over my head, and fastened my pearls around my neck. As the cool necklace came in contact with my skin, my confidence rushed back.

I would never be one of the world's beauties like Viola, but since its brushing, my hair was a darker shade of chestnut, and it had a shine in the light of the kerosene lamp. The soft glow of the pearls and the green glints in my eyes were my only other assets. I would have to be content with them.

I needn't have worried. The dining room wasn't crowded, and people were concentrating on their dinners and their own conversations. Most of the patrons were men, but I wasn't the only woman in the room.

Nearby was a merry party of four ladies, each one in gorgeous attire, with painted faces that enhanced their natural beauty. They appeared to be celebrating an event. One woman sat alone at her table. She wore black as I did, but her gown was more elaborate than mine and brightened by glittering jewelry at her throat. She had the impervious air of a queen, and the waiters gave her every possible attention.

I was seated at a secluded corner table, where I had an excellent view of my fellow diners and the surroundings. The hotel décor was a comfortable blend of the East and the West, mixing familiar and frontier touches. Soon I felt at home, especially when my dinner of savory meat and biscuits arrived.

I hadn't tasted food this good in a long time, certainly not since I'd left Michigan. For a while, I forgot about everything except the tasty repast in front of me, but gradually I became aware that someone was watching me.

He sat alone at a table across the room. I recognized the man I'd seen earlier in the day sitting with the Confederate veteran in front of the Silver Palace Hotel. The interest and admiration on his face were apparent. Although I felt uncomfortable to be the subject of his scrutiny, I looked directly at him and did the unthinkable. I smiled.

He was really quite handsome, although this hadn't occurred to me when I'd seen him previously. He appeared to be older than I'd first thought, in his late thirties, I decided, or early forties.

He lacked the finely chiseled features and dark perfection of Nicholas Breckinridge, but his was a roughhewn kind of attractiveness. Based on my brief glance, it seemed to me that he was a personification of this rugged land with which I had fallen in love.

He didn't look at me again but divided his attention between his meal and the newspaper unfolded at his elbow. I wished he would join me, but this didn't happen. Nor did he look my way again.

The dining room was more crowded now. I finished my dinner and, with no reason to linger, made my way past his table to the lobby and climbed the stairs to the second floor. Here all was shadowy and silent. I might have been the only guest in the hotel. Resisting the urge to look back over my shoulder, I hurried down the hall to the safety of my room.

I was uneasy about the coming night and its possible attendant horrors. Although I had slept for several hours during the day, I was still tired. I couldn't sit up all night, like a child afraid of dreaming. Centering my thoughts on the man in the dining room instead of the nightmare Indian, I exchanged my black dress for a nightgown and lay down.

As it turned out, I slept peacefully, while fresh, sweet-scented air flowed in through the half-opened window. Once I thought I heard drums, but they were faint and faraway.

During the night I woke to remember fragments of a short, pleasant dream about a man with brown, sun-streaked hair whose bold appraising eyes were neither gray nor blue. It was strange, but since meeting Nicholas, I'd forgotten that I'd always favored men with light hair.

Four

I awoke before sunrise, rested, hungry again, and happy in the knowledge that something wonderful was going to happen soon. The room was chilly, but I wasn't in the least tempted to stay under the blanket, especially since the fragments of my dream about the man in the dining room were already dissipating.

I splashed water on my face, brushed my hair, and dressed in a plaid skirt and a ruffle-bedecked bodice. Then I hung my watch around my neck. It was officially time to start the day.

I locked my room and went down to the first floor where I found Andy at his post with a biscuit close at hand and the cat on the desk, washing her paws. She interrupted her grooming to hiss at me, and I resolved to ignore her henceforth.

"Good morning, Andy," I said. "Mr. Brown will be in his office today, I hope."

"Should be. You sure look pretty this morning, Miss Marsden. Bright as a silver nugget."

This was, I imagined, his highest compliment. He offered me a scrap of paper covered with lines and drawings of miniature stores.

"I drew you a map. You can't miss Jeremiah's place. It's right on Main Street."

I thanked him and entered the dining room where more people were having breakfast than I'd seen during last night's dinner hour. I devoured a large morning meal consisting of wheat cakes and a thick slice of ham. I couldn't understand why I was so hungry. I'd never eaten so much at any one meal before.

Afterward, with the crude hand-drawn map clutched in my hand, I walked slowly down Main Street, savoring the sights and the early morning air. With every step, I saw something I hadn't noticed yesterday. The farther I wandered from the hotel, the more I felt as if I already belonged in this town.

I wasn't the only pedestrian abroad at this hour. The wood plank sidewalk was crowded with people, most of them with an apparent destination. In the street, the traffic was heavy as horses trotted by, sending dust particles whirling through the air.

I stopped to watch as two small boys, who resembled each other in build and coloring, ran past me in pursuit of a honey-brown puppy. Another canine, large and shaggy, crossed the street seconds before a wagon passed by, almost smashing him. I wished I knew the outcome of the chase, but boys and runaway puppy were long out of sight.

I could easily have found Mr. Brown's office without Andy's map by walking for five minutes in a straight line from the hotel. He was just arriving, turning the key in the lock, taking no notice of me until I came to a stop next to him.

"Good morning," I said in a soft voice to avoid startling him. "If you're Mr. Jeremiah Brown, I'd appreciate a few minutes of your time. My name is Mara Marsden. I'm in need of information and legal advice."

Although apparently surprised by my sudden appearance at his side, Mr. Brown smiled warmly. "I hope I can be of help to you, Miss Marsden. Just give me a minute to get settled."

He unlocked the door, ushered me into a cluttered office, and offered me a sturdy wooden chair. I watched as he opened the windows and cleared a space on his large desk by moving papers and books to the towering stacks on nearby tables.

Jeremiah Brown was tall, lean, and dark with a bushy brown moustache. While he hadn't been blessed with the handsome features of Nicholas Breckinridge or the rugged attractiveness of the brown-haired man in the Palace dining room, he was by no means ill-favored.

"I've been out of town for a week," he said. "Papers tend to pile up. Now, Miss Marsden, what can I do for you?"

"I came to the Territory to claim property that was originally willed to my late mother, Mrs. Adam Marsden, in 1866. I wrote to Mr. Joshua Johnston about my intention to travel to the West, not realizing that he had passed on. I don't know what happened to my letter."

He glanced at the stack of mail on his desk. "That's easy. It would have been delivered to me. Specifically, to what property are you referring, Miss Marsden?"

"A ranch known as Trail's End, at one time owned by Mr. Jules Carron."

"Trail's End," he said. "You're late in claiming your inheritance, Miss Marsden. That place has been deserted for years, since before my time."

"Haven't you lived in Silver Springs long?"

"I came to the Territory in 1870. The house at Trail's End has been unoccupied for at least ten years."

As he looked at me, I thought I detected a flicker of doubt in his eyes and suspicion as well. Quickly I produced Mr. Johnston's letter, offering it as proof of my identity, but I saw no need to give him every detail of the strange affair.

"My mother died the same year the letter was written. I don't know if she ever received it."

"Still, you've waited an unusually long time to investigate the inheritance," he said.

This was an easy statement to counter. "I was a child then, Mr. Brown, and for some time my father wasn't very strong. He needed me at home. He died this year."

I wouldn't like to be cross-examined by Jeremiah Brown. Although he seemed to be an easy-going gentleman, obviously he found my brief explanation lacking.

"Did you say that your mother's name was Mrs. Adam Carron?"

"I said Mrs. Adam Marsden. Jules Carron must have been a distant relative, one I never met. I didn't learn about the inheritance until some years later."

Gradually the doubt left Jeremiah Brown's eyes. I was relieved that he didn't find my lack of knowledge about my mother's legacy surprising, but I realized that children are seldom aware of the secret aspects of their parents' lives.

"Did you ever meet Mr. Carron?" I asked.

"No, and I didn't know Joshua Johnston either. I inherited his unfinished business. I suppose you fall into that category. I came West because of the opportunity for a young lawyer here. Now I have more work than I can manage."

"In that case, I'm very grateful for your help. Do you know how Jules Carron died?"

By his shrewd look, I knew that a sliver of his previous suspicion had returned.

"I never wondered," he said. "I assume it was of natural causes. I have no reason to think there was anything unusual about the manner of his passing."

"Can you tell me anything at all about him?"

"Very little. He was one of the first ranchers in the area, but he didn't live here long. In eighteen sixty-two he left the Territory for Texas and joined the Confederate army."

Pieces of the puzzle began to dance about in midair, tantalizingly beyond my grasp.

"He may have been killed in the War then."

"No, I heard he came home after the Surrender but died soon after."

My father had served in the Union army, but my mother never left Michigan, or so I had been led to believe. How could she have met a soldier from the South?

"Jules Carron was probably a Texan," Mr. Brown said. "I remember hearing that he'd been wounded. Carron was something of a recluse. He had a foreman or partner who used to come to town for supplies, but he rarely ventured off his own land. I don't think he had any close friends."

Did the trail end here, or was Mr. Brown telling me everything he knew? He impressed me as being an honest man. I reasoned that if he knew these few details, I might later encounter someone who possessed more information about the mysterious Mr. Carron.

"There must be at least one person in town I could ask," I said.

"You'd think so. Around four thousand people call Silver Springs home today. They can't all have come here after Carron's death. He's buried in the cemetery outside town. You could visit the grave, but that's a dreary activity for such a pleasant day."

"Riding out to my ranch would be more to my liking," I said. "I want to see the house and the land."

"You can view the property, but any additional exploration is impossible. The outlying buildings are crumbling. Who knows the condition of the house?"

He went to the safe and drew out an old iron box. My heart took a great leap upwards. Surely he was about to bring out another letter or paper explaining the connection between Jules Carron and my mother. Inside, however, an ancient key rested on the deed to the property. Only that.

Mr. Brown handed both to me. "You'll want to sell the place, of course. I know of a buyer who would be interested. He owns the neighboring land. Since Carron has been gone for so many years and no one ever came to take over, I think he considers your property an extension of his own."

"Has he? He will soon find out differently."

"This gentleman has been paying the property taxes for several years," he said.

"He will have to be reimbursed then, as soon as possible."

I was unprepared for the feeling of possessiveness that swept over me. That this unnamed buyer would probably offer me a considerable sum for Trail's End was immaterial. The place was mine, no matter how long it had been unclaimed, or who had been paying property taxes. I think I must have felt this way from that very first night, when Mr. Cameron told me about my inheritance.

"I saw a livery stable on my way to your office, Mr. Brown. If you would draw me a map to my ranch, I could rent a horse and ride out this afternoon."

He made no attempt to conceal his horror. "You're not serious. You're unfamiliar with the terrain and with horses too, I'll wager. You couldn't possibly make this trip without an escort."

For all his youth, the lawyer reminded me of Mr. Cameron, when I had told him of my intent to travel West. Or was this part of some unspoken agreement among men to shelter women from the harsher aspects of life on the frontier?

"All I need are directions," I said. "I've traveled this far on my own. I'm certain I can make it the rest of the way."

Jeremiah Brown said, "I'll be happy to escort you. In fact, in my capacity as your lawyer, I insist on it."

I didn't object. This would be a wiser course, and I suspected I would enjoy Mr. Brown's company.

I thanked him and asked, "When can we leave?"

"After lunch. I have to see what's in this pile of correspondence."

"There's one additional matter. As part of my inheritance, I have a certain sum in a Denver bank." As I spoke, I wrote the information Mr. Cameron had given me, together with his name and address. "Will you transfer the contents of the entire account into the bank in Silver Springs, except for this amount to repay a debt I owe Mr. Douglas Cameron?"

"I'll take care of it. Is there any other matter you'd like me to handle?"

"Except for reimbursing the gentleman who has been paying the taxes on Trail's End, for now, this is all. Shall I return at noon?"

"If you like, or I could call for you."

"I'll come back," I said. "I can't tell you how much I am looking forward to this excursion, Mr. Brown."

~ * ~

Instead of returning to the hotel, I wandered up and down Main Street, familiarizing myself with the various shops and businesses. An exploration of the general store occupied the better part of an hour.

This appeared to be a popular place where people came to meet and talk to one another as well as shop. I surveyed the shelves, noting that I could buy whatever necessity or luxury I had been accustomed to finding back in Michigan, although the items were more expensive here.

After purchasing a handsome book with long blank pages on which I could record my adventures, I resumed my tour of the town. I considered walking to the cemetery, but decided against it, since the time set for meeting Mr. Brown was approaching. As it happened, he was late, and I had a short wait in front of his office. At last he came around the corner in a large wooden wagon, pulled by two dark horses.

As he brought the vehicle to a stop, he said, "I apologize for the delay. Have you ever ridden in a buckboard, Miss Marsden?"

"No, this will be the first time."

He helped me up, and I settled myself beside him, eager for my first western ride to begin.

"Can you manage the reins?" he asked.

"I'm not sure, but I can learn."

As I reached for them, he laughed. "Not today. There's no need. I was only inquiring. I can see you're not the tenderfoot I was. Can you ride?"

"A little, but I haven't been on horseback lately." I paused, deciding to be strictly honest. "It's been several years."

"Western horses are different from what you're used to, but if you aren't afraid of falling, you shouldn't have any problems. That sun is warm. It's going to be a hot day."

"I love the weather here," I said. "Everything about the Territory is more wonderful than anything I could have imagined."

We were moving now, leaving Main Street, riding away from Silver Springs into the countryside. The breathtaking scenery made me long for a paintbrush and the talent to capture the landscape on canvas. Jeweled color veined the rocks, wildflowers splattered the ground with bright splashes of blue, and the sky was a vivid shade of cerulean filled with immense white clouds.

I was going to my home. A small part of this land was mine.

~ * ~

"We're on your property now," Mr. Brown said. "In a short while, you'll see for yourself the sad state of the house, but this is magnificent land. If you're serious about wanting to make a home here, my advice is to have the present structure torn down and build a new, modern one."

"That's a good idea for the future."

As we drew nearer, I saw that Mr. Brown had spoken the truth. Jules Carron's house was a desolate log structure set down in a virtual wilderness. The outbuildings were a collection of ruins, and the entire scene was reminiscent of a settlement lost in time.

World's End might be a more appropriate name for the place. Had Jules Carron's life ended within its walls? I wasn't so fanciful as to think that the house was haunted, but I sensed something unhappy about Trail's End. It hovered in the very air. I could almost believe that a shadowy presence beckoned to me.

What an absurd notion! Perhaps I would discover the nature of Jules Carron's connection with my mother here, but surely nothing more.

"I hope the key still works," I said.

"Are you certain you want to go inside?" Mr. Brown asked. "Please reconsider. The structure is uninhabitable, and it may be dangerous. The roof may collapse on us or the flooring give way."

"We don't have to go far inside. If you wish, you can stay in the buckboard."

"You know I won't do that, Miss Marsden. Prepare yourself for cobwebs and vermin then, and maybe a nest of snakes."

I said, "I'm not easily dissuaded, although that tangle of vegetation around the house looks dangerous."

Mr. Brown helped me down from the buckboard, and we plowed through a veritable jungle of high grasses and weeds, managing to reach the sagging front porch without mishap. He preceded me up the stairs, taking cautious steps and avoiding areas that looked unstable.

At last I was about to enter my future home. "This is the gloomiest house I've ever seen, but when it was new, it must have been handsome. It's no ordinary cabin. I detect a trace of style in the design."

Taking my hand, Mr. Brown said, "You have a lively imagination, Miss Marsden. I see a ruin. Watch where you step. Follow me."

I waited behind him, as he struggled to turn the key in the rusty lock and push open the heavy door. As we went inside into a rush of stagnant air and dust, I heard a faint scampering away at our approach.

"Mice or rats," he said. "I hope you won't be afraid."

"No, unless one bites me. Andy at the Silver Palace has a cat. Maybe I could borrow her."

Jeremiah Brown brushed a handful of cobwebs from his face. "It's like walking into a tomb, although I've never done that. There's an unpleasant odor here."

"It's nothing that soap, water, and fresh air can't remedy, but I hope no animals have ventured in here to die through the years."

"Have you seen enough, Miss Marsden?" he asked.

We hadn't taken a dozen steps inside, but already I felt as if a hundred dust particles were clinging to the exposed areas of my skin.

"Not really. I suppose the rest of the house is like this one room."

"Or worse."

I had expected to find the furniture covered with sheets but saw no sign of any such care. If Jules Carron had died alone here, who would have packed away his possessions and preserved his furniture for the heir? All appeared to be as he had left it, only covered in a decade's accumulation of dust.

But Jules Carron hadn't lived alone. What happened to the foreman or partner? Had he died as well or moved on?

"You'll agree that the house should be torn down," Mr. Brown said. "I think some of it is ready to fall now. Shall we go?" He took a few tentative steps toward the door and stood there, waiting for me to join him.

"It doesn't look as if it could be easily renovated."

"I'd say it can't be salvaged at all."

"I don't agree, Mr. Brown, but there's nothing to be done today. I think I'll leave further exploration for a later date."

I felt that the solution to the mystery that haunted me lay within these walls. I had drawn my own mental map of the way we'd come and intended to return tomorrow, as it was growing late. It wouldn't do to linger in such an isolated place with a gentleman, even if he was my lawyer. We had a long ride back to Silver Springs and Jeremiah Brown was obviously anxious to leave and not place me in a compromising situation.

Where did that thought come from? I reminded myself that nobody knew me in this town. Who would notice or care that I'd stolen away with an attractive man to a house at the end of the world?

Nevertheless, with the greater part of the day gone, I was loath to remain at Trail's End. I followed my escort through the door, over the forest of grass and weeds, to the waiting buckboard and thanked him warmly for his time and company.

As he helped me up, he asked, "May I call on you in the near future, Miss Marsden, not as your lawyer, but as a friend?"

"Why, yes, of course, Mr. Brown. That would be lovely," I said.

I hoped he wouldn't realize that his request had come as a surprise to me, that I thought of him only in the most casual sort of way. Perhaps friendship was all he intended. At some time, I would have to acquire more experience in affairs of the heart. I suspected I had come to the perfect place to accomplish this.

Five

That evening, in my room at the Silver Palace, I occupied myself with more mundane matters, such as dressing for dinner. Wishing I had a larger, more varied selection, I took my green silk out of the trunk and laid it on the bed.

I would wear my pearls tonight. They always looked new and elegant, and the misty shade of the gown would complement my coloring, especially the dark chestnut of my hair and the flecks of green in my eyes.

When I'd finished dressing, I was pleased with my appearance and ready to venture again into the dining room, which was no longer an unknown territory for me.

I waited until six o'clock and then walked down the stairs to the first floor. Moving through the bustling lobby, I searched for a familiar face but didn't see anyone I knew. That was all right. With every solitary entrance, I would gain more confidence in moving through my days as an independent woman.

As I settled myself at my table, a less secluded one tonight, I felt as if I were at home.

You are, I told myself. *You belong in this town now.*

No sooner was I seated than Jeremiah appeared at my table with the brown-haired rancher of last night. I noted that my lawyer's companion was wearing his camel vest again, although his shirt was a deeper shade of blue than the one he'd had on yesterday. And how I could be so certain of that?

Forcing my gaze away from the rancher, I said, "Good evening, Mr. Brown." To my dismay, my feelings of insecurity came rushing back, along with a shyness I thought I'd left behind years ago.

"Good evening. Will you join us at our table, Miss Marsden? My friend is Mr. Emmett Grandison. I'd like you two to get acquainted."

"I'd be happy to," I said and looked up at the man who had observed me intently on two occasions.

Since he stood so close to me, I could study his face at leisure. He certainly was handsome in a rugged, thoroughly western way. I felt myself especially drawn to his eyes.

I couldn't decide whether they were gray or blue. Most likely they changed their color as his mood or position shifted. Tonight, he stood under an elaborate crystal chandelier, and they held glints of gold. I imagined they could also grow as dark as a stormy sky, but I had been staring at Mr. Grandison far too long. Jeremiah Brown was waiting for me to rise.

"I've already ordered my dinner," I said.

"It doesn't matter. The waiter will find you."

He pushed back my chair and, with his hand on my shoulders, gently steered me to a larger table in the center of the room.

"There," he said. "Emmett is your neighbor, Miss Marsden. His ranch adjoins your property."

So the man I'd been admiring was the antagonist who coveted my land. His interest was in Trail's End.

I was unprepared for the pang of disappointment that struck like an unexpected thunderbolt, but I rebounded instantly. Mr. Emmett Grandison couldn't possibly have known my identity or my reason for coming to Silver Springs yesterday. He had looked at me with admiration then, or so I fancied.

No sooner had I completed this thought than another, less flattering one formed. Now that this man knew who I was, he might think of me as a naïve woman from the other side of the country who could be cajoled out of hundreds of acres.

Don't count on it, Mr. Grandison, I thought.

In a pleasant, even voice I said, "You'll be close by. That's good to know. You must call me Mara, Emmett, and you too, Jeremiah. I feel as though we're already friends."

I summoned a smile for my newfound neighbor. I was certain that Jeremiah had given him what few details he knew about my background, but I resolved to be careful about revealing anything more.

Jeremiah said, "Mara and I drove out to Trail's End today, Emmett. She made it more of a visit than I would have liked. I think I still have cobwebs on me."

"Did you ever go inside the ranch house, Emmett, living so close to it?" I asked.

For a man who I assumed wanted to meet me, Emmett Grandison hadn't uttered a single word yet. Now he said, "Was never any need to, Miss Mara. My own ranch keeps me busy."

As he spoke, I tried to identify his accent. It sounded Southern but wasn't quite a drawl. I wasn't sure. My knowledge of different ways of speaking wasn't extensive, and people came to the Territories from all over the United States and other countries as well. Perhaps when I knew Mr. Grandison better, I could ask him.

"When you're ready to sell Trail's End, Mara, Emmett will take it off your hands," Jeremiah said. "How soon will that be, do you think?"

I tried to hold on to my smile. How sure of himself he was, this too-attractive rancher with the gray-blue eyes. He must be wealthy already, although his way of dressing didn't suggest affluence. At the moment he had the smug look of a man who has completed a successful business deal.

"Oh, but Trail's End isn't for sale, Mr. Grandison," I said. "I've decided to fix it up and live there. It's my home now."

They didn't believe me. In truth I surprised myself, for my present plans hadn't gone beyond a second, more thorough exploration of the house. However, I didn't care for the expression of incredulous surprise on Emmett's face. I imagined I also detected a flicker of delight in his eyes, but it left so quickly I might have been mistaken.

"But you decided to build a new house, if you stay," Jeremiah said.

"I considered it, but renovation might still be possible. Perhaps all Trail's End needs is soap and water. And a hammer and nails."

"You can't be serious," Jeremiah said. "A woman from back East on her own could never take on such a project."

"Technically, I'm from the Midwestern United States, and I might have to hire help. But I'm fairly certain that in time I can transform the place into a home."

"It's a preposterous notion," he said.

Emmett, who had been so silent at first, didn't hesitate to speak now.

"Jeremiah's right, Miss Mara. You can't live alone in a derelict old house out in the middle of nowhere. You saw it for yourself today. Besides, a woman needs a man alongside her in this country." So saying, he looked down at his plate, as if he had said more than he'd intended.

Once Mr. Cameron had said something similar to me. Even a former lieutenant in the Union army had spoken in a less commanding tone. I had proved him wrong. I would do the same with Emmett Grandison.

"You're my neighbor, Mr. Grandison," I said. "How could I be afraid with a man like you living nearby?"

"I'm nowhere near Trail's End."

Emmett was working himself up into a near rage. His eyes had more gray than blue in them. They seemed to contain miniature storm clouds.

"My ranch is neighborin' to yours, yes, but I'm a good hour's ride from Trail's End. More. Can you ride a horse?"

"Of course, I can. I'm an experienced horsewoman."

"Can you fire a gun?"

"Not yet, but I'm going to learn. Where is the town gunsmith located?"

Emmett banged his cup down on the table, and coffee spilled out onto the white cloth.

"Whoever let you out to roam around unattended?" he demanded. "You don't know the first thing about livin' in the West."

I struggled to hold onto my temper. "I'll learn everything I need to know. Let's not argue. I wonder when they'll bring our dinner."

Jeremiah said, "Whether you keep the old house or have it torn down, it's fortunate for our town bachelors that you plan a long stay, Mara. Women are a scarce commodity in the Territory. We aim to keep the ones we have."

Emmett stared at him. He had mopped up coffee with his napkin. Now he held the wet cloth in midair as if unsure where to place it.

"Isn't there a man back East waitin' for you?" he asked.

"I came out West alone, and this is my home. But I already said that. You'll have to look elsewhere for more land. Mine isn't for sale." I added, "I understand you've been paying the property taxes. Jeremiah will see to it that you're reimbursed."

I was braced for a thunderous rejoinder from the stormy Emmett Grandison, but it didn't materialize.

Instead he said, "You have the prettiest eyes I ever saw on a person, Miss Mara. They're like the green grass growin' over on the ranch."

"Why, thank you, Mr. Grandison."

"You were goin' to call us Emmett and Jeremiah."

"Yes, of course. Emmett, then."

Our food finally arrived, and we suspended conversation while we ate the meal. The mood grew progressively lighter, and Emmett was soon in so convivial a mood that I decided to tease him.

"Since you have the most prosperous ranch in the Territory, Emmett, perhaps you'll sell me a few head of cattle so that I can start a herd. I'd like one of your horses, along with the loan of a cowboy or two."

Hastily Jeremiah said, "In the meantime, while you're making a final decision, we have a few respectable houses right here in town where you would be welcome. I can think of three fine ladies who would be happy to have you join their households."

I couldn't imagine a more dismal prospect. "I have a comfortable room in the hotel. I don't see the need to be a paying guest in another woman's house."

"The Palace is a good, safe place for you, but even in town, you'd better let me or Jeremiah escort you," Emmett said. "You can't go strollin' out like you do back East."

"I'm from the Midwest, remember, and I'm not afraid."

This wasn't strictly true. I hadn't yet forgotten my most recent fear.

"There is something though," I said. "On the train I heard some terrifying stories about Indians. One of my fellow passengers assured me that they live on reservations now."

"That's true," Jeremiah said. "You might run into one who strayed away or a rough man lonely for company. As a general rule, cowboys are respectful of women, but Emmett's right. You can't go roaming around alone."

Entering the spirit of the discussion, Emmett added, "And there's the Swinging Lady Gang. Don't forget them, Jeremiah. They're making themselves heard lately. Outlaws, I'm talkin' about, Miss Mara."

"If this is an attempt to subdue me by frightening me, it isn't fair," I said. "And it won't work."

Jeremiah looked stunned. "We would never do such a thing, Mara. We're only giving you an adequate picture of a woman's life on the frontier."

"A slightly slanted one, I think."

"We don't want to see you carried off by a gang of outlaws or, worse, captured by Indians," Emmett said.

His eyes were like storm clouds still. Thunder speaking with a drawl—that was Emmett Grandison. Fortunately, gun belts weren't part of his attire tonight, as I wasn't sure whether he wanted to court me or shoot me. Or perhaps he'd prefer to strangle me with his coffee-soaked napkin.

During the rest of our meal, we conversed civilly, and eventually I had the pleasure of seeing the dark look leave Emmett's eyes. This man was an electrifying blend of sunshine and storm. With a mere look, he made me feel more alive than I had ever been. That was a desirable state, but it was also a dangerous one.

It was time to end the evening. I needed to be alone to reflect on the new emotions that made my heart race and flooded my body with warmth.

"I'll say goodnight to you both now. Thank you for your company. It's been a very enjoyable evening."

"Shall I escort you back to your room?" Jeremiah asked.

"Oh, no, thank you. I'll be fine."

With a smile and one last look at the glowering Emmett Grandison, I rose and walked out of the dining room, hoping my companions hadn't noticed the change that had come over me. Usually I prided myself on being even-tempered and serene, two qualities my mother said every lady should possess. Tonight she wouldn't have known me.

~ * ~

The next morning I prepared to strike out on my own, as Andy would say. Jeremiah would be working in his law office, and Emmett would probably be at his ranch, leaving no one to wonder where I'd gone or question the propriety of my expedition.

I remembered Emmett's warning about a gang of outlaws but didn't believe he was serious. Both men had spoken of Silver Springs as a civilized town where law and order were respected, along with education and even culture.

My plan was to hire a buckboard and drive out to Trail's End. I remembered the way Jeremiah had taken us yesterday. With the key in my possession, I would be able to let myself into the house. I intended to spend the entire day at Trail's End and would be back in Silver Springs long before sundown. Jeremiah and Emmett could disapprove all they liked. Chances were they'd never learn about my day's activity.

I stopped at the desk to ask Andy if he'd ever met a man named Jules Carron.

"I was out here in fifty-nine but away in the mine," he said. "I never saw Carron. Where are you off to so early, Miss Marsden?"

"I'm going exploring again. Would you be willing to lend me your cat for company?"

Before Andy could reply, she leaped off the desk and raced down the hall.

Well, a reprieve for the vermin of Trail's End. "I see she isn't interested in being sociable."

"Cats are like that," Andy said. "You have three gentlemen friends already. You won't be living in the Silver Palace long, Miss Marsden."

"I've only met one person and his friend. If you'll recall, Jeremiah Brown is my lawyer."

"Even so."

On my way out of the hotel, I remembered the third gentleman, Mike, who had helped me with my trunk. I hadn't seen him since my arrival. But how did Andy know about Emmett, and why would he think Jeremiah was my friend?

I concluded that Silver Springs was not a private place. I'd have to remember that.

~ * ~

Everything went according to plan. With a few leftover breakfast items wrapped in a napkin, I walked to the livery stable and arranged for the rental of a buckboard. Even the young man at the stable wanted to protect me.

"It's real rough country, ma'am," he said. "You oughtn't to go out alone. You sure you can handle horses?"

"I can manage these."

Yesterday on the way back to town, Jeremiah had allowed me to take the reins, and I'd driven us several miles without a problem. I had confidence I could do the same today. There must be something in the mountain air, an unknown quality that energized me and told me I could do anything I desired.

With a deep breath, I lifted myself up into the buckboard and took the reins in my hands. First I had to find my way out of town, and that proved to be the most difficult part of my venture.

Once I set myself on the road to Trail's End, however, I discovered that my memory of the route and its landmarks was accurate. The entire trip was unremarkable, except for the fact that I didn't encounter a single other traveler on the road. After an hour of solitary driving, I reached my destination.

My second glimpse of the house was much like my first. Wrapped in a silence that was almost tangible, this was an unhappy, abandoned place. Still, it seemed to beckon to me. I was determined to unearth whatever secrets might be hidden within its walls, but I had a sinking feeling that Trail's End would never be a home to me.

I left the buckboard in the shade of a massive, ancient tree and set my lunch on the porch. Taking out the key, I unlocked the heavy door and stepped across the threshold. Now, what should I do first?

A careful investigator would be sure she wouldn't be trapped inside. The air was still, without even a mild breeze. All the same, I wasn't taking any chances. Spying a heavy stool, I dragged it across the room to use as a doorstop.

Next I opened a window. The added light seemed to magnify every speck of dust that had collected during the last ten years. Soon I would have to return with a broom, rags, and soap. As for a water source, the property must include a well. I would have to locate it.

Housecleaning was not my immediate concern. I turned at once to the task of investigation. I thought I could create a picture of Jules Carron based on the objects with which he had surrounded himself.

In a corner was a roll top desk similar to the one in my father's study. The drawers were jammed with papers and small articles of every description. Here was the place to begin. Evidently Jules Carron had saved everything that came his way, but the writing appeared to relate to items associated with running the ranch. Some of it was in French.

When I came across a Bible, I felt certain that the solution to the mystery was at my fingertips, but I couldn't find a family tree inside, or even the name of an owner. It looked as if it had never been opened.

The next book I examined was a well-worn botanical guide printed in English and containing descriptions of the Territorial flora and their pictures. Now this was something I could use. Whenever I went walking or riding through the countryside, I would take it with me.

Suddenly a sound broke into my thoughts. Faint and indistinct, it was different from the insect chirrups that were so much a part of the outdoors scene that I didn't even hear them anymore.

Setting the book down, I listened, but there was nothing to hear now, not even the scampering of mice or rats. Nevertheless, I sensed that I was no longer alone. Someone was watching me, outside the house or perhaps in one of the rooms.

Emmett's warning came back to me. Had I been followed to this lonely place by someone who wished me harm? I'd been too self-assured, even arrogant, and now I was going to suffer for it.

I remembered to breathe. Outside the horses were quiet. That should be a sign that all was well. I could account for whatever sounds I heard. Gradually, the feeling of being watched receded, but I decided to make a hasty search of the rest of the house and head back to Silver Springs, just in case something was lurking outside the cabin.

I thought of Emmett and his gray-blue eyes filled with merriment. He would roar with laughter if he could see me now.

~ * ~

I found the portrait inside a massive, ornate armoire that was large enough to conceal a person during an Indian raid. As I pulled open its right door, I came face to face with a likeness of myself.

The girl in the painting was wearing a simple blue gown in a style that had been in vogue before the War. Since she so closely resembled me, I surmised that I was looking at the face of my mother when she was younger.

She stood on the lawn of a pillared Southern plantation house under a tree dripping with Spanish moss. Her hand rested on the head of a large white dog. She was a long way from Pineville.

I took the portrait over to the window to study it by daylight. It was medium in size and framed in an oval made of material that resembled twisted cords of silver. It appeared to be work of a skilled artist who had captured her loveliness on the canvas, along with her grace and gentle nature.

I recalled that my mother had often expressed her aversion to travel. If she had ever gone down South, I thought she would have told me. But she had kept other secrets. A slim possibility existed that whoever painted the portrait had set his subject against an imaginary background.

I knew that my mother could never have come to this house in the Colorado Territory. In 1860 the structure was already standing or in the process of being built. In that year, my mother had nursed me through pneumonia. She couldn't have been in two places at the same time, living separate lives.

Or could she? In this house, her presence seemed real to me and near. In one more minute, I would be imagining the scent of roses.

I forced my thoughts back to present concerns. The portrait represented one more mystery. By my watch, I had been searching for almost two hours and hadn't found any answers. It was time to leave.

I pushed the stool to one side, locked the door, and noticed my lunch that I'd forgotten to eat. I tossed it into the high grass for the birds or whatever hungry creature was the first to discover it. A glance at the sky told me it was later than I thought, and I started moving faster. The ride to Silver Springs was long, and I wanted to reach my destination before dark.

I took my mother's portrait with me. As I drove along, I became so distracted by memories and wild speculations that I could hardly force myself to concentrate on the route. I only hoped I wouldn't give Emmett Grandison the satisfaction of knowing I'd gotten lost.

Six

I arrived in Silver Springs at a respectable hour and without incident. As soon as I returned to the hotel, I locked the portrait in my trunk. Then I attempted to restore my appearance by bathing my face in cold water and brushing the dust of the trail from my hair.

Revived and dressed in clean clothing, I went down to the lobby where I sat alone, pondering the significance of the day's major discovery. Jules Carron might have met my mother in any number of ways and held on to her portrait as a sentimental remembrance of the past, or he might have been in love with her. I had no way of knowing.

How did she feel about him? Again, I had no answer. I remembered my childhood as an endless stream of happy days. My mother's activities were largely of a domestic nature, her great joys being needlework and roses. I couldn't imagine her pining for a lost lover, but it wasn't an impossibility.

Had Jules Carron hoped that one day she would be the one to travel to Trail's End and find the portrait? This sounded more like the plot of a romance novel than life.

Countless other questions clamored to be answered. Did he know of my mother's marriage? I would have to search in the cemetery for the exact date of his death, but it was reasonable to suppose that when he named her in his will, he didn't know she had died. Was my father aware of their connection? Could he have known Jules Carron?

No one was left alive to answer my questions. In my frustration, I resolved that if ever I had children, I wouldn't keep secrets from them.

Delving into past mysteries soon grew tiring, and I longed for a new diversion. Perhaps a short walk would be the best way to fill the time remaining until dinner. With a welcome sense of purpose, I drew my shawl closer about my shoulders and slipped quietly out the door.

The day was perfect for a leisurely stroll. Since my arrival in Silver Springs, the weather had been ideal, with moderate temperatures, warm sunshine, and no heavy rainfall. I thought about Nicholas' sister. This was the best possible climate for a woman who was in poor health, or for someone like me, looking for a new part of the country to call home.

I'd never intended to heed Emmett's warning about venturing out alone in Silver Springs. Without the encumbrance of an escort, I could take any direction I chose and stop when I grew tired or desired a change of activity. Glorying in a heady sense of freedom, I walked on, more intent on seeing sights than memorizing directions. Gradually I wandered into a rougher part of town.

Coming to a standstill at a corner, I made an attempt to orient myself. From a saloon named the Lost Duchess, the merriest music imaginable spilled out into the air, along with laughter and shouting, all of these sounds mixing together to suggest that the people inside were having a rousing good time.

The Lost Duchess was a tempting destination, but I wasn't reckless enough to venture inside unescorted. Turning to walk in a different direction, I almost stumbled over a bundle of fur blocking the middle of the sidewalk. The obstacle was a small black and white dog, a bony and filthy creature that whined and stared at me with a wary, yet beseeching look in its dark eyes. I reached down to touch it, but it rose awkwardly and limped down the street.

While I was occupied with the animal, two brightly dressed and bejeweled women emerged from the Lost Duchess. Entranced by their glittering attire, I watched as they approached two cowboys who were tying their horses to a post. After a few seconds of talking and laughter, the women went back inside, taking their new friends with them.

Wishing I could follow them into the light and the music, I took a step forward. At that moment, I saw Nicholas.

He came out of the Lost Duchess and paused to consult his pocket watch. Without looking around, he walked off briskly in the direction taken by the dog.

The man was definitely Nicholas. I, who had studied his features discreetly during the long hours on the train, could never mistake him for another. Obviously he hadn't seen me, and something about him was different. He had changed his way of dressing. Now he wore the same kind of clothing as most of the other men in Silver Springs.

What was he doing here? Setting aside the axiom that a lady doesn't pursue a gentleman unless she is in the profession of doing so, I set out to overtake him. He had a head start, however, and moved much faster than I could. Eventually, he turned down a narrow side street where the shabby dwellings were draped in shadows.

Pausing to catch my breath, I saw that I had wandered even farther away from the more populated area of town. The sounds of shouting coming from a building above me were more indicative of a brawl than revelry. I heard a woman's scream, a burst of tipsy laughter, and a child's wail. I couldn't see Nicholas.

Slow down, I told myself. Think. Nicholas was emphatic about his two-week stay in Denver. Could he have changed his plans, his way of dressing, and, most important of all, his intention of contacting me when he arrived in Silver Springs? Was it possible that I was mistaken, that the man wasn't Nicholas after all?

As I pondered my next move, I noticed two strangers approaching me. They were rougher in appearance than any of the men I'd seen thus far, with heavily bearded faces and malice in their manner. An Indian stood behind them.

According to Jeremiah, cowboys were respectful of women, but lonely men looking for female companionship were a force to be reckoned with. I, of course, had blithely ignored the warning.

My heart beat rapidly, and my thoughts spun around in a mad fashion. I wasn't afraid of the cowboys, who now addressed me in a familiar manner, but the Indian terrified me.

How could I have been so foolish to follow Nicholas into peril?

The dangerous situation I anticipated didn't materialize. The men invited me to accompany them into the Lost Duchess. When I didn't respond, they simply laughed and went into the saloon without me.

That left me alone on the street with the Indian who might still pose a threat. With his long black hair and burning eyes, he looked ferocious. My imagination, always ready to take off in a gallop, added a tomahawk and garish face paint.

One step at a time, at first slowly, then rapidly, I began to walk away. A quick glance over my shoulder told me that the Indian wasn't following me. My main priority was to find my way back to Main Street, which I thought I would be able to do.

Then I saw Nicholas again, ahead of me, about to round a corner. I called his name. In the sudden stillness, my voice sounded unnaturally soft.

He kept walking, and that was the end of the matter for me. I couldn't follow him. I wouldn't. Surely he had seen or heard me, but had failed to recognize me, or, more likely, had done so and chosen to ignore me.

That was so painful a conclusion that I reached blindly for another one.

Maybe the man wasn't Nicholas at all but his double. The real Nicholas Breckinridge was still in Denver, where he said he would be. I grasped for an explanation that wouldn't show me in such a foolish light, but I felt it wasn't true.

All I had for my efforts was a thoroughly muddled idea of my present location. I set off in a few wrong directions but soon recognized the buildings that lined the way to the Silver Palace. I hoped that Emmett, who was undoubtedly savoring his dinner in the hotel dining room, would never know how foolish and shameless I'd been.

At a fast pace, I set off for the edge of town. With my eyes fixed on my destination, I didn't see the small missile until it crashed into my legs, its agonized yelp lost in the slamming of a door. The black and white dog bounced off my body and landed in the dust. Whimpering in pain, it made a frantic, futile attempt to get up and lay down again, panting but otherwise very still. She was a female, and her distress tore at my heart.

In my softest voice, I said, "You poor little thing. Don't be afraid. I'm going to take care of you."

She whined but didn't move.

Although I knew the danger in approaching a wounded animal, I couldn't keep away from her. She, however, had other ideas. Still whimpering, she managed to rise on three shaky legs and one damaged one and limp away. Where she had lain I saw a small pool of blood.

With no thought of my recent misadventure, I set out after her.

From somewhere behind me I heard pounding hooves. I felt my arms close around fur barely stretched over bone just as a sharp pain exploded on the side of my head. The world came to a shuddering halt.

Through darkness and pain, I was aware of the soft bundle slipping out of my arms. A familiar voice shouted my name. I rolled over in the street and came to rest against a hard wooden surface.

Strong arms lifted me up. The hoof beats were now distant echoes, but I heard my name spoken in a voice I thought I recognized. A sense of safety wrapped itself around me. Everything was going to be all right now.

I whispered, "Nicholas?"

From the faraway place to which I'd gone, I heard the name repeated in a voice that sounded like thunder.

"Nicholas!"

The voice was filled with scorn, and I drifted away from the approaching storm, but I took my last vivid realization with me. Nicholas had led me into this danger and walked away.

Seven

I awoke to find myself looking into the dark gray-blue eyes of Emmett Grandison. I wasn't lying on the ground, but in a soft, warm bed. My head ached, and I thought I could still hear the pounding hoof beats.

For some unknown reason, Emmett was berating me soundly. I wondered what I had done to anger him. With a great effort, I willed myself away from the raging storm.

Above and around me swirled a deep male voice with a drawl and another one, much softer and smoother. It reminded me of sun-warmed syrup and honey.

"Emmett, quit carrying on so. Let her rest. Go home."

I agreed. That was a good idea. I slept; but when I woke up again, Emmett still sat at my bedside in the pool of light cast by the kerosene lamp on the table. It must be the middle of the night.

He was staring into space. Next to him, an older lady sat at her sewing, her skirts almost hidden by lengths of deep pink material. She was a pretty woman, silver-haired and blue-eyed. I thought she might be Emmett's mother.

When she became aware that I was awake and watching her, she set the rosy folds of fabric aside and came to the bedside.

"You're awake at last, child. How do you feel?"

"Not very well."

I reached for my watch and saw that it was half past ten. As I did this, I realized that I was wearing a white nightgown. My face grew warm as I wondered whether Emmett had been banished from the room at any time.

The lady said, "I'm Miss Eulalie Langlinais. You're going to stay with me for a few days until you recover, but you'll be fine."

I was in a small cozy room that was plainly but comfortably furnished. Emmett still glowered at me from the shadows. I was thankful that he was silent.

Memories came back to me, tumbling over one another in a confusion of noise, darkness, and pain. I saw again the shadowy, unfamiliar street and myself following Nicholas, trying to capture the wounded dog, and landing in the path of what must have been a runaway team of horses. I could surmise what had happened and feel the inevitable effects as I tried to sit up.

"No, honey," Miss Eulalie said. "Lie back down now."

"Was the dog killed?" I asked.

Emmett jumped up, and I could almost see storm clouds gathering around him. He towered over me, appearing to have grown to a height of seven feet.

"You almost died tonight because of that mutt, and you're asking about him?"

"She was a female," I said. "Were you there?"

I didn't remember seeing Emmett, but someone with strong arms had lifted me out of the street and held me, a man who wasn't Nicholas.

"Did you rescue the dog, too?" I asked.

If he replied, I didn't hear him. The room suddenly turned into a churning sea on which Miss Eulalie and Emmett slowly floated away.

"You can't get out of bed tonight, honey," Miss Eulalie said. "Doctor Westbrook would be furious with me."

Emmett added, "The doctor thinks you're a fool, but you'll live, if you get some sense."

"Now, Emmett, he didn't say any such thing."

Miss Eulalie was right. It was far easier to rest my head on the pillow than attempt to rise. Since I'd awakened, my headache had grown worse. Now my entire body hurt as well.

I found the strength to ask one question. "What happened to the dog?"

In the long pause that followed my inquiry, I thought no one was going to answer me.

Then Miss Eulalie said, "You could go back to that street and look for it, Emmett."

"All right, I will." He was shouting again. "It's almost eleven, but I'll go look for the dog in the dark." He stamped out of the room. Minutes later I heard the front door slam shut.

I couldn't believe what I had heard. Who would shout at a kind lady like Miss Eulalie or at someone who was lying helpless in bed, recovering from a nasty accident?

"Don't mind Emmett, child," Miss Eulalie said. "He's a trifle upset. I've been wanting him to find a wife for years now. If only I were ten years younger, I'd marry him myself. Any girl around here would wed him in an instant, but he's only interested in that ranch of his."

What possible answer could I make to this speech? I wondered if I had been brought to a madhouse.

As Miss Eulalie rambled on in her slow Southern manner, she revealed her affection for Emmett in everything she said. Not appreciating his domineering manner toward me, I didn't share her feelings.

She said, "Then tonight, he appears on my doorstep with you in his arms, and I know why he hasn't found a wife before. It wasn't destined to be."

So I had been brought here by fate in the guise of Emmett Grandison. The idea was unlikely, but amusing. I suspected that I would soon be asleep, lulled by Miss Eulalie's soothing voice. That would be preferable to listening to a recitation of Emmett's virtues.

For the first time I noticed the teapot on the table beside my bed and the empty cup and saucer. My mother had always brought me tea when I was ill. I felt as if I were eleven years old again. To my horror, my eyes filled with tears.

I willed myself to think about Emmett instead of weeping. Having saved my life, he undoubtedly thought he had the right to rail at me. As soon as I was stronger, he would learn that he was mistaken.

"He's so dictatorial, Miss Eulalie. His shouting has made my headache worse."

"It's his way, child. He's a good man, the best in the Territory."

"Is he your son?"

"Oh, Emmett is no actual kin of mine."

Belatedly, I remembered her remark about marrying him.

"Emmett hails from Texas, and I'm from Louisiana. We found each other after the War when I came out to the Territory. He is like a son to me, though."

Since Miss Eulalie had come from Louisiana, I thought she might be able to answer a question for me, but I couldn't remember what it was. Then I was asleep.

~ * ~

The next morning, I insisted on getting up and was relieved to know I could do so, although at first every move I made caused me pain. My trunk had mysteriously appeared in my room. That was Emmett's doing, Miss Eulalie said.

He'd gone to the Silver Palace and brought it back late last night. His presumption amazed me, but I was glad to have my possessions. I opened the trunk at once and, lifting out the portrait, set it on the floor against the table.

"That scene fairly makes me homesick," Miss Eulalie said with a sigh. "I miss those oaks above all. How pretty you are, Mara. But no, of course that isn't you. Is the lady a relative of yours?"

"It's a likeness of my mother painted many years ago when she was young."

"Yes, before the War. You resemble her. Was she from the South?"

"No, but the portrait was painted there." That might be true, for all I knew.

Miss Eulalie let the matter drop there and said she'd see me for breakfast in twenty minutes, if I felt strong enough to get dressed and go downstairs.

"I'm sure I will," I said. "I don't want to lie in bed a second longer than necessary."

The long rest had revived me, and I was able to put on a dress, although it took me twice as long as usual. By the time I brushed my hair and tied it with a length of green ribbon, I felt new and fresh. To be sure, every one of my motions reminded me of last night's accident, but since I was alive and able to take care of myself, at the moment I wasn't going to ask for more.

My long sleeves covered my battered arms, but nothing could hide the large bruise on the side of my face. Miss Eulalie said the horses hadn't trampled me, only knocked me to the side of the street.

I glanced at my reflection in Miss Eulalie's small oval mirror and frowned. The accident was entirely my fault. I should have looked where I was going before dashing after the dog. If I intended to survive my first days in the Territory, from now on I would have to be more careful.

Emmett voiced a similar sentiment later, when he joined us for breakfast with the dispirited little canine in his arms. He had knotted a rope around her neck as a collar. When I reached out to touch her, she whined in a friendly manner.

Emmett showed me his hands. They were liberally covered with scratches.

"Both of you were lucky you're not dead. You've got to look at what's comin' before you run out in front of a wagon. This young pup's a right mean one. She snapped at me and scratched me, too. Her leg isn't broken, but she'll favor it for a while. It sure was a struggle breakin' her."

He set the little creature on my lap.

"She isn't a horse," I said. "Do you suppose she belongs to somebody?"

"It was after midnight when I found her, Miss Mara. I didn't go knockin' on doors to inquire if someone lost a dog. You almost paid for her with your life. I reckon she's yours."

"A dog in the house is nice," Miss Eulalie said. "I had one myself until last year. The poor thing."

She poured Emmett a cup of the dark rich brew she was drinking.

"This is real Louisiana coffee," Miss Eulalie said. "Emmett brought it all the way from New Orleans last year. Would you like some?"

She had already made a pot of tea for me, and I was drinking my second cup.

"Later, perhaps," I said. "When I'm stronger."

She poured milk into a bowl and added bits of broken bread for the puppy. We watched in fascination as the mixture rapidly vanished.

"I'm going to keep her," I said. "You found her around midnight, Emmett? That's what I'll name her."

"She'll be a pretty little creature when she's fattened up," Miss Eulalie said.

I lifted her and she settled down happily on my lap, licking drops of milk from her chops. "A thorough washing will make a difference, too. Didn't Mr. Grandison feed you last night, Midnight?"

"I took her home with me," Emmett said. "Of course I gave her somethin' to eat. She slept in the bunkhouse, so likely she had two dinners. Miss Eulalie, you can fatten up both of them."

He turned to me, and his tone changed. "What were you doin' out alone in that particular part of town, Miss Mara?"

I poured more tea in the cup. "I went for a walk and lost my way. Yes, I know what you said. I was regretful as soon as I remembered your warning, but by then it was too late."

My concession silenced him. It occurred to me that it would be an easy matter to handle this volatile man, but he wasn't finished with his tirade.

"You shouldn't have gone anywhere near the Lost Duchess."

"You were there."

Before he could reply, I hurried on. "Then I thought I saw a friend of mine, but I was mistaken."

"I thought you didn't know anyone in town, Miss Mara."

This man sounded more lawyer-like than Jeremiah Brown.

"I don't remember saying that. I've met a few people, but this person wasn't a native of Silver Springs. He was a gentleman I met on the train."

I didn't want to talk about Nicholas. Now that I was feeling better, I remembered every detail of the incident that had preceded my accident. Last night I was convinced that he had led me into danger. In the morning light, I realized how unlikely this was.

Assuming the man was Nicholas, he couldn't know that I would follow him and rush out into the path of a runaway team in an attempt to catch a dog. How convenient that Emmett had been on hand to come to my rescue, which was, now that I thought about it, a great coincidence.

"What were *you* doing in that part of town, Mr. Grandison?" I asked.

Quickly, Miss Eulalie broke into our conversation. "Have some more coffee, Emmett. I'll expect you back for dinner promptly at six. Mara is going to stay with me indefinitely. I *do* like her. You were right."

For the first time since I'd known him, Emmett looked ill at ease.

"I'm grateful for your offer, Miss Eulalie, but I couldn't do that," I said.

"What you can't do is live in that hotel alone, Mara, honey, a refined young lady like you. It simply isn't done. Emmett tells me you have an idea of fixing up Trail's End and living there. That's even worse than the Palace. There are other possibilities."

"At the moment, I can't think of any."

"I have a big house," she said. "Why, I have four rooms I never use, and I get so lonely. Oh, Emmett is a dear, but sometimes I want so much to have another woman to talk to about little things. Besides, Doctor Westbrook says you have to rest. You can't do that in a busy hotel."

Not wishing to appear ungrateful, I gave in. "If you're sure it won't be an inconvenience, I'd like to stay, but it'll only be for a few days."

"Of course," she said.

As I finished my tea, I pondered my new living arrangements. Only yesterday I had been driving through the Territorial countryside, following my own pursuits. Today I was installed in a respectable house in town. Jeremiah's suggestion had become a reality.

~ * ~

After Emmett left, Miss Eulalie fetched her sewing and settled herself in the parlor. Midnight lay down at her feet and promptly went to sleep. I made myself comfortable in a chair in front of the window with a view of the street outside, but for some reason, I felt like crying again. The house was quiet, the atmosphere tranquil, but some vital force appeared to be missing.

Miss Eulalie loved to talk. Her softly accented voice was the most soothing sound I'd ever heard. Listening to her, I thought of fruits and flowers that were rich and smooth and warmed by the sun. Gradually, my melancholy fell away.

As if she could read my thoughts about Emmett, she said, "He's really taken with you, honey."

I didn't believe her. A gentleman who wanted to impress a lady would surely speak to her with civility, as Nicholas had, but I didn't want to think about Nicholas today.

"I don't agree. Emmett thinks I'm a fool. He said so. He wanted to buy my land. I'm sure he still does."

"He was real upset last night. I don't think he knows how to take you. You're different from the girls around here. There aren't many of them."

Miss Eulalie held up the garment she had been fashioning from the pink material. Since this morning, it had taken on a definite shape. She was sewing lace trim to the bodice.

"This dress is for Annabelle Westbrook, the doctor's granddaughter. She set her cap for Emmett ages ago, but he never looked her way, for all that she's a pretty little thing. I couldn't see her on his ranch, though. I guess he can't either."

This talk of Emmett Grandison and his romantic aspirations was growing wearisome. I searched for a safer topic. "Are you a seamstress?" I asked.

"I sew for a few ladies in Silver Springs. It's a pleasant way to pass the time and have a small income."

"I'd like to have a few dresses made, perhaps three. The one I wore yesterday is ruined. I'm glad my shawl survived the accident."

"You shall have them then. For you, we'll need blues and greens. Pink is for the Annabelle's of the world."

"The colors of the grass and sky will suit me admirably," I said.

Although Miss Eulalie didn't talk much about herself, a few stray facts found their way into our conversation. She had come to the Colorado Territory because she was alone and the idea of a new life in an adventurous place appealed to her. In that one way, we were alike.

"My family were all dead," she said. "The gentleman I might have married was killed in Mississippi. At the time I wanted nothing more than to leave the South, but every now and then, even after all these years; I get homesick for New Orleans."

I learned more about Emmett. According to Miss Eulalie, who might be prejudiced in his favor, he was the most successful and the richest rancher in the Territory. He was the one who kept the property surrounding her house neat, and he was always on hand when repairs needed to be done.

"He's like a son to me, the one I never had," she said.

I began to see another side of Emmett Grandison. Although he was busy running his ranch, he had time to help Miss Eulalie and to find a lost dog because it mattered to me.

"Don't cross Emmett," she said. "I can tell you're a headstrong young lady. Women today have so much freedom. I can't bear to think about you wandering unattended in that deplorable district. I do hope things work out for you and Emmett."

"You're a dedicated matchmaker, but I don't think that's likely. I've heard that women are scarce in Silver Springs. Couldn't you find a husband for yourself and give up the dressmaking business?"

She set down her needle and laughed. "Why, honey, I do have a suitor, but he's much too old for me. You'll see him soon. He's Doctor Westbrook."

"You're the most delightful of landladies, Miss Eulalie. I can see why Emmett has established himself as your special protector."

"You're going to stay then? I'm so glad."

"For a while," I said. "A few more days. Then I have something I must do."

~ * ~

That night Emmett appeared for dinner, for the first time dressed in clothes such as Nicholas had worn on the train. Although he looked fine and handsome, his suit wasn't strictly modern in style. As I studied him discreetly, I decided that I preferred him in his camel vest and shirt, with his gun belts strapped on.

He was in a congenial mood, offering me a bouquet of wildflowers, complimenting Miss Eulalie on her dinner, and even making a fuss over Midnight.

"That dog looks improved, Miss Mara," he said. "Still all bones, though. You're lookin' right pretty tonight, too."

Miss Eulalie had found a green dress for me to wear. Simple but elegantly styled, it was all the more charming because it was slightly out of fashion.

As she had helped me with the row of tiny buttons, she'd said, "I made it for Miss Allegra Brimston, but she eloped to San Francisco before it was finished. It's been hanging in the closet for these five years. The fit is perfect, and the color brings out the green in your eyes."

Now I touched the green ribbon I'd twisted into my hair and decided I felt much better. Emmett's compliment had set my spirits soaring. Nicholas Breckinridge was a distant memory walking down a dark street, a man I hadn't truly known.

"Will you have some more pie, Emmett?" Miss Eulalie asked.

Emmett handed her his empty plate. "Yes, ma'am, thank you. There's no better pie baker in all of Silver Springs than Miss Eulalie."

"The berries grow wild on the Grandison ranch," she said. "I only made the crust."

Emmett said, "The beef came from my spread, too. Did you ever see a real working ranch, Miss Mara?"

"No, we have only farms in Michigan."

"I built the Grandison spread from two acres and a few cows. Your Trail's End isn't a ranch at all. Never was. Carron didn't do much but camp there, before the War and after. He wasn't a genuine rancher."

"Did you know him?" I asked.

"I never set eyes on him. When I came to Silver Springs, he was already dead. I was wonderin', Miss Mara. How did you come to inherit his place?"

"That's complicated, Emmett. It's a tale with many twists and no real end."

"It sounds like a good campfire story," he said.

"That's where I'll tell it, sometime in the future, if you build the fire."

"How exciting!" Miss Eulalie's enthusiasm was contagious. "Mara has brought new life to this old house. I can't thank you enough for bringing her here, Emmett."

"I'll take you ladies to the X Bar G on Sunday," Emmett said. "You can meet the hands, and we'll have some real Texas cooking. I have a special horse for you to see, Miss Mara. She reminds me a little of you."

A new sparkle seemed to dance amidst the gray-blue flecks in Emmett's eyes, piquing my curiosity. "Oh? In what way?"

"You'll have to wait till Sunday."

Miss Eulalie said, "I think I know the one. You're right again, Emmett."

"I'm going to look forward to it. Maybe one day Trail's End will be a real working ranch, too."

"You have a right wild imagination, Miss Mara," Emmett said.

"So I've been told. Thank you for the compliment. Now, Miss Eulalie, did you ever happen to meet Jules Carron?"

"I didn't have the pleasure," she said. "I knew who he was, but after he came back from the War, he didn't encourage company. To my knowledge, he never came to town. There was no way we could have gotten acquainted."

I couldn't believe that in a town of four thousand people, I couldn't find one person who had known my benefactor. It was almost as if the whole of Silver Springs was involved in a conspiracy to keep Jules Carron a mystery.

Eight

I couldn't wait to return to Trail's End. The long hours of forced inactivity quickly turned from tiresome to unbearable, but I endured my two days of prescribed rest and dreamed of my ranch.

I began writing in my journal, recording my impressions of the town and the countryside, Trail's End, and the people I'd met. For my accident I used an entire page. But my mother's portrait was a constant reminder to me that I had scarcely begun my investigation. I had at least a hundred blank pages still to fill.

Sitting in Miss Eulalie's parlor on the second day after my accident, I thought about the gloomy old house and the secrets it held. Jules Carron might have kept a journal of his own or saved his correspondence. I had to make a more thorough search of his desk and also the armoire. Knowing what Emmett would think of my plan, and that Miss Eulalie would agree with him, I decided not to tell them.

On the third morning, I was wholly recovered. If I didn't reassert my independence soon, Miss Eulalie would smother me with attention. Since my unconventional arrival on her doorstep, we had become friends. This was an unexpected and welcome development, with certain drawbacks.

She called into the room as she passed through the hall.

"I'm taking the dress to Annabelle for a fitting. I'll be gone until after lunch, but there's meat in the kitchen and pie, whenever you get hungry. We're expecting Emmett for dinner. You might like to plan tonight's menu."

That I could do in a few minutes. My main endeavor would involve several hours.

Alone in the house with only Midnight to observe my perfidy, I slipped into a serviceable dark dress, wound my hair into a thick bun, and hung my watch around my neck. In the kitchen I wrapped a slice of pie in a napkin for a light lunch and wrote a note to Miss Eulalie explaining that I was going out with Midnight for a short excursion and might be late returning. I'd think of a more detailed explanation on the way home from Trail's End.

Since my accident I'd only been out of the house once for a moonlight stroll with Emmett. The sunshine and fresh air had the effect of a restorative tonic. At some point, my pain had diminished to a tolerable aching sensation, although the walk to the livery stable was more of an effort than I'd anticipated.

With a feeling of freedom and exhilaration, I ordered the buckboard and set out for Trail's End, once again my own mistress. Since I'd passed this way twice, the route to the ranch was familiar, although the trip seemed to take twice as long as it had on previous occasions. Perhaps I wasn't fully recovered as I'd thought.

"It's too late to turn back now, Midnight. We're almost there."

Bringing the little dog along was an inspiration. When I reached Trail's End, a canine's keen sense of smell and sharp teeth would be indispensable.

She was alert long before I spied the house in the distance. As we drew nearer, she set her ears high at attention and stared at the place as if she knew that something or someone was there, waiting for us. This wasn't a good sign.

As soon as I stopped the horses, she jumped down from the buckboard and ran up to the house, her small body almost sinking into the high grasses. I followed, and as I struggled to open the door, she made a thorough exploration of the porch, sniffing and wagging her tail. Once inside, she fell into a frenzy of yipping and soon disappeared down a dim hall.

I went straight to the armoire and started my search. There I found the relics of Jules Carron's years in the Confederate army: A tattered gray uniform retired with love and care, rust-encrusted pistols neatly lined up on a shelf, and a sword. His civilian clothes were here as well, none of them in wearable condition. The armoire had served in a strictly utilitarian capacity, although this was where he had kept my mother's portrait.

Next I moved to the roll top desk and examined his papers, eventually sorting them into two categories: One for those written in English and the other for French documents. The records supported Emmett's claim that Jules Carron had never managed Trail's End as a successful working ranch.

He had saved old receipts, maps, and sketches of the Territory, as well as battle scenes and fragile, old newspaper clippings giving news of the War from the Southern point of view. I set his drawings aside in their own stack. They were realistically detailed. I suspected that he was the artist who had painted the portrait of my mother.

I didn't see any personal correspondence, but found an enchanting silver nugget, apparently used as a paperweight. Holding it in my hand, I studied it with pleasure. At one time, Emmett said, silver had been more valuable in the Territory than gold.

"*That's how the town got its name*," he'd added.

The eerie feeling of being watched by unseen eyes came upon me gradually. When I thought I heard a muffled sound, almost a sigh, I held my breath and waited. Then I called Midnight's name.

Although I couldn't have said where she was at the moment, I thought that, being a canine, she would naturally sound the alarm at the approach of danger, whether from the real world or the one beyond. Maybe I was putting too much faith in her abilities.

I called to her again, more loudly. This time she was at my side in an instant with a few cobwebs attached to her coat and a playful sparkle in her eyes. As she awaited my bidding, her tail wagged enthusiastically.

I felt reassured. Of course Midnight would let me know if we weren't alone. That was what dogs did.

"Come," I said. "Outside."

She followed me to the porch where I looked around, hoping I wouldn't find anybody or anything lurking in the vicinity. All I could see was blue sky, a desolate green landscape, and horses resting in the shade. The hidden watcher must be a figment of my imagination or a fancy inspired by the dark, secretive rooms and old documents. In any event, the feeling was gone.

I shared a few bites of pie with Midnight and leaned against the railing, thinking about the items Jules Carron had left behind and trying to form a picture of the man. He had kept his uniform, pistols, and sword. According to Miss Eulalie, he hadn't encouraged company. Had he returned from the defeated South an embittered man with no future, content to wait for death? Perhaps he'd been gravely wounded or had some dread disease.

I considered Emmett. He had also served in the Confederate army, in a Texas unit. With pride, he'd told me that he came to the Territory to begin a new life. In the West he'd turned his few acres and cows into a prosperous ranch. Even in defeat, he'd looked to the future.

After the war, what had Jules Carron felt, and what had he done?

I wished I had a likeness of him. From my first glimpse of his name in Mr. Johnston's letter, I'd imagined him as a dark and handsome man, a Louisiana version of Nicholas Breckinridge. In my view, if I were to truly understand the man, I had to know his features.

Thinking that he might have drawn a self-portrait, I turned my attention to his artwork. I was absorbed in examining his sketches of battle scenes when an approach of soft footsteps and breathing pulled me abruptly back to reality and the vulnerability of my position.

Dropping the sketch, I whirled around. Midnight ran to the window, a little late, but no less present.

Someone or something was outside the house. Through the glass I saw a man who at first glance appeared to be a Confederate soldier. He was gray all over, with long straggly hair and eyes that burned with a disturbing intensity. In his hand he held a sword so new and shiny it might have been fashioned yesterday.

I stepped back. He uttered an ungodly yell and dashed away. Wildly excited, Midnight leaped at the window.

Although a more fanciful woman would think she had been visited by a ghost, I knew I'd seen a living person. I recognized him as the man who had been sitting with Emmett in front of the Silver Palace the day I arrived in Silver Springs. Almost certainly the unfortunate soldier was delusional, but as he had merely shouted at me and gone away, it was unlikely that he posed a threat.

It occurred to me that the man I had seen was Jules Carron, not dead, but a madman, protected by the townspeople. That would make an exciting story, but it wasn't very likely. And how could I then explain the inheritance? Living men didn't will away their belongings, and I chose to believe that lawyers didn't lie.

Whatever the answer to this latest mystery, I realized the folly in lingering in the house with only a small dog for protection. I'd take the botany book, a handful of sketches, and the silver nugget and drive back to town. When Emmett came to dinner tonight, I'd ask him what he knew about the man in gray.

~ * ~

I saw the material on my way out of the house.

At first I thought it was an article of clothing, a coat perhaps, left in an untidy, wrinkled heap in the chair. But as I drew nearer, I realized that it was something else entirely.

Without thinking, I lifted it and felt revulsion well up in me. Paper thin and shriveled, the yellowish gray fabric shed particles of dust as I moved it and seemed to shiver at my touch.

"When I was a girl in forty-nine, the Indians captured a white man and they skinned him alive."

As if my hand had suddenly caught fire, I dropped the stuff. Hideous images that had once haunted my dreams rushed back with the speed of a westward moving train. I remembered every word Mrs. Haskins had uttered and every grisly detail of her stories.

Could this possibly be human skin? Had an unspeakable deed been done in this house? Before these ghastly imaginings took control of me, I'd better rein them in and think rationally.

I couldn't remember seeing anything on the chair before. Someone might have placed it there while I was preoccupied with my search, but had an intruder come into the house, I thought Midnight would have alerted me.

Before continuing in this vein, I needed to know exactly what the material was. Although the only way to determine this was to take it with me, I didn't want to touch it again.

Leave it, I told myself. The material isn't likely to move itself away.

In the end I called to Midnight and left the premises with only the sketches, the book, and the nugget. The next time I visited the house, perhaps I could persuade Miss Eulalie to accompany me.

All the way back to Silver Springs, I kept hearing Mrs. Haskins' voice and remembering the way the thin, gritty material felt when I touched it.

It was there all along, I told myself, a *remnant of clothing that should have been in the armoire. You didn't notice it because it wasn't what you were looking for. There isn't a chance in a million that it's human skin.*

Still, a trace of my old fear remained. To my surprise, I discovered that I was positively longing for Emmett. It was the first time I'd thought about him in this way. When I saw him tonight, instead of quizzing him over dinner about the rebel soldier, I resolved to be more of a lady, serene and obliging.

The evening didn't turn out as I planned though. When I arrived, Emmett was sitting in the parlor with Miss Eulalie. I could tell that he was angry again.

I set the articles I'd brought from Trail's End on a table and pushed them to the back, close to the wall. Midnight bounded into the room ahead of me, going directly to Emmett, where she sat at his feet, trying to attract his attention.

"Oh, Mara, honey," Miss Eulalie said. "I've been getting worried. Where have you been?"

Emmett was frowning, but his voice was mild enough. "You went off to get yourself run down again, I'll warrant. You look like you met up with a whole herd of horses this time."

Ignoring his ungallant observation, I started to talk about the wildflowers I'd seen on my excursion, but Miss Eulalie interrupted me.

"We've been waiting for you for hours, Mara. You have a visitor, Miss Viola Courtenay."

As I tried to absorb this unexpected news, Viola came quietly into the room in a swirl of purple. She was as beautiful as ever, but her blue eyes were disturbed, and when she spoke, her voice was unsteady.

"Oh, Mara," she said. "I'm so glad to have found you at last. I'm in such great trouble."

Nine

After dinner Viola and I shared a pot of hot tea in the parlor, while Emmett and Miss Eulalie drank their strong Louisiana coffee. From time to time, Miss Eulalie glanced at Viola, no doubt taking in every detail of her elaborate purple dress and extraordinary beauty.

I hadn't mentioned Nicholas and Viola to my new friends. Clearly, Emmett had made up his mind about Viola already. Fortunately, he was silent as she recounted her adventures after our parting.

"I was stranded. That night while you went to the hotel with Nicholas, I went to my brother's boarding house. The landlady was out. I waited hours for her to come back, only to learn that my brother had moved. It was too late to go to his new dwelling, so I rented a room from her for the night. I was beginning to be frightened. How I wish I'd gone with you."

I remembered that night well, with Viola disappearing down the street, Nicholas saying goodbye, and my vivid nightmare. All this time I had been imagining Viola safe and happy in her brother's company, acting in one of his plays, never guessing at the desperation of her situation.

"The next morning, I discovered he'd moved again," Viola said. "To end my story, I finally learned he took the company to San Francisco."

"But he was expecting you!"

Viola looked down into her teacup. "Well, not exactly. He didn't know I was coming, but he would have welcomed me. I'm sure of it. I didn't have enough money to follow him to San Francisco or even to remain in Denver.

"I remembered that you were going to a ranch, and I wanted to see you. I came to Silver Springs and found out that you were staying at the hotel. They sent me here. This has been an unexpected setback, but I do have other talents. I'm told I have a good voice. I can find work in a saloon."

Emmett's glower returned, and Miss Eulalie gasped.

"That is unthinkable," she said.

"I'm so sorry, Viola. I do have a ranch, and I wish I could offer you hospitality, but at present, the house is unlivable."

Emmett nodded in approval. What would he think if he knew where I'd spent most of the day?

Miss Eulalie said, "You're welcome to stay here with me, Viola. Don't even think about singing in front of strangers. It may be that we can find a way to help you join your brother in San Francisco."

"That's kind of you. I have a little money left, and I'll find some kind of work. As soon as I can afford a train ticket, I'll be on my way."

Miss Eulalie set down her empty coffee cup. "It's settled then. I'll get another room ready, if you all will excuse me."

We three were alone, and the silence would have been awkward had it not been for Viola who, apparently having sensed Emmett's disapproval, set out to charm him. She was an accomplished actress. I observed her carefully, hoping to learn her techniques.

In no time at all, Emmett's frown disappeared, and he was speaking kindly to her. He might still have reservations, but being a man and therefore susceptible to feminine wiles, he appeared to be won over.

Now that we were all awash in goodwill, I decided to ask Emmett about the Confederate soldier.

"I happened to be at Trail's End today looking at wildflowers, and I saw the strangest person on the property. I think you know him."

I described the man and his startling actions, but, to my surprise, Emmett remained calm.

"That'd be Silver Jake you saw. You say he didn't hurt you?"

"Not at all. He stayed outside the house and didn't frighten me. Not much anyway. Who is he?"

"I don't know his real name. He was Carron's partner. Sometimes he comes to town, and we sit and talk about the War. Probably he's harmless, but you stay away from him."

"I can't promise that."

"I don't think he would hurt you, but I don't know. I told you, and I'll tell you again. Don't go to Trail's End unless I'm with you, or Jeremiah, if I'm not around. Anything could happen. You ought to know that. You should have been resting anyway, not riding all over the Territory."

I ignored Emmett's domineering manner and his directive and instead told Viola about my mishap with the runaway horse and explained how I came to be staying with Miss Eulalie.

To Emmett I said, "Now that Viola is here, we can go to Trail's End together."

"Then there'll be two of you to look after."

Apparently Viola had abandoned her plan to charm Emmett, for she said, "I'd love to see the ranch, Mara. We'll go tomorrow."

The conversation came to a standstill. Surreptitiously I contemplated Emmett, trying to read his mood. I sensed there was something he wasn't telling me.

"Why would Silver Jake want to harm me?" I asked.

"For the same reason he wears that Confederate uniform and carries a sword. He thinks it's eighteen sixty-three, and he's still fightin' in the War."

"Here in the Colorado Territory?"

"No, Miss Mara, in his head."

I had been right then. The man in gray was a deluded Southern veteran lost in time. He hadn't bothered me today, but he was Jules Carron's partner. Could he have seen me searching the roll top desk and leaving with Carron's possessions? More to the point, did he mind?

He might have been the one who had brought the loathsome piece of matter into the house, but no one knew about my secret fear or could have predicted my reaction. How could anyone be certain I would even notice it?

Still, Silver Jake might be important to me, but in another way. "Maybe he can tell me something about Jules Carron."

"He's a madman, and you're not going to talk to him," Emmett said.

"Not unless I happen to see him again. I found a silver nugget among Jules Carron's papers. It's a pretty thing, and I have some interesting sketches of war scenes and a book that identifies flowers in this party of the country."

"How lovely!" Viola said. "Let's see how many we can find tomorrow."

"We'll make our walks educational and safe."

"I'd like to see the sketches," Emmett said. "That's sometime, Miss Mara. I've got to go home now."

"I'll walk with you to the door, if you'll excuse me, Viola."

In the hallway I handed Emmett his hat. He touched my hand as he took it and let it linger there for a fraction of a second.

"You're looking recovered, Miss Mara, but don't overdo the travelin'. That was a bad fall you took. You sure Silver Jake didn't scare you none?"

"I'm not easily frightened," I said.

I would have liked to tell him about the material I'd found in the house, but then I'd have to include Mrs. Haskins and her stories, and we didn't have time for a long narration tonight. He had his hand on the door.

Sometime soon, though, we'd talk, and I'd ask him again about the Territorial Indians. I had a feeling that he and Jeremiah had told me what they wanted me to believe. I needed to know the true situation.

~ * ~

After Emmett had gone and Miss Eulalie retired for the night, I visited Viola in her room while she unpacked her few belongings. She spread out her brush and comb on the dresser, as well as various toilet articles and finally her book.

I had intended to ask her about lip color but instead found myself talking about Nicholas.

"Did you see Nicholas Breckinridge when you were in Denver?" I asked.

She was quiet for a moment. She looked away, rearranging her comb and brush.

"Denver is a big town, Mara, and Nicholas isn't the kind of man to seek the company of an actress. Why do you ask?"

I gave her the unedited version of the events that had preceded my accident.

"I was so sure it was Nicholas. He was so very handsome I couldn't have been mistaken. I called out to him, but he walked on. There couldn't be another man in Silver Springs who looks exactly like him, could there?"

Viola smiled in amusement. "Ah yes, Mara, you were so infatuated with the handsome Nicholas. Here is some free advice. Ask yourself what lies beneath a handsome appearance. Silver has a way of tarnishing. It's unattractive in that state."

She spoke as if she didn't like Nicholas. Or was a warning for me buried in her words? Perhaps it was only the resentment of a young woman who wouldn't be sought out by a respectable man because of her profession.

I didn't know what to think.

Viola said, "Nicholas told us he was going to Denver to find a house for his sister. Well, then, he must be there. Now, if you think he has a double in Silver Springs, you'd better search for him instead of this Jules Carron who has been dead and buried for so long. But Mara, that rancher who was here tonight—I think he's in love with you. Why look further?"

With consummate skill, she turned my thoughts from Nicholas. I considered what she said.

"I don't think Emmett is in love with me, and Nicholas is more..."

I broke off, my words, like my thoughts, in a jumble of confusion. I didn't really know what I wanted to say.

"Your rancher doesn't approve of me," Viola said. "He thinks I'm a lady of easy virtue come to lead you astray. With your permission, I'll continue to charm him. I'll use all my wiles, and we three will be true friends for life."

"I think I'd rather let come what may."

"My way is better, but you must do what you think best. Thanks to Miss Langlinais, this has been a fortunate end to our journey. Forget silver. Think about fools' gold tonight, and tomorrow we'll ride out to your ranch. Goodnight, Mara."

I left her brushing her hair in front of the mirror and humming a strange, haunting air.

She had given me a great deal to think about.

~ * ~

With Viola's coming, life speeded up considerably and acquired rich new colors. As planned, we visited Trail's End together the following morning. Viola agreed with me that the house was uninhabitable at present but could be aired out, washed, and fitted with new furnishings.

I knew that Trail's End would show a calm face today because I hadn't come alone. No unseen watching presence lurked in the quiet rooms, and no lunatic pierced the stillness with rebel yells.

Since Viola was already familiar with Mrs. Haskins stories, I told her about finding the skin.

"I want to know what you think. It's right over here."

But it wasn't. I looked behind the chair and under it and finally through the entire room.

"I'm sure there was something here. Where could it have gone?"

Viola tried to calm my agitation. "Come now, Mara. Of course I believe you found something, but it couldn't be what you think. You were far too affected by Mrs. Haskins' ramblings. I'm sure she enjoyed scaring you. If your gruesome find is gone, I suspect an animal took it away."

"I locked the door when I left."

"Something living inside the house then."

"Now you're frightening me. I wish we'd brought Midnight with us. She was here before, though, and she didn't find anything."

"She's only a puppy."

"I'm glad I didn't tell Emmett about the skin. He already thinks I'm a fool."

"How unkind of him to say such a thing. Has he offered you a generous price for your property yet?"

"My lawyer mentioned a possible sale the night he introduced us, but I said I wasn't interested in selling my land."

"He never will," she said. "He's counting on marrying you instead."

"I don't think so, Viola, but I don't have your gift for seeing into the hearts of men."

She only laughed. At times, she could be exasperating. Viola was determined to turn my thoughts away from Nicholas. I wondered if she wanted him for herself. Certainly, if that were the case, I would be no competition for her, unless Nicholas felt that an actress wouldn't be a suitable consort for him.

When we returned to Miss Eulalie's house, we found Jeremiah Brown waiting for me with some legal papers to sign. Soon I abandoned the notion that Viola might be interested in Nicholas. The attraction between Viola and Jeremiah was instant and mutual. To me, they seemed an unlikely pair, but it was obvious that each was dazzled by the other.

Seeking to break the sudden spell, I said, "Jeremiah, I never asked you about my silver mine."

"It isn't worth much, I'm afraid. I'll do some investigating. You can visit it one day, if you like."

He didn't elaborate, and soon he and Viola were engaged in a lively conversation about the theatre. I stood outside the invisible circle they'd woven around themselves. Would Viola be so eager to earn her fare to San Francisco now that she had met Jeremiah Brown?

As Miss Eulalie said when I told her about the new development, time would tell.

~ * ~

A disturbing occurrence clouded that afternoon. I'd gone to the general store to buy headache powder for Miss Eulalie who lay in a darkened room, felled by a throbbing pain in the back of her head. Jeremiah had returned to his law office, and Viola had taken over the sewing Miss Eulalie was compelled to set aside for the day.

Unaware of Viola's skill, Miss Eulalie had protested, but Viola prevailed.

"I've been designing and sewing my own dresses since I was fourteen," she said. "I know what I'm doing."

I knew very little about Viola's past, as she seldom spoke of it.

"My mother was a seamstress," she added. "Don't worry, Miss Eulalie. Go lie down. I'll continue with this, and no one will be able to tell the difference."

I had just stepped into the street with the headache powder and a new dime novel clutched in my hand when I saw Nicholas again. As on the night of my accident, he was dressed as a rancher.

He emerged from the barbershop and walked slowly down the street in the direction of Jeremiah's office.

He hadn't seen me, and this time, I didn't call out to him. In the bright daylight, with a clear view of his face, I knew for certain that I'd seen Nicholas himself and not his look-alike.

As soon as I reached Miss Eulalie's, I found Viola and told her about the incident.

"The Nicholas double," she said. "If you come across him again, perhaps you can contrive a ladylike encounter; but remember what I said. You will never have to chase Mr. Grandison."

The house was quiet. Viola held the needle up to the light and threaded it.

"Now, *I've* found the man I want," she said, as she bent her head over Miss Eulalie's sewing.

"Jeremiah Brown?"

"Yes, Jeremiah."

"That's—good then. He seems to be a solid citizen, and he's a nice man. I'm happy for you."

When I took the medication to Miss Eulalie, I said, "Viola is doing magnificent work on the dress. She's an expert."

"She's a great help to me. I'm so glad you girls are living with me, and Midnight is here too, asleep in the corner."

"I'll leave you alone now. I hope the powder works."

As I walked down the hall, I glanced at my watch. Emmett was coming to dinner, but many long hours stretched between now and the time we could expect him to arrive. Everyone, even the dog, was occupied. I was restless, but the prospect of leaving the house for a walk didn't appeal to me. I might see Nicholas again, and that was the last thing I wanted to happen.

Finally I decided to leaf through the botany guide I'd brought from Trail's End.

Emmett's wildflowers were in a jar on the bedside table, only now beginning to droop. Deciding to identify each one and surprise him with my knowledge of Territorial flora, I opened the book and turned the pages, trying to find an illustration that resembled the first flower I'd chosen.

As I did so, an old letter fell out and landed in my lap. Ironically, the clue for which I had so diligently searched had made its appearance while I was looking for something else.

Ten

Unfortunately the writing was in French, but the signature was clearly that of Jules Carron. He had penned these pages in his own language many years ago. I doubted if anybody in Silver Springs could translate them for me, with the possible exception of Miss Eulalie. Since she was from New Orleans and of French descent, there was a good chance that she read the language.

I couldn't disturb her at the moment, but I didn't want to wait either. Taking the letter over to the window, I examined the unfamiliar words carefully, willing them to give up their secret. In the salutation, I recognized a variation of my mother's name, Margaret, but aside from the signature, nothing else.

I hurried back to the room where Viola was sewing and set the letter down on the table. The light from the kerosene lamp drowned the uneven lines in a dim yellow pool.

"I found this marking a page in the botany book," I said. "Are you familiar with the French language?"

Viola set her sewing aside. "Not very. Maybe Miss Eulalie can read it."

"I hope so. I'm going to ask her as soon as she wakes up."

"I do know a few words. I played the part of a French maid in a play once. Jules Carron is the man who owned your ranch originally, isn't he? To whom did he write?"

"Possibly my mother, Margaret."

"Ah, a love letter. Wasn't Jules Carron your relative?"

"I'm sure he wasn't, but there's so much I don't know."

"Now I can see your fascination with Trail's End. You want to solve old mysteries."

"I'll admit I am curious. Something about the place haunts me."

"A ghost, you mean?"

"Not exactly. Somehow the past is still alive in the house. There's a sense of lingering sadness there or a deed left undone. As I'm the new owner, I've inherited the legacy."

"That all sounds very strange to me," Viola said. "It's like the story of a play. Let's see if we can translate a few words of the letter. Then we'll let imagination take over."

I held the letter closer to the light and pointed to the salutation and signature. "Here are two names: Jules Carron and Margaret."

Viola ran her finger along the lines, stopping when she thought she recognized the English counterpart of a French word.

"'Love', 'always', 'forever'. This is like a game," she said.

"Here's 'treasure'."

Hastily I counted. "We have four words and two names already."

"But several more we can't translate. Let's go through the letter again."

"I wonder why Jules Carron never mailed it," I said. "There's no date. Let's assume he wrote it during the War from the Territory or some Southern state. Would it have reached the North?"

"My mother received a letter from her cousin in West Virginia in 1864," Viola said. "It was delivered by a friend."

"I didn't see an envelope. Maybe he never intended to post it or was prevented from doing so. I don't think my mother read French. This is such a strange affair. One questions leads to another one."

On the day I'd found the emerald ring in my mother's jewelry box, I thought I'd seen her at the window with an unknown letter in her hand. Certainly it wasn't this one. Did she ever wonder what had become of Jules Carron, while these, his words to her, were trapped inside the botany book?

Wherever I turned, new mysteries rushed out to greet me, but in the end, did any of this matter now?

Yes, of course it did—to me. The story was part of my heritage.

"It's a fascinating puzzle," Viola said. "Maybe Jules Carron was telling your mother about a hidden treasure."

"Now you're the one spinning a plot for a play."

"The word could be an endearment or a reference to gold or silver. I have a rudimentary knowledge of French grammar. He used the form *le*, as in the treasure. I know I'm right, Mara. All we need now is a map."

I considered her idea, but on closer examination, it fell apart.

"That's extremely farfetched, Viola. Jules Carron would have given any resources he had to the Southern Cause. I think it's more likely that he used the phrase as an extravagant endearment."

"Weren't you and Jeremiah talking about a silver mine today?" she asked.

"Yes, and he said it was practically worthless."

"What if Mr. Carron had a real treasure in silver to leave your mother and hid it at Trail's End? You found one nugget.

There might be more, a whole chest filled with them. Surely he didn't mean for your mother to inherit only that depressing house and the land."

"There's also a sum of money and the mine."

Viola turned back to the letter. "Here's another word. *Emeraude* for emerald. Silver and precious stones. Wouldn't it be exciting to go on a treasure hunt?"

Emeraude. I remembered the exquisite emerald ring pushed to the back of my mother's jewelry box. Even before I had the evidence of the letter, I'd thought the jewel was a gift to my mother from Jules Carron. He must have given or sent her the ring and afterwards written this letter. She had the symbol of his love but not the message.

I was now more determined than ever to know the whole story, but I decided not to mention the ring to Viola. Not just yet.

"A treasure hunt would be fun, but your theory is based on two words and your limited command of French grammar," I said. "Let's wait until we have the letter translated."

~ * ~

It was late in the evening before Miss Eulalie felt well enough to join us in the parlor. She was pale, but the look of pain was gone from her eyes. I made us all a fresh pot of tea and poured the first cup for her.

She said, "I've lost the whole day. I'm awake just in time to go back to bed."

Viola pushed the needle into the pincushion and laid the pink garment in her lap. "But your sewing is done. You're not behind at all."

"You've finished Annabelle's dress already? Oh, my! She'll be overjoyed."

"If you're feeling better, and after you've had your tea, I found a letter I hope you'll be able to read, Miss Eulalie," I said. "It's in French."

When I told her about my mother's mysterious connection to Jules Carron, she set her teacup down immediately.

"How enchanting to have a romantic mystery to solve! It's even better than a novel. Now, you understand that I haven't read French in years, but I'm sure I'll be able to translate your letter. Do you have it here?"

I handed it to her, watching with growing curiosity as she read the foreign words silently.

"Can you read it?" I asked.

"Yes, Mara. It's very simple. This is a love letter to a woman named Margaret. Was she your mother?"

"Yes. That was my mother's name. What did Jules Carron write?"

"In my own words, he's leaving in the morning to fight for the Southern Cause. If he should be killed in the War, the ranch is hers, along with everything he possesses. He tells her that his love for her will endure in this life and the next, and he prays for her happiness forever. He asks her to remember him always, even if she doesn't wear the emerald ring, and ends by saying that the map will lead her straight to the treasure."

Frowning, she turned the paper around.

"The map?" I asked.

"That's all. There's nothing written on the back. There must be another page somewhere."

"Oh, no!" Viola said.

Quickly, I opened the book and began turning its pages, while Viola stood behind me. "There's nothing more here. If he originally included a map with the letter, it's missing."

"But there is a treasure," Viola said. "He says so."

"So it would seem, but we don't know what or where it is, and we don't have the map. There was an emerald ring, though. I found it just before I left."

"Maybe he sent your mother the map along with the ring."

"No. If he had, I'm sure she would have kept it. There was no map."

"We can still look for the treasure."

"I'd rather know the truth about my mother and Jules Carron," I said.

"Since they're both dead, that may not be possible," Miss Eulalie pointed out.

I was still idly turning pages of the botany book, hoping that somehow I'd missed the map. I wondered if it was the same size as the letter. Perhaps Jules Carron had tucked it into another book, possibly his Bible. If so, that wasn't a very reliable way to make sure that my mother would find it, but he might not have had a choice.

I said, "When I first came to Silver Springs, I didn't know this letter existed. Maybe I'll stumble on another clue."

"This is going to be an exciting summer," Miss Eulalie said. "I'm so glad you girls came to town."

~ * ~

That night I dreamed I was looking through Jules Carron's desk again, finding a key I'd overlooked during my previous search. The next morning in Jeremiah's office I learned that my mine was located in a deserted camp once known as Carron Creek. Although it wasn't a proper town and at present no one lived there, I found the information exciting.

"Why didn't you tell me about this before?" I asked.

Jeremiah's look was reproachful.

"I didn't know myself until last night. Jules Carron named the camp after himself, probably thinking it would grow into a town. That didn't happen. At some point, he abandoned the mine and moved on. Either he or someone else dynamited it. Old Andy at the Palace told me the story."

"If Jules Carron lived near the mine, he might have built a house there."

"I said it was a camp, Mara. The Territory is filled with places like Carron Creek. Ghost towns, we call them. You won't find them on any map except the one in Andy's memory."

"Do you know where it is?" I asked.

"According to Andy, about eleven miles from Silver Springs to the northwest."

"I want to see it," I said. "Maybe Andy can draw me a map."

In my mind, I was already exploring a mysterious settlement that was now left to the ghosts. If Jules Carron had lived there for a time, he might have left personal belongings behind or hidden the hypothetical treasure nearby.

I felt as if Jeremiah had just handed me the key from my dream. I was eager to return to Trail's End and resume my search. When I told Viola about Carron Creek, she said she'd join me. The next day was Sunday, however, the day Emmett had invited us to visit his ranch. Also, we were going to church with Miss Eulalie. Our expedition would have to wait.

~ * ~

Viola came slowly down the stairs the next morning, for once looking self-conscious and uncertain.

"I don't think I should go," she said. "My clothing is unlike what I've seen other women wearing."

"Nonsense," Miss Eulalie said. "Your blue dress is very becoming, and you certainly can't stay home on a Sunday morning. Jeremiah always goes to church, as do scores of other bachelors in the vicinity."

"Does Emmett attend services?" I asked.

"Sometimes," she said. "Now, both of you girls look lovely. Come along. We're going to be late."

She had an elegant little buggy that looked as if it had never been driven down the dusty main street of Silver Springs, but because the distance to the church was short and the morning was so fine and warm, we walked.

I had never ventured in this direction and, hence, hadn't seen the plain white building with the adjoining cemetery. It occupied a spacious, serene section of land, with a few cottonwood trees and a vast grassy expanse for outside church activities.

Several groups of people waited outside for the service to begin, many of them families with young children, but I saw only a few of the bachelors Miss Eulalie had mentioned. Probably the others were already inside.

"The church is only a year old," she said. "The last one burned. Our Reverend Winters is an unmarried man. I see Doctor Westbrook with Annabelle and Arabella. You probably don't remember him, Mara."

"When he attended me, I was unconscious, but I'd like to meet him. Isn't he your suitor, Miss Eulalie?"

"Really, Miss Eulalie?" Viola said. "You never mentioned him."

"Now, hush, Mara—Viola. Sometimes the Doctor and I have Sunday dinner together. That's all."

They waited for us to catch up to them, although the slender, fair-haired girls with the doctor looked restless, especially the younger one who seemed not to care for her frilly dress. The dapper silver-haired gentleman smiled warmly and kissed Miss Eulalie's hand.

"You look beautiful as always, Eulalie," he said. "And Miss Marsden, you're recovered, I see. I don't believe I know your friend."

Miss Eulalie performed the introductions and complimented Arabella on her Sunday finery, causing her to tug nervously at the ribbon of her bonnet.

Doctor Westbrook said, "It's all right, Arabella, if you want to sit with your friend. You, too, Annabelle."

"Thank you, Grandfather, but I'll stay," Annabelle said.

She wore the pink dress Miss Eulalie had made for her. As we walked along, I remembered that, according to Miss Eulalie, Annabelle had set her cap for Emmett. She'd also called her a pretty little thing, but that was inaccurate. Annabelle was tall and truly beautiful with pale blonde hair and a fair complexion.

Miss Eulalie and Doctor Westbrook were engrossed in their conversation, and Viola, who had spied Jeremiah in the crowd, was moving sedately away from us and toward him. Left alone with the doctor's granddaughter, I smiled at her and made an attempt at light conversation.

"Have you lived in Silver Springs long?" I asked.

"My sister and I came to live with Grandfather five years ago when our parents died," she said.

"Do you go to school here?"

Annabelle hesitated a moment before answering. "Not any more, Miss Marsden. I'm out of school. I help my grandfather with his practice."

I wanted to continue our conversation and possibly learn more about her, but she said, "Excuse me, Miss Marsden. I see a friend of mine."

Very politely, very smoothly, she walked toward another young woman, and I was left alone to follow Miss Eulalie and Doctor Westbrook into the church.

Don't feel slighted, I told myself. *You're not going to a social occasion. You don't need an escort or companion at your side.*

Nonetheless, I had the impression that Annabelle Westbrook wasn't going to become one of my dear friends. That didn't surprise me. If she was interested in acquiring Emmett as a husband, she wouldn't welcome competition.

Most likely, her grandfather had told her about Emmett Grandison's interest in the new woman in town, the one he'd saved from a runaway team of horses. That was reason enough for her to dislike me. In her place, I would have similar feelings.

But if women were indeed scarce in Silver Springs, why would a willowy, fair-haired girl, the granddaughter of the town doctor, be pining for one irascible man? The answer was simple: Because he was Emmett Grandison of the X Bar G, a wealthy and attractive bachelor.

I had a feeling I had just met my chief rival, but that was an ungodly thought for a woman to have on her way to a place of worship.

Just then, Miss Eulalie turned around to look for me, and I quickened my pace. It was time for serious and reverent thoughts, but all through the service, Emmett was very much on my mind. When he picked us up at Miss Eulalie's house after church, I felt as if my day were only now beginning.

Having joined Miss Eulalie's household, Viola was included in Emmett's invitation to visit the X Bar G. As he helped her up into the wagon, she flirted outrageously with him. He looked so uncomfortable that I wished she'd quit acting, since she had accomplished her purpose, at least superficially. I had a suspicion that Emmett knew her true intent.

Eventually, though, Viola turned her attention to the miles of pristine Colorado scenery, often exclaiming over a particularly awe-inspiring sight.

Finally Emmett said, "We're on the Grandison spread now. Today the X Bar G is the largest and best ranch in the whole Territory. I started it with only two acres."

"Don't forget the few cows, Emmett," Miss Eulalie said.

"Sure, Miss Eulalie. They were the most important part."

"Wherever you look, there's a spectacular view," Viola said, with a sweeping gesture that appeared to include the sky. "This is the most beautiful part of the West I've ever seen."

"It's God's country, Miss Viola."

"So, if you own all this, you must be a wealthy man, Mr. Grandison."

"Maybe. What's important is the land," he said.

"And the house," Miss Eulalie added. "Emmett built a fine, large house. It's very comfortable. I helped him furnish it."

"That you did, ma'am. Miss Eulalie gave me some of her lamps and pictures. You'll find it right homey, Miss Mara."

I was quiet, listening to the others and looking at Emmett's strong tanned hands firmly gripping the reins.

As we traveled across his acres, he continued to talk about his ranch in warm and glowing terms. He spoke with pride of his herd, the horses he owned, and the men who worked for him.

By listening carefully to all he said, I was able to find a balance for his blustery, dictatorial side. He defended the law of this new land as fervently as he had the vanquished Confederacy. Now he promoted the growth and welfare of Silver Springs and the entire Territory. At the heart of this powerful enigmatic man of the future was the X Bar G.

I could easily see my land joined to his and myself sitting beside him as we came home to our ranch house, sat together at the dinner table, or enjoyed each other's company in a variety of warm and exciting scenes. On such a morning as this, it all seemed possible.

However, these moments in the present had a vast appeal of their own. After we'd toured Emmett's house, enjoyed a hearty Texas barbecue under the hot July sun, and met those of his men who were around, Emmett escorted me over to the corral to see a horse called Star.

"She's pretty and spirited, with a shiny chestnut coat," he said. "Except for that star on her forehead, she reminds me a little of you, Miss Mara."

Star trotted up to the fence, and Emmett stroked her head. She watched me with large dark eyes that were both grave and inquisitive.

"I think I'm flattered. I wonder, Emmett, would you let me purchase Star? I need a horse, and I'd like to have one who's like me."

"I might be willing," he said. "First, you'll have to prove to me that you can ride her."

"I can do that. My friend back in Michigan had a pony, and we learned the rudiments of horsemanship together."

He nodded his approval. "Good enough. You'll need a clean place to keep her, not one of those dilapidated old stables at Trail's End."

No, for a horse like Star, only the best accommodations would do, but that presented a problem.

"Could you keep her here temporarily?" I asked.

"Sure thing."

"But let me take her for a long ride in a few days?"

Miss Eulalie and Viola were making their way over to the corral. They reached us in time to hear my question.

"Where do you want to go?" Emmett asked.

"To Carron Creek to see the mine Jules Carron left me. Viola will come with me."

"Oh, Mara, that's much too far," Miss Eulalie said. "You girls will get lost on the way, and suppose you encounter outlaws?"

"It would be better if we had a guide and companion," Viola added. "Jeremiah might offer to take us. Shall we ask him?"

During this exchange, Emmett had remained silent, but his eyes were stormy.

"Jeremiah's too busy with his law practice to go on a fool's errand. Miss Lally's right. You two go ridin' alone, and you'll be sure to head straight into trouble. There's danger of snake bite and attack by wild Indians..."

"But you and Jeremiah said they were on reservations," I said.

"There's always the renegades. You don't know the country, Miss Mara. You'll likely lose your way and end up in Wyoming Territory. I'll ride over with you, but not till later in the week."

His willingness to take my plan seriously and the prospect of his company filled me with a quiet happiness. "We accept your offer and thank you; but why do we have to wait?"

"Oh, my dear!" Miss Eulalie said. "Are we all forgetting the Fourth of July is coming up? For some people, there is so little entertainment out here that we celebrate every holiday we can. This year it's also the Centennial and the tenth anniversary of Silver Springs, all three together."

Emmett added, "There'll be food and dancin' all day in Silver Springs and fireworks at night."

"How exciting!" Viola said.

I glanced at her, wondering if these homespun frontier festivities really appealed to her. Then I remembered her interest in Jeremiah Brown. Being the town's lawyer, he would certainly be at a July Fourth celebration.

"For me, it'll be my first territorial entertainment on a grand scale," I said. "I wouldn't miss it."

Emmett cast me an approving smile. "I'm countin' on you to save a dance for me, Miss Mara."

"I will. One dance."

Already I was planning to wear the new green dress Miss Eulalie had made for me. With Viola's help, I would add a little color to my lips, and Emmett would court me for one day.

Slow down, I warned myself. It was only a dance he asked for, nothing more.

Still, there would be fireworks. On this exciting, celebratory night, anything could happen.

Eleven

As soon as darkness fell, the first firecracker of the Centennial Festival exploded in a dazzling configuration of light over Silver Springs. I looked for Emmett in the milling crowd. Throughout the day, he had been often at my side, although not as an escort. When I mingled with the townspeople, I was always aware of him, never too far away.

Now I spared a thought for Midnight who was fearful of gunfire and other loud noises. Since she had been easy to housebreak, we'd left her in the kitchen where she was probably cowering in some dark corner. Just as I wondered whether I should go back to the house and check on her, the next firecracker burst the safe and happy life I'd been building for myself into bright rainbow colors.

Nicholas was walking toward me. Dressed like a fine Boston gentleman, as he had been when I'd first seen him on the train, he looked out of place among the rough frontier folk to whom I'd grown accustomed.

As he lifted a gold pocket watch to the sky, the light generated by the explosion danced off its shining surface. Then he smiled at me, and all my suspicions vanished.

He was exactly as I remembered him with black hair, clear blue eyes and skin deeply tanned, by far the handsomest man I'd ever seen.

When he was near enough to be heard, he said, "Mara, at last. I've been looking for you for hours."

Unable to conceal my delight at this unexpected encounter, I said, "I'm so happy to see you, Nicholas. Where have you been all this time?"

He looked slightly taken aback, not at my obvious pleasure, but at my inquiry.

"Why, in Denver, Mara. I told you about my business there. The house is now bought and furnished. I wanted to see you again, and I must say, except for those marvelous green eyes, I would hardly have known you. You are even more of a beauty than I remembered."

My face grew warm. Of course I didn't believe him. Nicholas had never said that he thought me beautiful. I knew he was only being gallant to a friend, but the compliments were pleasant to hear.

I remembered that words came easily to Nicholas. All those smooth, flattering, cajoling phrases were like a second language to him. Also, no matter what the answer, there was a question I had to ask him before we could proceed.

"When did you arrive in Silver Springs, Nicholas?"

"On the morning train. I checked into the Silver Palace Hotel, where I plan to stay for a while."

"Were you in town last week, by chance?"

"Mara, my dear, can't you hear me with this infernal racket? I told you I've been in Denver. I only arrived this day."

We stood together beneath a lone cottonwood tree, apart from the crowd who watched the celestial display.

"I didn't expect to arrive in the midst of a festival," he said. "Are they celebrating the Fourth of July?"

"Yes, that and the nation's Centennial, along with the town's tenth anniversary, all in one. This is a special evening for Silver Springs."

"It will be for us as well. We'll enjoy the rest of the night together," he said.

I hesitated. I thought of Emmett somewhere in the crowd. Then I saw him. From as great a distance as twenty yards away, I could feel the impact of stormy gray-blue eyes. He moved toward us in a rapid stride. I, who hadn't yet had a serious suitor, was about to be caught in the crossfire between two men, but I was determined to meet the challenge. It wasn't as if I were Emmett's property. We hadn't come to the affair together.

I waited for fireworks to explode closer to the ground.

When I introduced the two gentlemen to each other, though, Emmett surprised me by being congenial. Gradually, however, the awkwardness thickened in the air, as powder from the explosives. I looked for Viola, whose presence could lighten any mood, but I didn't see her. She and Jeremiah had attended the celebration as a pair and kept to themselves, apart from the crowd, but not too far from the watchful eyes of Miss Eulalie.

Although Emmett and Nicholas had little to say to each other, they remained civil. In every way they were different, and in ordinary circumstances, the two men would never have met. Seeing them together allowed me to make comparisons. I liked both of them very much, but Nicholas was more genteel. Was that what I wanted a man to be? At this moment, I didn't know.

Emmett's voice had a gruff, no-nonsense edge. "What's your business in Silver Springs, Mr. Breckinridge?"

Nicholas drew my hand into his. "I've come to see Mara. She and I are old friends."

Before I could agree or protest, Nicholas led me away. I glanced back to see Emmett glaring after us in anger.

"You shouldn't have said that, Nicholas. Emmett has quite a temper, and he carries a gun."

"But it's true, Mara. We are friends. I've come to visit you. Your friend *did* ask."

Nicholas led me to the bench in front of the general store. Since the fireworks display was at the edge of town, this area was deserted. We might have been in a compartment on the train again.

"You have another old friend to see," I said. "Viola is here, and we are staying together. She couldn't join her brother as planned, but she has found a new gentleman friend."

For a fragment of a second, I thought he looked startled.

"Viola here and with a young man! Well. My lovely companions are together in one place. This would be too much of a coincidence if we hadn't both promised to visit you at Trail's End."

His voice lingered over the name of my ranch, almost caressing it.

"The house is in need of repair and renovation," I said. "I'm staying with a kind lady with whom I became acquainted."

At that moment Miss Eulalie appeared, no doubt extending her chaperone duties. She had never minded leaving me alone with Emmett, her favorite, but Nicholas was unknown, a handsome stranger from beyond the Territory.

I said, "Miss Eulalie, this is Nicholas Breckinridge, a gentleman I met on the train on my journey out West."

Nicholas kissed her hand. "I'm so pleased to meet you, Miss Eulalie. Since I came to the Colorado Territory, I've found one beautiful lady after another."

Nicholas could charm anyone in Silver Springs, with the obvious exception of Emmett Grandison. On Miss Eulalie, he had an additional effect.

"I believe I've seen you before, Mr. Breckinridge. Oh, I'd remember such an exceptionally fine looking man, I know. Only, where was it?"

Nicholas smiled at the compliment. "I don't think so, ma'am. I come from Boston. Some years ago, I visited Denver, but I'm sure we never met. I wouldn't forget you."

Miss Eulalie blushed but looked unconvinced.

"I'm concerned about Midnight, Miss Eulalie," I said. "With all the noise, she might tear the kitchen apart."

"I'll be going home soon. Doctor Westbrook will accompany me. Don't stay out late, Mara. Have you seen Emmett? Annabelle was looking for him."

"I saw him recently."

I knew what Miss Eulalie was doing, and it made me uncomfortable. Looking toward the fireworks, I saw a flash of yellow and pink that could only be Annabelle. She was talking to Emmett. Miss Eulalie must have seen her, too. I frowned, wishing I knew what Emmett and Annabelle were discussing.

"I'll take care of Midnight, dear," Miss Eulalie said. "Don't stay out late. Mr. Breckinridge, goodnight."

~ * ~

As the evening progressed, I was aware of Emmett always nearby, one of a crowd or standing alone, always glowering. Once I saw him with Annabelle, dancing in the candle-lit square in front of the Silver Palace. He didn't look my way.

With a pang, I remembered my promise to save a dance for him. I wanted to go to him, and at the same time, to stay with Nicholas. Fortunately, I didn't have to choose between the two gentlemen. Nicholas made the choice for me.

The fireworks were over, the festival drawing to an end, and the crowds dispersing. Only stars were left to light the sky. Nicholas and I walked back to Miss Eulalie's house, away from the others, into the darkness.

Nicholas said, "I almost forgot." He took a small box out of his pocket and opened it. "I brought you a souvenir from Denver, Mara." He lifted a green jewel suspended on a fine gold chain from its snowy bed.

Not an emerald, I thought, with a rush of fear.

"It's an emerald to match your pretty green eyes," Nicholas said.

He fastened the clasp around my neck, and his hands rested on my shoulder.

The jewel lay lightly on my throat. I looked up to thank him. In the next second, he kissed me. I was so surprised that I didn't have time to wonder at the suddenness of his passion.

We stood in front of Miss Eulalie's house. The oil lamp in the window sent out a stream of light onto the grass.

I knew that I shouldn't have accepted the present or the kiss. I could give one back, but not the other.

"The pendant is beautiful, Nicholas, but we hardly know each other," I said.

"We will. When I come back to the Colorado Territory to stay, we'll become well acquainted."

I opened the gate. Nicholas followed me into the yard and pulled me close again.

At that moment, Midnight bounded out into the night. Delirious with joy at being released from her captivity and seeing me, she ran around us, sniffing the leather of Nicholas' boots and barking.

"Good dog," Nicholas said.

I pulled away from him. "Come here, Midnight."

I lifted her and held her, while she struggled to be free. She wanted to make friends with the tall stranger who didn't share her enthusiasm. Curiously, my own enthusiasm for Nicholas' embrace was rapidly cooling.

I didn't intend to invite Nicholas into the house. I wanted to take the pendant from around my neck and return it to him. My hands wouldn't move.

"Do you ever dress like the other men in the Territory, Nicholas, in a Stetson hat and gun belts?" I asked.

Nicholas laughed. The sound carried in the night silence, finding its way into the house, where Miss Eulalie would hear it, and surely back to Emmett in the heart of town.

"If I stay in the West long enough, I may begin to dress like the natives, but I don't wear gun belts. Ever. Why do you ask?"

"I was trying to picture you dressed like—say, Emmett Grandison."

"That ill-mannered admirer of yours?"

"He has a temper, but..."

Something happened then with the suddenness of a firecracker bursting. This explosion, however, was reserved especially for me.

I had set Midnight down on the ground. Rebuffed by Nicholas, she'd run back into the area behind the house. Nicholas was about to reach for me again when we heard someone walking down the street. The sound of footsteps shattered the illusion that we were alone in the world.

Hoping it wouldn't be Emmett, I again backed away from Nicholas.

The newcomer was Annabelle, strolling down the street with a young man I'd never seen before. When she noticed us in the shadows beyond the gate, she smiled. As Nicholas nodded to her, she came to glittering life. What broke the spell, though, wasn't her intrusion but her words. She reached over the gate and touched Nicholas gently on the hand.

"Why, Mr. Breckinridge," she said. "I'm so glad you came back to Silver Springs."

Twelve

That night I wrapped the emerald pendant in a handkerchief and laid it in the drawer of the table at my bedside. I had a fleeting memory of an emerald ring similarly wrapped and pushed out of sight. In some unfathomable way, could history be repeating itself?

In my mind, Nicholas' gift was mixed up with Annabelle's words and the doubt that wouldn't leave me. Last night, with his usual courtesy, Nicholas had smiled at Annabelle and made a conventional remark about the success of the festivities. Annabelle, looking confused, bade us good evening, and walked on with her escort.

When they were gone, Nicholas said, "That young lady is under the impression that she knows me. She's mistaken."

"Then how did she know your name?" I asked.

He shrugged. "Someone might have told her."

"Who, Nicholas? You said you just arrived in town this morning. Annabelle implied that you've been here before."

He stared down the quiet street, as if the answer could be found in the darkness.

"One of your friends; maybe that cowboy. He must have mentioned my name to her. You introduced us, if you will remember."

"Yes, but..."

Nicholas took my hand again and let it rest in his own, caressing my palm with his finger.

"This is the first time I've set foot in this town, Mara." He paused, looking deeply into my eyes, and frowned. "Anyone would believe you're doubting my word."

Although I was loath to admit that this was true, I said, "Well, it's strange."

"As I said, the young lady is mistaken."

I said goodnight to Nicholas after that, unconvinced but not wanting to continue the discussion on Miss Eulalie's doorstep.

That night, unable to sleep, I relived the events of the celebration: Emmett's anger, the emerald, Nicholas' kiss, and finally Annabelle shattering the spell, followed by Nicholas' unlikely explanation.

Turning on the bed, I tried in vain to find a comfortable position that would induce sleep. I couldn't keep mulling over the mystery that Nicholas had become. I needed to be rested because Emmett wanted us to be ready to leave for Carron Creek at sunrise.

As soon as I fell asleep, however, the night was virtually over. Although it was still dark beyond the window, Viola was in my room, already dressed and urging me to hurry.

When I joined her ten minutes later, she was in the kitchen packing the food we'd prepared yesterday. Midnight followed me and watched the picnic ingredients disappearing into the basket, undoubtedly hoping to be a part of our newest expedition.

I started to tell Viola about Nicholas' arrival, but she'd already heard the news from Miss Eulalie.

"Apparently Annabelle thinks she knows Nicholas," I said, repeating her puzzling statement.

Viola had not one explanation but several.

"It might have happened as Nicholas said. You introduced him to Emmett and Miss Eulalie. Doctor Westbrook is Miss Eulalie's friend, and Annabelle is his granddaughter. One of them may have mentioned Nicholas to her, or Emmett might have asked her to say something incendiary."

I wanted to believe Viola, but I couldn't. "On the other hand, Annabelle may have met Nicholas when he was here before."

"He told you he was in Denver and that he hadn't been in Silver Springs before yesterday. You'll have to decide whether you want to believe Annabelle or Nicholas."

That was something I couldn't do at this hour of the morning, but I suspected that if I had to choose one version, it would be Annabelle's. I had to break through her unfriendly shell and question her. That would be later, though, after our trip to Carron Creek.

I noticed that Viola had laid a large pad of paper and pencils on the table next to the basket.

"These are my drawing materials," she said. "If we see something interesting at the mine, I'll do a little sketching."

"I didn't know you were an artist."

"I draw for my own pleasure. Now, do we have all the food? Should we take anything else?"

I reviewed the contents of the basket. "We have fried chicken, cake, pie, biscuits, beans..."

"That's enough for a week-long excursion."

"I'll add a bone and a bit of meat for Midnight," I said.

"The dog? You're not taking her."

Emmett said the same thing, more forcefully, when he arrived moments later. I searched his face, looking for the familiar storm clouds, but he was in a genuine good humor this morning. He had brought Star with him and a sandy-haired young cowboy named Tyler, who led a mount for Viola.

"This is Miss Mara, your new owner, Star," Emmett said. "She's promised to take good care of you."

"I haven't paid you for her yet."

"There's time for that later. The dog stays with Miss Eulalie. It's a long ride to the mine and back. She can't run all the way, and you can't carry her."

Midnight was already whining in anticipation of a morning outing with us.

"She was alone last night," I said. "I don't like to abandon her again. I could carry her."

"You'll be holding the reins, Miss Mara."

Because it made no sense to argue the matter further and I knew they were right, I shooed the little dog up the stairs, telling her to find Miss Eulalie, and we were off.

~ * ~

It was a day made for a long ride on horseback. Viola and Tyler rode ahead. From what I could hear of their conversation, Viola was entertaining her escort with stories of her days on the stage. I would ask her to tell me about them sometime. With me, she was always reticent about her past.

Our route took us through gently ascending foothills where the air was thin and clear and the blue sky seemed to be moving toward us. Dark trees lined the trail, but the sun was warm and bright. I had never felt happier and more alive.

Every now and then I glanced at Emmett. I assumed he'd forgotten about last night, but I was wrong. After we'd ridden for an hour and exhausted conversation about the weather and scenery, he alluded to the events of the previous evening.

"I take it Nicholas Breckinridge is an old friend of yours, Mara."

"Not exactly. We met on the train coming West."

I hoped Emmett hadn't seen Nicholas give me the pendant or, what would be much worse, witnessed our kiss. It appeared he hadn't, and I added, "At times Nicholas Breckinridge can be presumptuous."

"You met him on the way to the Territory? You've hardly known him longer'n me."

"That's true, but it was a long, tedious train ride. We had nothing to do but talk and become acquainted with each other."

"He never did say what he's doin' here."

I told Emmett about Nicholas' desire to see his ailing sister settled in the West.

"He's an Eastern dandy. Has money, I reckon."

"I never asked him. Nicholas doesn't talk about himself."

"He rented the best suite in the Silver Palace. What I want to know is, why is he here?"

To see me, he had said, but I didn't believe this. Although I didn't have the vaguest idea of Nicholas' agenda, I said the first thing that came to my mind, although I knew it to be the least likely of reasons.

"Viola was on the same train. We three were often together. Perhaps he came to see her."

"He didn't last night."

We had talked about Nicholas long enough. "Viola and Tyler are so far ahead of us, we'll lose them."

"Then we'll catch up to them and let them follow us," Emmett said. "Hold on tight to those reins. I don't want to have to collect you up from the trail."

~ * ~

Emmett thought that, allowing for the journey to and from Carron Creek, we would have ample time to eat, rest, and explore the site. We hadn't ridden long, however, before I fervently wished myself out of the saddle. When Emmett called for a rest, I slid to the ground, grateful for the support of his arms around my waist.

All too soon, we were moving again. Shortly after noon, we reached a quiet area in the wooded hills where the scent of pine was strong in the high, clear air. Walls crumbled into ruins suggested that this had once been a town.

Emmett helped me down from the horse and tethered his mount and Star to a sturdy tree. "We'll wait for Tyler and Viola here."

"How do you know this is Carron Creek?" I asked.

"This is it, all right. I talked to Andy last night. Your mine is over a way to the south. It was blasted years ago. Carron was in these mountains only five or six months."

Emmett took my hand and we walked down what had once been a main path.

"Watch where you step," he said. "The ground's rough."

It was hard to imagine that Carron Creek had once been a boomtown. Ghosts lived here now, holding fast to their broken dreams of silver strikes. Did they resent the intrusion of those who came to disturb the dust, rock, and shadows? In the dark shade of the tall trees I shivered. Emmett put his arm firmly around my waist.

Beyond a green screen of leaves, three walls still stood, although I suspected that the next strong wind would bring them down.

"Doesn't that shack look like a scaled down version of Trail's End?" I asked.

"Not to me, Miss Mara. All I see is rotting wood. Here are the others. We thought you were lost, Tyler."

Tyler chuckled. "Not a chance, Boss. We let you be the first to arrive."

"I am so tired of riding, and I'm hungry," Viola said. "Is anyone else ready to eat?"

~ * ~

After we had eaten lunch and explored the site, Viola took out her sketching pad, and Tyler sat down to watch her. Emmett and I walked back to the three-walled structure.

"Viola and I could never have done this on our own," I said. "But is there really danger?"

"Could be."

"I know there are always snakes, but you weren't serious about the Indians, were you?"

"Dead serious. We won't have to be afraid of 'em if we leave 'em alone."

I needed more reassurance. "We couldn't get scalped or..." My voice trailed off. I couldn't bring myself to mention the unspeakable horror that had befallen Mrs. Haskins' white man.

Emmett squeezed my hand. "Not with me'n Tyler here."

My nightmares, the sound of drums, an Indian in the heart of Silver Springs, and the suspicious material in the chair at Trail's End—I thought I had left them behind. With this powerful man of the West by my side, they should have no power to harm me. I must have trembled because Emmett was immediately solicitous.

"You're not afraid of Indians, are you, Miss Mara?" he asked.

"I might be."

"You came West at the exact right time. You got me. I been savin' you practically since you got here, and I aim to keep on doin' it, but I won't need to save you from Indians. We won't likely meet any."

"I know."

A feeling of security enveloped me. I could see my life consisting of one glorious day after another, filled with good times in the outdoors, friendship, and, most important of all, love.

As we came to a shack that had survived the years and elements and still retained a semblance of its original shape, Emmett said, "Here was another house."

"I wonder if any furniture is left inside."

I stepped through the space where a door had once been. As soon as I crossed the threshold, I stumbled over a loose board and would have fallen if Emmett hadn't caught me.

"You don't need to worry about Indians, Miss Mara. You can hurt yourself without any help from them. Let's call an end to this exploration. I see a nice shady spot ahead where we can rest."

Six or seven yards from the structure, we found a clearing where a fallen tree provided a natural bench. Bright blue flowers covered the ground, and a little silver stream wound away into the woods.

As I sank to the soft earth, I said, "This is an enchanted place. It's perfect for just about anything."

Emmett's slow smile found its way directly to my heart. "That it is, Miss Mara. I've been wonderin'. Why are you so interested in the past? I think the future is more excitin'."

"I like to think about the years to come." Suddenly, I found myself telling Emmett the entire story of my inheritance, although I didn't include my fancies and fears. "Viola and I think Jules Carron may have hidden a treasure at Trail's End or even here at Carron Creek."

Emmett's laughter rang out across the countryside. Viola and Tyler, who were too far away to hear what we were saying, looked our way.

"Why is that humorous?" I asked.

"Sure there's treasure, Miss Mara. All Silver Springs knows about it. Silver Jake has been talkin' about it for ten years."

"Why didn't you tell me?"

He was still laughing, merriment coming to him as easily as anger.

"You always talked about fixin' up the ranch and livin' there, not about riches. You know Silver Jake. You met the gentleman."

"Didn't anyone ever look for the treasure?"

"Could be. Folks around here know it's just a story."

"I may have proof. There's a letter in Jules Carron's hand in which he mentions a treasure and a map."

Emmett was unimpressed. "You've been at the house twice now, maybe more. Did you see any sign of treasure?"

"No, but I was looking for something else. You're probably right, though."

In a sense, I felt as if I had reached the end of the trail. There was nothing at Carron Creek to find. Whether or not I solved the mystery, my life would go on. As Emmett had reminded me, the future was more exciting than the past. I felt all my concerns slip away and set my thoughts on the flowers, the stream, and the man beside me.

"You sure look pretty with the breeze tossin' your hair, Miss Mara."

"You look fine and handsome yourself, Mr. Grandison." I couldn't believe I had spoken in such a bold manner.

Emmett appeared to be surprised at my compliment. For the first time since we'd met, I thought he was a little shy. But I must be entertaining fancies. Emmett Grandison was a straight-speaking man who didn't hesitate to take what he wanted. The next instant he wrapped his arms around me and pressed his mouth to mine in a new proprietary way.

This was unlike the kiss Nicholas had given me last night. It was nothing I could have imagined, and I felt myself surrendering entirely to the wonder of the moment.

When Emmett released me, he sat back, looking at me, as if to brand the kiss and my face on his memory.

"You have a blade of grass in your hair, Miss Mara. Maybe more than one."

Self-consciously, I raised my hand to my head, but he was there before me, stroking my hair lightly, brushing the grass back to the ground. All too soon this pleasant interlude came to an abrupt end.

He glanced at the sun. "We'd best hit the trail for home, Miss Mara." In a louder voice, he added, "Tyler, you ready?"

One of the horses whinnied, and Tyler called back, "Anytime you are, Boss."

While Tyler brought the horses, Viola folded her sketching pad, and we gathered the remains of our picnic to disperse to the wildlife. Although I was still reeling from the power of Emmett's kiss, I made an effort to return to the real world.

"It seems our secret treasure is common knowledge in Silver Springs, Viola," I said. "All we had to do was ask."

"In that case, someone must have found it by now. I have some good sketches. I'll show them to you when we get home. I have one of Emmett..." She froze. "What's that?"

In the deep silence, a new sound insinuated itself. From somewhere near, I heard hoof beats.

Emmett and Tyler were instantly at our side.

"Company," Emmett said, as his hand dropped to his gun.

The horseman rode up the trail, brought his steed to a halt, and said, "Whoa, hold your fire. I'm a friend."

It was Nicholas, dressed in rancher's clothes, riding a massive dark horse. Beside me, Viola took a few steps backwards and whispered his name.

"You sure as hell turn up at unexpected times, Breckinridge," Emmett said.

"What are you doing here, Nicholas?" I asked.

He looked directly at me. Mounted on the horse, he seemed more powerful, almost menacing, but when he spoke, his tone was mild and conciliatory.

"I was out riding, enjoying this beautiful countryside. I heard voices." He looked at each one of us in turn, but his gaze lingered on Tyler. "Since I know all but one of you, do you mind if I join your party?"

"We're on our way back to Silver Springs," Emmett said. "Sure you can ride along with us. It's a free country."

Nicholas appeared to hear nothing but a friendly invitation, and so we became a party of five. Our trip home proved quieter and less enjoyable. I'm sure that not one of us believed that Nicholas Breckinridge had been on a pleasure ride.

Thirteen

I thought it would be a simple matter to call on Annabelle Westbrook and ask her a few questions about Nicholas, especially since our accidental encounter on the night of the festival. But nothing in life is as easy at it seems, not even a social visit.

When I mentioned my destination to Miss Eulalie, she promptly derailed my plan. "Annabelle is in Denver this week visiting a friend. When she returns, I'll be visiting her myself, and you can accompany me. She wants to have another dress made, something fancy."

I remembered a past observation of Miss Eulalie's about the freedom enjoyed by modern young women.

"Doctor Westbrook must allow his granddaughter to come and go as she wishes," I said.

"He is fairly lenient with the girls. He wants them to have every advantage. Sometimes he frets about the responsibility of raising two young women. His dearest wish is to have them happily settled."

"They both appear to be thriving, although Annabelle isn't very friendly."

"She may be a trifle reserved. The doctor is mainly concerned about Arabella. That child is a little hoyden. She's always in some kind of trouble."

I decided to tell Miss Eulalie the real motive for my visit to Annabelle.

When I'd related the Fourth of July incident, she said, "Well, isn't that strange? If Annabelle says she knows Nicholas Breckinridge, I'm sure she does. Or maybe she knows someone who resembles him."

It was the theory of the Nicholas look-alike again, one I had examined and long since discarded.

"No, Miss Eulalie. Annabelle called Nicholas by his name."

"Then I don't know what to say."

"That's why I want to talk to her."

"Mr. Breckinridge is a man of mystery. I wish I could recall where I saw him before. I know I did."

"It would help if you could remember."

"Ah, yes, but I can't, not at the moment. If he was in Silver Springs, someone besides Annabelle must have seen him. With his singularly attractive features, he's quite memorable."

I couldn't resist teasing her. "Except to you, it seems. Seriously, Miss Eulalie, I've thought of that, but I can't interrogate the townspeople in the hope of finding someone who remembers seeing him."

"Certainly not. That would be unseemly."

"I'm still going out. Viola was in bed when I passed by her door. Imagine sleeping away one of these rare summer mornings."

"Are you going to the store?" she asked.

"No. Because I can't call on the living, I'm going to visit the dead."

At her look of horror, I added, "I'm going to walk over to the cemetery. I've been meaning to visit Jules Carron's grave.

~ * ~

I didn't have the cemetery to myself. A child with hair like a golden cloud knelt at a grave, unmindful of the proximity of her full skirts to the dust.

This was an unusual place for a young person to come, although, as I walked deeper into the cemetery, I noticed that many of the graves were those of children. Some had died when they were mere infants. Others had reached their teen years before succumbing to disease or fatal mishap. Apparently the West was inhospitable to the young.

I turned just in time to see the child at the grave rise from the ground and brush the dust from her skirts. As she did so, I noticed that she was no child but a young woman. She was petite and pretty with a fair complexion enhanced with artificial coloring. She smiled briefly in my direction and hurried past me, not saying a single word, but leaving a trace of spicy perfume to linger in the air.

This was the second woman I'd met in Silver Springs who wasn't particularly friendly. One would think that the situation was reversed, with a surplus of females in town competing for the hearts of a few bachelors. I thought myself fortunate to have found a compatible companion in Viola.

I soon discovered that the cemetery was divided into two sections, and it was in the older part that I found the grave of Jules Carron. According to the roughhewn headstone, he had died in April of 1866. Under his name, someone had carved the letters C S A, for Confederate States of America, I assumed.

I now had enough information to answer one of my earlier questions. My mother had died in June of that year, on the last day of the month. Most likely, she had received the letter that told of the inheritance but decided not to act on it.

Perhaps the emerald ring was a sufficient remembrance of Jules Carron. Lost in the tale of the past I was constructing was my father. How I wished I could ask him how much he knew of the connection. I also didn't understand how my mother could ignore the inheritance, if indeed that was what she'd done.

I was back in mystery country again, floundering in unknown waters. In both past and present, questions I couldn't answer surrounded me. Nicholas was a prime example of my confusion. I thought that by now I would know whether or not he had visited Silver Springs before the Fourth of July. Until Annabelle returned from Denver, I had only his words and my suspicions.

It was maddening. In exasperation, I sent the mysteries on their way. Kneeling at the grave of my never-known benefactor, I said a prayer for his soul and added petitions for the eternal rest of my parents. For myself, there were my main desires: Continued good health, a happy life in the West with a husband I could love forever, children and...

I paused to think. That was all. It would be sufficient. However important the rest of my wishes seemed to me now, in the end they were only diversions.

When I left the cemetery, I felt at peace. The gleaming white church and these quiet graves where the departed slept were the heart and soul of Silver Springs. I intended to remember that.

~ * ~

Although it was the last development I could have anticipated, that evening I had dinner with Nicholas Breckinridge in the dining room of the Silver Palace.

He had come to the door, asking to speak to me alone in the parlor. Viola quickly found a task that required her immediate attention. Although Miss Eulalie was polite, she spoke to him in a cool manner. When she left us alone, I hoped he would elaborate on Annabelle's remark.

Instead he said, "I'm asking you to forgive me for the liberty of a stolen kiss. I presumed that our friendship had progressed further. That was my error. I see you're not wearing the emerald. It was too intimate a token, I know."

As I searched for a response worthy of this grand speech, all I found was the truth.

"There's nothing to forgive, Nicholas, but I'd feel more comfortable if you'd take back the pendant."

"Very well. I will. I came to tell you I'm leaving Silver Springs in the morning."

"Are you going back to Boston?"

"Eventually I will, but not yet. There's been an unforeseen complication in Denver that requires my immediate departure. Will you join me tonight for a farewell dinner?"

I didn't hesitate. Annabelle might be out of town, but Nicholas was here, giving me another chance to interrogate him—subtly, of course. Where was the harm in saying goodbye to him over a meal? I would return the pendant to him then.

"I'd like to do that, Nicholas."

"I'll call for you at six."

As soon as I closed the door, Miss Eulalie materialized behind me, waving a feather duster at the hallway table. She couldn't have gone very far.

"I don't trust that man, Mara. He's too handsome and smooth. I thought you didn't either."

"I don't. Not entirely. He's asked me to have dinner with him tonight, and I accepted. He won't be in town very long. He's leaving tomorrow."

"That's a relief," she said. "Here is some unsolicited advice for you, my dear. Never put your faith in a drifter. A woman needs a man who is solid and stable, like our fair Territory."

"Like Emmett, you mean?"

"He's a good example, yes."

"This is only one evening, Miss Eulalie. Nicholas might still explain what Annabelle meant, and Emmett isn't coming to dinner tonight."

"No, I believe he'll be at the Lost Duchess."

"The saloon?"

"Yes, he goes there sometimes. Gentlemen need their distractions."

"Oh."

Until now I hadn't thought much about what Emmett did in his spare time. On occasion I pictured him sitting around a campfire, listening to old trail songs, swapping stories about the War with his men, and visiting us. All of these were safe activities but they were, unfortunately deeply routed in fantasies—mine. It occurred to me that about some matters I was incredibly naïve.

I said, "I wonder what the attractions at the Lost Duchess are?"

Miss Eulalie blushed. "Emmett has friends there, I'm sure. Now, shouldn't you start getting ready for your dinner engagement?"

"I have plenty of time."

"Well, I have to return to my sewing. Don't let Mr. Breckinridge keep you out late."

With that, she swept out of the room, effectively terminating our conversation. I was frustrated for I felt that we had much more to discuss.

~ * ~

As it turned out, Emmett dined alone at the Silver Palace that night. He greeted me cordially when he passed our table, but a certain spark I had come to expect was gone from his eyes. Since I couldn't see Emmett from where I sat, I gave Nicholas my full attention and plied him with inquiries designed to elicit the exact date of his arrival in Silver Springs and the true version of his association with Annabelle. Not surprisingly, he was elusive.

Whether or not he knew my intentions, he gave nothing away. I kept the conversation focused on the unsurpassed beauty of the Territory and the advantages of living in a growing town like Silver Springs.

Midway through the meal, Nicholas said, "Your friend would like to shoot me, I believe. It's a good thing I'm leaving tomorrow, but I hesitate to leave you unprotected in the proximity of such a rough man."

"I'll be fine, Nicholas. Emmett would never harm me."

Emmett passed by our table then with a brief word of farewell. I watched him as he paid his bill and disappeared through the door. I wondered about his next destination. Would he visit Miss Eulalie, go home to the X Bar G, or stop at the Lost Duchess Saloon?

My dessert, a plain but tasty cake, lost much of its flavor as I imagined Emmett in a company of painted ladies. *Go home, Emmett*, I pleaded silently.

I tried to think of him at the ranch, imagining him visiting his men in the bunkhouse, taking a solitary ride around the ranch, and sleeping alone under the stars.

"I'll always remember these few days in Silver Springs with you," Nicholas said. "They have been extraordinary. If I'm able to, Mara, I'll return, and we'll have many more."

~ * ~

The next morning Nicholas left on the Denver-bound train, undoubtedly taking the pendant he'd given me with him. Andy waylaid me on the street that afternoon to give me the news. With Nicholas gone and Emmett apparently keeping his distance, my thoughts turned once again to Trail's End.

I planned to exorcise the ghosts of the past with mop, soap, and water. I believed that the treasure existed. If Jules Carron had hidden it in his house, a thorough cleansing would uncover it. My decision was inspired by a dream I had one night of washing a begrimed wall, only to discover that it was made of silver.

"Why are you dressed like that?" Viola asked, as she joined us at breakfast.

I wore a plain garment of gray and white and had an apron in my hand.

"It's time I did some work at my house. I'm hoping you'll offer to join me."

A familiar pounding on the door interrupted us.

"That'll be Emmett," Miss Eulalie said. "Will you let him in, Mara?"

I had a minute to wish I'd chosen one of my new dresses to wear this morning, but Emmett appeared not to notice my garment. He stood on the doorstep with his Stetson in one hand and a bouquet in the other.

"You're up bright 'n' early after bein' out so late last night, Miss Mara," he said. "Aren't you going to invite me in?"

Miss Eulalie set the special cup she kept for Emmett on the table. "Come have coffee with me, Emmett. What pretty flowers! Are they from the X Bar G?"

"Close enough. I picked 'em on the way. They're for your table."

I took the bouquet and put them in a glass of water, wishing he'd said they were for me. But how could I expect such a display of regard from Emmett after dining with another man last night?

He watched me arrange the flowers, all of his good humor restored, making no attempt to mask an infuriatingly smug look.

"I heard your Eastern friend left town this morning, Miss Mara," he said.

"That was his plan. I'm going to ride over to Trail's End, do a little cleaning and throw the trash in a bonfire. Viola is coming with me."

I glanced at her doubtfully. She, too, was plainly dressed, but her dark blue garment looked stylish and almost regal.

"As soon as she changes clothes and finds an apron," I added.

Miss Eulalie looked from Viola to me and finally to Emmett, as if in supplication. "Oh, my dear, who knows what you'll find in that dreadful place?"

"I hope it'll be something good."

"I washed my hair last night," Viola said. "I thought I'd help Miss Eulalie with her sewing today."

"You can cover your head. Say you'll go with me. It's too nice a day to sit inside."

"Of all the dam' fool schemes," Emmett said. "Why clean a house that's goin' to be torn down?"

I glared at him. "I may not do that. I have a notion to entertain my friends in my own home."

"Your friends are welcome here, Mara," Miss Eulalie said. "Yours too, Viola."

"Thank you, Miss Eulalie, but I have a yearning to be mistress of my house, if only once. I'm not sure who I'd invite to a party, or if I even will, but I want to have the house in good condition for any activity."

"You got another motive, Miss Mara," Emmett said. "Are you still hankerin' after that make-believe treasure?"

"What I want is to have everything that's mine clean and neat," I said. "Also, I want to be sure I'm not destroying something of value."

"That sounds reasonable," Miss Eulalie said.

"We could make a room or two livable," Viola added. "Will you lend us some sheets and blankets, Miss Eulalie?"

"Of course, dear, and some rags for washing."

"What an adventure it would be, spending a night or two at Trail's End," I said.

Emmett finished his coffee and rose, setting the cup down none too quietly on the table. "Miss Mara, I told you I don't want you to go there. Did you forget Silver Jake prowlin' around with his sword?"

"You told me he was harmless."

"I said that?"

"Maybe it was the Indians you were talking about."

He smacked the table with his Stetson. "If you want to do some honest work instead of flirtin' with Boston millionaires, I have no objections. I'm goin' to send over Tyler to help you. You goin' along, Miss Viola?"

"I guess I've been drafted," she said. "I'll go back upstairs and change into something more suitable for the occasion."

"I was only having dinner with Nicholas, Emmett," I said. "I am not a flirt."

Emmett set his hat on his head and rose. "My mistake, Miss Mara. I'll see you ladies soon."

~ * ~

When Viola and I arrived at Trail's End later that morning, Tyler was already there, pacing through the high weeds that grew around the porch. With him was an older, stouter man with a gray-streaked ginger beard. They had come in a wagon that was loaded with boards.

"This is Mac," Tyler said. "Mr. Grandison sent us to help and see that you're safe."

"How thoughtful of him. You must wish you were doing whatever you usually do on the ranch instead."

For some reason, both men found this amusing.

"No, ma'am," Mac said. "This is like a vacation for us."

Emmett's unexpected contribution to my effort moved me. As guards, Tyler and Mac were superfluous, but they were both strong enough to move furniture around, and I suspected that the boards would be put to good use.

"Let's start by opening all the windows," Viola said. "Then we'll clean one room at a time."

"As we go through them, we can decide what's to be taken outside to burn. We'll dust or scrub everything else."

"Don't forget to look for a treasure map," she added. "That's why we really came, isn't it?"

"It's one of the reasons."

That was how we began our project, with energy, a clear plan, and sufficient help, but it wasn't long before we were tired and in a state of dusty disarray.

In the meantime, Mac and Tyler concentrated their efforts on the outside of the house. With the hammers, nails, and boards they'd had the foresight to bring along, they soon had the place well on its way to being mended and secure.

"You don't have to tear the house down," Mac said. "It was built to last. When we're through, all it'll need is a good cleaning. Is there anything more for the trash pile?"

"These old clothes," I said, "but not the Confederate uniform and the weapons. I'm going to keep them."

As Mac carried the remnants of Jules Carron's wardrobe out of the house, Viola said, "Playing the part of a maid on stage was much more fun."

"You're getting tired. We can quit anytime."

"So are you, but anything worth doing at all is worth doing well," she said.

That was a wise saying, one I was going to remember and act upon.

As Viola worked, she hummed to herself and frequently burst into snatches of song. She mentioned once that she could sing, but I hadn't realized until now how clear and beautiful her voice was.

When I told her how much I enjoyed listening to her, she said, "I'm going to be a featured attraction at the Silver Palace Hotel, beginning this Friday. It's all arranged."

"That's not a saloon, but..." I trailed off, imagining a cloud of disapproval descending on Viola's debut.

"You're afraid Miss Eulalie won't think it's suitable," she said.

"I'm not sure. Have you told her?"

"Not yet."

"Does Jeremiah know?"

"Again, not yet. You're the only one who does. I'm not used to sitting inside sewing, although I'm so grateful to Miss Eulalie for taking me in. It's time I moved ahead."

"Then you've found an ideal solution to your financial problem. The Palace is a respectable hotel, but it seems a waste of your talent."

"The day will come when I won't have to sing for my supper," she said. "Until then, I'll do what I must."

~ * ~

Toward the end of the afternoon, Emmett rode over in time to see the last smoldering remnants of the bonfire and to join us for a plain meal consisting of handouts from Miss Eulalie's larder.

"I take it you ladies didn't come across any gold pieces or chunks of silver, Miss Mara," he said.

"We haven't gone through the entire house yet."

"What's on the bonfire?"

"Old clothes and papers, nothing significant. Only useless things. I kept Jules Carron's Confederate uniform and his weapons."

"That's right and fitting," he said. "You did well. The old place should stand for another ten years or more now, but you still can't live so far from town. It isn't safe and it's not proper either."

It heartened me to see the look of approval on Emmett's face, and it was a pleasure to bask in his compliments. I chose to let his ideas about my future living arrangements pass by unchallenged.

While the men were outside examining the exterior of the house, Viola and I surveyed the cleaned rooms one last time.

"There's a different atmosphere here now," Viola said. "Do you suppose the ghosts have been exorcised?"

"I don't think so. In spite of everything we've done, this is still a sad house. When we were all together, the mood was festive, but it's changing back again. Can't you feel it?"

"All I know is that it's easier to breathe with all the dust swept away."

"Maybe I'm the only one affected this way. I didn't admit it to Emmett, but I can't see myself living in this house. I may sell Trail's End to him and let him tear it down or do whatever he wants with it. I'll find a small place for myself in town."

"I haven't heard Mr. Grandison make an offer for your property," Viola said.

"Nor have I, but I'm sure he still wants the land."

"He has another way to get it."

Because I had no doubt of her meaning, I set the conversation in another direction. "If you're going to begin singing at the hotel on Friday, won't you have to practice?"

"I know my songs as well as my own name. *Sweet Betsy from Pike*, all the music Mr. Stephen Foster wrote, and ballads everyone knows. I'm well prepared for what I'm going to do."

In spite of her confident words, though, she didn't appear to be looking forward to her singing engagement. I decided that if she was unhappy, the probable cause was Jeremiah.

Although Viola and Jeremiah had attended the Fourth of July celebration together, I'd observed that Jeremiah had a way of immersing himself in his books and law practice. Viola wasn't the kind of woman who liked to be overlooked.

If she and Jeremiah didn't get married, one day she would leave Silver Springs. When that happened, I was going to miss her.

Fourteen

Now that the house at Trail's End was clean and livable, my next project was to spend a night there, alone or with Viola.

As I made my announcement, I looked at Viola who was unfolding a length of shimmering gray material on her lap.

"I want to do this," I said, "but I'd be happier if I had a companion."

"So you're afraid of renegade Indians, marauding outlaws, and the ghost of Jules Carron come back to haunt you for destroying his possessions. I wouldn't have thought so," Viola said.

Her spirits were soaring again. Late yesterday afternoon, when we returned from Trail's End, she'd gone walking with Jeremiah. Already today she'd mentioned his name several times.

"I'm not afraid of anything much, Viola," I said, wishing that it were true.

Miss Eulalie swept into the room with an armful of blue material. "You should be, Mara. I've never heard of such an outlandish plan. A young woman staying by herself out in that ungodly wilderness is pure and simple trouble."

"You're talking about my land."

"Emmett won't like this."

"He won't know, unless you tell him. Now, Viola, can you join me?"

"I think so, but it's going to be complicated. I don't have to rehearse for my opening night, but I'm making a new dress. I'll need at least a morning to finish it. Can you go on ahead alone?"

"Certainly. I've done it before."

"Then later in the afternoon, Jeremiah and I will ride out together. We'll all have dinner. Afterward, he'll return to town, and you and I will spend the night there."

"This is the height of folly," Miss Eulalie said. "Jeremiah will never go along with such a dangerous plan."

"Viola and I don't answer to these men. We make our own decisions. Why don't you go with us, Miss Eulalie?"

"I have my own comfortable home and bed to sleep in at night."

"We'll have Midnight for protection."

"She's a puppy. I haven't even heard her growl yet."

"It doesn't matter. There won't be any danger."

Miss Eulalie was usually easy going, but on this occasion, she was determined to have the last word. "It isn't right. Something is going to happen to you. That isn't an ordinary house."

~ * ~

So I took off for Trail's End the next morning alone, with Miss Eulalie's words echoing in my mind, and the long spell of fine weather changed without warning. Midnight and the horses showed signs of restlessness long before I noticed the gathering darkness on the horizon.

The ride had never before seemed so long. I kept looking at the sky. It was the color of Emmett's eyes when he was angry. I wasn't afraid, as I loved thunder and lightning, but rain was another matter. I didn't want to arrive at Trail's End with my clothing drenched.

As it happened, I reached the house before the rain came; and when I opened the door, the first object I saw filled me with pleasure. On the table where we had recently enjoyed a makeshift supper was a chipped glass containing a bouquet of wildflowers.

This had to be a gift from Emmett. Miss Eulalie must have informed him of my plan, and instead of making his disapproval known, he'd come ahead of me to arrange a surprise welcome.

Soon afterward, my day at Trail's End began to take on ominous overtones. The rain held off, but thunder rumbled in the distance, bringing a disturbing sensation of something about to happen. Midnight's annoying behavior added to my apprehension. She kept running through the house in search of a place to hide.

To take my mind off the weather, I unpacked my basket of provisions and started preparations for a quick meal. When I was halfway through, the thought came to me with the suddenness of a lightning strike. If the developing storm grew severe, Viola and Jeremiah might be late or, worse still, have to cancel their plans altogether.

As the afternoon wore on and my company failed to appear, I realized that this had happened. I was alone in an isolated house in the middle of a wilderness, with only a frightened dog for company, and I had myself to blame for this dilemma.

Had I actually said "Emmett won't know" in that flippant tone I rarely used? He was my nearest neighbor, but the X Bar G was so far distant from Trail's End that it might as well be in another territory.

I wasn't really afraid. Still, I took refuge in unnecessary activity that all too soon lost its appeal. Without my company, I wasn't hungry, and long before nightfall, I made the bed with Miss Eulalie's donations, brushed my hair, and donned my nightgown.

Why had I thought this would be a good idea? Here, alone in the house with the haunted past, I couldn't remember.

The storm was still brewing, but not yet over Trail's End. Let the rain come. As soon as it was daylight, I would head back to Silver Springs. But first, I had the long night to get through.

I climbed into bed and pulled the blanket up to my shoulders. Midnight lay down, then promptly got up and changed her position. Needless to say, I couldn't sleep. Outside, the rain began at last. It wasn't a full-fledged storm but a gentle, soothing pattering on the windows, with the thunder a long way off.

I lay still, thinking about a little silver stream where blue wildflowers grew, and added a remembered face with gray-blue eyes that were flecked with golden glints. Finally, lulled by the sound of water, images of Emmett, and his kiss that lived on in my memory, as vivid and stirring as when it was new, I fell asleep.

~ * ~

A crash of thunder directly overhead woke me. I opened my eyes, instantly and completely awake. The room was flooded with light, and I was no longer alone.

Standing on my threshold I saw a figure from my nightmare, a mass of bone, blood, and muscle in a vaguely human shape. This specter could only be the unfortunate man who had been skinned alive in forty-nine or another who had met with a similar fate.

In his hand he held the kerosene lamp I had so carefully extinguished, and on his face, or what would have to pass for one under the circumstances, was a look of unendurable terror and agony. He was as I had imagined and dreamed him, but he was real.

How could that be?

If I were nearer, I could have touched him, had that been my desire. Although I didn't think I was superstitious, it occurred to me that he might be a ghost.

For one terrible moment, I gripped the edge of the blanket and contemplated diving down into the relative safety of the bedding.

Don't be a coward. Ask him what he is. Find out what he wants.

I did none of these things. He stood on the threshold motionless for a second before backing slowly out of the doorway, taking the light with him.

Get up and follow him. No, don't. That would be foolish.

I called to Midnight, but she didn't answer. Apparently I was alone in the house, except for the ghastly apparition.

In the darkness I reached for the candle that should be at my bedside. Fortunately, it was there. I set it alight and held it high. A trail of bright red drops led from the doorway to what I could see of the hall beyond.

Although the door had no lock, I closed it and blocked the entrance with the few pieces of light furniture we'd moved into the room. The barrier offered little protection, but if the apparition returned, I'd have a warning.

Then I realized the futility of trying to keep the entity away. Assuming the skinned-alive man was a ghost, he could come through a wall and wouldn't make a sound.

Not wanting to make my situation worse with terrifying suppositions, I lay back down on the bed. I didn't intend to sleep. In the dark and quiet, I could lie awake and think. There had to be a rational explanation for what I had seen, and I was going to find it, if not tonight, then in the light of the day.

~ * ~

I planned to get up before daybreak and head back to Silver Springs, never to return to the house at Trail's End, but I didn't count on falling asleep. I dreamed I was on the train again, alone in the compartment, in perpetual motion, and knew that a man with stormy gray-blue eyes waited for me in front of the Silver Palace Hotel because this had happened before.

It must have been mid-morning when an ear-splitting pounding and a thunderous voice woke me.

"Miss Mara, are you in there? If you don't open the door, I'll break it down."

I pushed back the blanket and scrambled out onto the hard floor, but before I could dismantle my barrier, Emmett came crashing into the room. Splintering wood and assorted objects flew in all directions. Then I was in his arms. His voice was gruff with concern.

"Are you all right?"

"I'm so glad you're here," I said.

He all but squeezed the breath out of my body. I didn't mind. I didn't want him to release me.

No evil thing can touch me now, I thought. *Emmett is here.*

Without a word, he led me into the kitchen, where bright, blessed sunlight poured in through the window, chasing away the night terrors.

I saw Midnight then. She lay on the table beside the glass of wildflowers, as still and limp as a rag that had been tossed aside. Her eyes were closed. I touched her head. She felt warm, but she had an ugly wound above her right eye on her white marking.

"My dog is dead," I said.

"No, she's breathing. Let her rest. What happened here last night?"

Struggling to keep my voice from shaking, I said, "I don't know, but it was horrible. Like a nightmare."

Emmett drew me close to him again. I hadn't thought he could be so gentle. I laid my head against his chest, and the material of his vest was rough against my face. I wished I could freeze this moment for some future time when he wouldn't be with me.

"Tell me," he said.

Describing the skinned-alive man in a coherent and credible manner would be a true challenge. To complicate the matter, I wasn't sure what I had seen.

"There was an intruder in the house last night. While I was sleeping, a strange man came to my room."

Emmett looked as if he were contemplating murder. His eyes were almost black.

"What man, Miss Mara?"

"It isn't what you're thinking. He just stood and looked at me and went away. That's all. I think I saw the ghost of a man who had been skinned alive."

Said aloud, my statement sounded so preposterous that I hastened to add Mrs. Haskins' terror tales, my previous nightmares, and the piece of matter I'd thought was human skin, mixing all the elements together in a tangled, feverish jumble.

"So maybe he came from the other world," I said.

As Emmett listened without comment, he spilled the contents of his canteen into a cup "Drink this. It's good strong Louisiana coffee, cooled down some, but it should help."

I took two or three swallows. While the brew wasn't to my liking, still I found it soothing.

"Did you lock the door before you went to bed?" He fired the question at me, and I tried to think.

"I must have, but I don't remember doing it."

"This mornin' it was wide open. I came by because I found your dog dumped on the trail over by my spread."

"He must have taken Midnight out of the house. When I went to sleep, she was in the room with me."

"Are you talkin' about a man or a ghost, Miss Mara?"

"I don't know what he was."

"I never heard any story about a haunt in these parts. It wasn't a spirit that left blood on the floor by your room. I don't believe in ghosts. Do you?"

"I didn't think I did, but the other explanation is too horrible. If a real man was skinned alive..."

"Think, Mara. That'd kill a man. He'd be in no shape to go strollin' in and out of a lady's bedroom. You say he up and walked away. What happened then?"

"I barricaded the door."

"Why were you alone here last night?"

"Viola was supposed to come with Jeremiah, but they never arrived."

"A bad storm ripped through Silver Springs last night," Emmett said. "It was no time for travelin'. Anyway, alone or two ladies together, this was a crazy idea."

"Do you think it was Silver Jake? You said he might harm me."

He shrugged. "I wasn't thinkin' of anythin' like this. In or out of his right mind, Silver Jake wouldn't hurt a woman. Finish your coffee now and go get dressed. If Miss Lallie could see us now, she'd have the preacher here by this evenin'."

"Why?"

"You're wearin' a nightgown."

I hadn't forgotten, but set alongside the night's horrors, a departure from convention was insignificant. Nonetheless, I hastened to do his bidding. When I joined him in the kitchen, he was talking softly to Midnight. Her eyes were open now, and she was wagging her tail weakly.

"You'll come with me, Miss Mara. I'll send one of the men back for Midnight and the buckboard."

I laid my hand on the little dog's head, above the nasty wound. For the first time since my ordeal began, I felt like crying.

"I thought you'd be safe with me, Midnight, but you're going to be all right," I said.

"Sure she is. Now, let's you and me get on home, if you don't mind riding double on my horse."

~ * ~

By home, Emmett meant the X Bar G. I sat in his kitchen, watching him prepare breakfast and brew another strong pot of Louisiana coffee. It was strange that I could still be hungry after all the talk of blood, skin, and related unsavory details, but as Emmett set a plate stacked high with wheat cakes in front of me, I realized what ailed me. I was ravenous, and no food had ever tasted better.

"You're a good cook, Emmett," I said. "I wouldn't have thought so."

"I get by. Usually I eat in the bunkhouse with the men or at the Palace. Sometimes Miss Lallie invites me."

"I feel so much better now, but I wish I knew what happened."

"I don't like any of this. Someone wants to scare you and maybe do more. Could be next time it'll be you dumped on the trail instead of the dog."

"Or I'll be skinned alive. That's a hideous thought."

"You've been listenin' to foolish stories," he said.

"You really don't think Silver Jake had anything to do with what I saw?"

"He lives in his own world. I don't see why he'd concern himself with you, but I aim to have a good talk with him. If he's the one, I'll stop him."

"Silver Jake is tall and wiry. My apparition was stockier."

"I'm goin' to see him anyway."

"When you go, will you take me with you?" I asked.

"You don't want to go callin' on a crazy man, Miss Mara. I'll talk to him alone."

"Please, Emmett. This happened to me."

He smiled at me then, for the first time since he broke down my door.

"If I don't, like as not you'll try to find him on your own and get yourself in trouble. You'll be safer with me."

"When can we go?"

"Soon as I find out where he's stayin'. Sometimes he travels around the Territory."

On an impulse, I said, "You might look for an Indian, too. I saw one the night I was almost run over. Maybe they're connected in some way."

"Describe him."

I did my best, falling back on words like grotesque and gruesome, but my memory refused to yield any specific details.

"Never saw anyone like that in town," he said. "Nowhere else neither. If you're done eatin', Miss Mara, I aim to get you back to Miss Lallie."

I rose and followed him outside to the post where he had tethered his horse. He mounted, lifted me up into the saddle sideways in front of him, and we began the ride back to Silver Springs. I kept my arms around him, feeling warm and secure, almost sleepy, as my hands rested on his hard body.

We didn't talk much until I remembered something.

"Thank you for bringing me those beautiful flowers, Emmett. It was such a pleasant surprise to walk into the kitchen and find them."

Although I couldn't see his face, I knew by the almost imperceptible pause that he was puzzled.

"What flowers, Miss Mara? The ones on the table? I didn't leave them for you."

Fifteen

We found Miss Eulalie in the parlor sewing and Viola sitting quietly in a chair, reading her book. Miss Eulalie dropped her material and rushed over to take me in her arms.

"Mara! We've been so worried. Why is Emmett with you?"

"There was some excitement at Trail's End last night," Emmett said. "I brought Mara home."

"Where were you yesterday, Viola?" I asked.

As she turned her head toward me, I noticed the bruise on the side of her face.

"I'm so sorry, Mara. We started out, but the storm came, and lightning spooked the horses. I was thrown out of the buckboard, and Jeremiah brought me back here. I wasn't seriously hurt but didn't feel up to traveling."

"Colorado Territory is proving hazardous for women," I said. "You have to sing at the Palace tonight, Viola. How will you cover up that bruise?"

"I don't think I can conceal it completely, but there's no need to. I've changed my plans. Tell me about the excitement I missed."

As I related the harrowing events, I realized that my story sounded like an imaginary tale. Its chief weakness was my inability to explain the nature of the apparition. Left to interpret the incident without any help from me, Miss Eulalie and Viola both rushed to conclude that I had seen a ghost.

I said, "Maybe I did. After last night, I'm almost ready to believe in supernatural manifestations."

I thought Viola looked pale, or perhaps it was only the dark bruise that made it seem so.

She closed her book. "I'm so sorry, Mara. I should have been with you."

"Wrong," Emmett said. "Neither one of you should've been there, and you aren't goin' again. Do you understand me, Miss Mara?"

"I do, but there's no need for you to use that domineering tone. I have no desire to return to a place where I've acquired an enemy or attracted a ghost."

"Where's Midnight?" asked Miss Eulalie.

"She's recuperatin' at the X Bar G," Emmett said. "Mac will bring her home later. Now, if you ladies don't need me to do anythin', I'll be at the Lost Duchess for a spell."

Emmett was going to the saloon again? I hoped my face didn't betray the dismay I felt. I'd hoped he would stay a little longer. Not that I needed him, but his presence was so settling.

Maybe I should reconstruct that thought. Settled wasn't the best way to describe how Emmett made me feel.

"Don't stay at that saloon too long," Miss Eulalie said. "We're having a special dinner tonight. Jeremiah is going to join us, and of course you're invited as well."

Emmett laid his hand on my shoulder. "I won't. Get some rest, Miss Mara. You're safe now. I'll be back soon."

I walked to the door with him and thanked him one last time. "We still don't know what I saw last night. I don't think it was an apparition."

"More'n likely there's a man behind it, but so long as you stay away from Trail's End, you should be safe," he said.

~ * ~

I guessed there was a secret brewing around me that had nothing to do with the haunting of Trail's End. The air was charged with excitement, and the mystery deepened as Miss Eulalie brought out a crocheted tablecloth and her best china. In the meantime, Viola arranged a charming bouquet with flowers cut from the garden for the center of the table.

After dinner, Miss Eulalie made an announcement. "We're celebrating an engagement tonight. Jeremiah and Viola are going to be married."

I almost dropped the fragile crystal glass. "Viola! What a surprise! You and Jeremiah have only just met."

If Jeremiah hadn't been sitting beside her, I might have said more. I wondered what had prompted this sudden engagement and if it had anything to do with Viola's decision not to sing at the Silver Palace.

Emmett offered his best wishes, but he seemed less than enthusiastic. I suspected he still had reservations about Viola. Miss Eulalie, however, was oblivious of any undercurrents. She glanced at me and then at Emmett.

"They are going to be married right here in the parlor very soon. Viola will find a more enduring happiness in the home of a good man than on the stage."

I doubted that, as I knew Viola was serious about her acting. And what about her plan to join her brother in San Francisco? Could she have fallen so quickly and completely in love with Jeremiah Brown that she would be willing to abandon her career?

The hasty engagement seemed out of character for her. Although I thought Jeremiah a congenial, but dull, choice as husband for my vibrant friend, I kept the doubt out of my voice as I wished them happiness.

Viola bestowed a warm smile on Jeremiah. "The life of an actress isn't as glamorous as you think, Mara. I hope Jeremiah won't be disappointed in me."

"That will never happen," Jeremiah said. "I still can't believe my good fortune in finding you."

After dinner, Miss Eulalie asked Viola to sing for us, and she was agreeable. When I mentioned my fondness for the songs of Mr. Stephen Foster, she sang *The Voice of Bygone Days* and *Hard Times Come Again No More*. The melody and words had never sounded more melancholy. Before long, the festive mood generated by the engagement announcement had vanished.

"Let us pause in life's pleasures and count its many tears..."

What a jolly idea! I thought. *Let's do that.*

Leaning back in the chair, I willed myself to stay awake and listen to the music, but the next thing I knew, Viola was finishing a different song about dying and bells tolling.

A pall had settled over our little group, and Miss Eulalie's eyes were filled with tears.

"Can't you sing somethin' cheerful, Miss Viola?" Emmett demanded. "I was just at the Lost Duchess, where the entertainment was a whole lot livelier."

Jeremiah said, "I can provide a different sound. I brought my banjo."

This evening was brimming with surprises. "I wouldn't have guessed that you played a musical instrument, Jeremiah," I said.

"I'll continue Viola's program of songs by Mr. Foster, but I know some merrier selections."

Jeremiah's unexpected musical contributions saved the evening from descending into gloom. Later that night, however, when I was on the verge of falling asleep, I had a premonition that something unfortunate was going to happen to me soon. In spite of Emmett's care and protection, this disaster was making its way slowly toward my life. Even though I never set eyes on Trail's End again, it would find me.

~ * ~

Long uninterrupted hours of sleep in a familiar bed had a marvelous restorative effect on me, as did the bright sunshine. As soon as I opened my eyes the next morning, I saw a pencil sketch of Emmett on the chest of drawers. The artful work captured his mercurial personality and the look of storms that so often came to his eyes.

I went at once to Viola's room to thank her. She was already dressed for the day and brushing her hair in front of the mirror.

"I thought you'd like it," she said.

"You have another great talent. The picture looks exactly like Emmett."

"It did turn out well. I thought you'd like to have a likeness of him since you appear to be so enthralled by the man."

"He's very comforting," I said.

"Only that?"

"I feel at home with him."

"That's saying the same thing in different words."

"I suppose it is. The news of your engagement came as a surprise to me. You've only known Jeremiah for a few weeks."

Viola lay down the brush and held her left hand up to the light. As of yet, there was no ring on her finger.

"From the beginning, I knew I wanted Jeremiah but I didn't think he felt the same way about me. My life is going to be different now. I'm going to be happy."

"I'm sure you will be."

"Isn't that Midnight barking outside? There's someone at the door, I think."

"It might be Emmett," I said.

"I wonder when he runs his ranch. He is always in some other place. I'll go down and entertain him, while you get out of your nightgown."

It didn't take me long to get dressed because I didn't want to miss anything the others were saying in the kitchen. But when I joined them, I discovered that I'd interrupted a discussion about cattle.

The happiness and approval in Emmett's eyes sent a warmth coursing through my veins. I longed to be as near to him as I'd been yesterday, close enough so that his vest touched my cheek and my hands could move up to his brown hair and pull his face close to mine.

I called a halt to my rambling thoughts. That last part had happened only in my imagination.

"You're dressed more suitably for the occasion this mornin' than you were yesterday, Miss Mara," he said.

As Miss Eulalie looked confused, I added, "For the hot weather, he means. What occasion is it? Are we going somewhere?"

"I tracked down Silver Jake. He's at his cabin, and you can ride over with me, if you still want to."

"Of course I do. We can leave anytime."

"Right now then. I brought Star for you."

"Have another cup of coffee, Emmett," Miss Eulalie said. "Here's tea for you, Mara. Now, why are you two paying a social call on a gentleman in Mr. Jake's condition?"

"I want to be sure he's not the one who tried to scare Miss Mara," Emmett said.

"I thought it was a ghost who did that."

"Oh, Miss Eulalie, I don't think so," I said. "It must be a living person."

"This frightens me, Mara. If you must go, stay close to Emmett."

I thought her smile was a trifle sly, but I might have imagined it, because no one noticed anything out of the ordinary.

"I'll see she does that," Emmett said.

~ * ~

"This is a good, sunshiny day. I don't want us to go rushin' through it. After we talk to Silver Jake, we'll take the long way back to Silver Springs," Emmett said.

Riding alongside Emmett on my own horse, I could almost forget our mission and think that we were bound for a picnic or some other outdoor diversion. I let my imagination run amok and imagined us once again heading to our home at the X Bar G. It must be the lingering effect of Viola's engagement, for my thoughts were no longer in the realm of reality.

When we rode past a field of blue and yellow flowers, I remembered the bouquet, the one Emmett hadn't given me.

"Do you think somebody from the ranch left the flowers? I asked. "Tyler or maybe Mac?"

"They'd sure give you flowers, Miss Mara, but they were at the spread all day and night. Your gentleman friend from Boston was in Denver. He'd be more likely to give you jewelry than somethin' growin' free."

So Emmett had known about the pendant all along. Because the subject was a sensitive one, I decided to leave it alone.

"Do you think the apparition man did it?"

"No, Miss Mara. Makes no sense that he would."

"Maybe they were meant for my grave."

Emmett scoffed at this morbid notion. "Write 'em down, all the mysteries. Write the flowers first."

"I have a journal, but I haven't remembered to write in it in days."

"With all that's been happenin' lately, you should do that. You'd have a genuine dime novel when you got through," he said.

~ * ~

Our ride came to an end too soon, as is always the case when one is engaged in a pleasurable activity. But we were going to take the long way back. We were only midway through our adventure.

"There's the cabin up ahead and Jake, there out in front," Emmett said.

A large wolf-like dog with a handsome face and ferocious manner ran up to our horses with a grand display of barking and bared fangs.

"That's Wolf," Emmett said. "He won't hurt us."

Silver Jake, clad in shabby clothing and engaged in the ordinary chore of chopping wood, shouted at Wolf to be quiet. There was no sign of the sword today, only the hatchet. As soon as he saw us, he put it down and came forward to greet us. If I didn't know his history, I would think him as sane as Emmett or I.

We dismounted and approached him slowly, while Wolf growled and stationed himself beside his master.

"Afternoon, Major," Emmett said. "I brought a lady to meet you."

Silver Jake's eyes were bright and intelligent, and his smile was welcoming. But with his first words, the illusion of normalcy fled.

"I know this lady already, Mr. Grandison. She stepped down from the portrait and got away. You trapped her. You're a clever man."

"Did you see a picture of my mother in the house at Trail's End, Silver Jake?" I asked. "I resemble her, I think."

"No, the woman in the portrait has a dog, not a child. Her name is Margaret."

"The picture was painted a long time ago, before I was born."

"She's long gone," he said. "Since you've got her, it's all right, Mr. Grandison."

Emmett said, "You like to go back to the old place, don't you, Major? Been there lately?"

"I got to leave now to rejoin my regiment," he said.

I saw that we were too late. In his lonely world, he had already left us to ride to a War that had ended over ten years ago.

"Of course you do, Major," I said. "You have to fight for the Cause."

"Is the South winning?" he asked.

"Both sides are losing."

"I'm bound to go then. I'm needed. I've stayed in these mountains too long. You're a real fine lady, Miss Margaret. It's nice of you to come visit me."

He might have said so much more. All of the answers for which I'd been searching might be buried in his mind. I wasn't going to hear them today. In the meantime, I thought I'd solved one mystery.

"I came to thank you for the flowers, Silver Jake," I said. "They're so beautiful."

He smiled at me, but didn't admit or deny that he had left the bouquet in the house at Trail's End.

~ * ~

On the way back to Silver Springs, we came to a clearing. I pleaded exhaustion, and we dismounted. Tall dark trees were reflected in a stream so shiny and bright that I thought it must be lined with silver nuggets.

"This is like Carron Creek," I said.

"We have lots of places like this in the Colorado Territory. Like I always say, this is God's country."

We sat on the hard forest ground in a companionable way, and I watched Emmett as he lay back, using his brawny arms for a pillow. I trailed a flower through the water and wished I knew what he was thinking.

I didn't have to wait long to find out. Suddenly and without a word, he pulled me gently over to him and kissed me. I felt the roughness of his face on my skin and his hard mouth on my lips, while his hands pressed firmly on my back, bringing me closer to his body. A strong sweet smell of leather invaded my senses and set my heart racing like a wild colt crossing a plain.

"Emmett," I whispered, when I was able to speak.

He lay back down on the ground, this time using his arms to take me with him, and held me in a close embrace. He didn't say anything, but gradually he moved his hands up to my hair, stroking it in the same gentle way that he had touched Star. From the nearby aspens where he had tethered the horses, I heard a soft whinny.

He spoke then. "I'd best be takin' you back to Silver Springs, Miss Mara."

"Yes," I said softly. "Before it gets late."

He rose, pulled me to my feet, and kissed me again, a long, searing kiss that seemed more like a prelude than an ending. Emmett's ardor had so completely distracted me that I almost forgot the primary purpose of our visit.

As much as I would have wished to remain in that joy-filled state to which he had taken me, I knew that somewhere the real world waited for us, with a menace that was still as murky as it had ever been.

"I sure like bein' alone with you, Mara," he said. "When we get back to town, you can brush the pine needles out of your hair and put on that pretty green dress with the white stripes. We'll have dinner together at the Silver Palace and make the day last a little longer."

"Pine needles?" Quickly I moved my hand through my hair.

"One," he said. "No, two. Here, I have 'em."

As he helped me up on Star, I said, "I'm sure Silver Jake wasn't the intruder, and I'm not ready to believe it was a ghost. Where does that leave us?"

"With someone else, a real man, passing through, wanting a place to stay for the night. Could be you imagined some of it."

"I didn't. Not any of it. As impossible as it sounds, he was as I described him."

"I don't know, Mara. Let me think on it."

He mounted his horse, and we set out on the trail to Silver Springs, riding toward home and the end of the day.

"That talk about my mother's portrait was unnerving," I said. "As Jules Carron and Silver Jake were partners, he would have seen it."

"Sometimes you can talk to Jake and get a sensible answer," Emmett said. "Others, you're talkin' to yourself. We might learn somethin' more later."

"In the meantime, all I can do is wait and see what happens next."

"And be ready for it. That's where I'm goin' to come in."

Emmett's last words replayed themselves in my head all the way back to Silver Springs. I felt my anxieties leave me, let them blow away in the breeze. We were only at the beginning of this journey to our possible future. He wanted our time together to continue, as did I. We were going in the same direction. Some night soon, we wouldn't have to part.

This feeling of happiness and anticipation stayed with me throughout the ride home and our dinner in the hotel dining room.

I was devoting all my attention to a piece of berry pie when I heard Emmett exclaim angrily under his breath. I looked up to see what had annoyed him.

"That Easterner," he said. "He's back in Silver Springs."

Sixteen

"Nicholas is here?" I said. "That's strange. He left only a few days ago."

Emmett frowned into his coffee cup. "I thought he was gone for good."

"Is he alone?"

"The banker's with him. If you're finished with your pie, Mara, I should be takin' you home now."

"Yes. We've had a long day."

The sight of Nicholas, as handsome as ever, nodding to us as we left the dining room, disturbed me. Annabelle still hadn't returned from her trip. Before I saw Nicholas again, I wanted to talk to her.

The pressure of Emmett's hand on my shoulder suggested possession and reminded me how safe I'd been with him all day.

Stay close to him, Mara, and you'll never be in danger again, I told myself.

And are you thinking of Nicholas as a source of peril now? If so, it would be advisable to tread warily.

It was dark outside, and my long day with Emmett had dwindled down to minutes. As we walked back to Miss

Eulalie's house, he held my hand, and, when we reached the gate, he turned me around to face him.

"You're right skittish tonight, Mara. Is somethin' wrong?"

"No, nothing. What could be the matter?"

He tightened his grip on my hand. "I reckon you're still lookin' for that skinned man in the shadows?"

"I'm not. I was terrified for a few minutes. Now I'm curious. I was hoping we'd learn something from Silver Jake today."

"There's always another time. You do like I tell you and stay away from Trail's End. Someday we'll learn the truth."

I longed to touch him, wished he would seal our evening with another searing kiss. But I kept my hand on the top of the gate, and he only said, "Goodnight, Mara. Don't you fret. I'm goin' to be close by."

~ * ~

On Sunday I accompanied Miss Eulalie to the little white church, and four of the Silver Springs bachelors came to town. Because Doctor Westbrook had driven out to a ranch to tend to a boy who had been bitten by a snake, Miss Eulalie had ample time to gossip.

We stood outside the church, where the congregation lingered to discuss the events of the past week, their plans for the rest of the day, or the sermon delivered by the affable Reverend Winters. His homily echoed in my mind, along with the strains of the last hymn we had sung. I felt confident that I was going to defeat the evil force in my life and find my way to place of true happiness.

Miss Eulalie called my attention to pair of tall, rugged men who stood talking to the Reverend. "Cade and Clay Mallory are Southerners from Georgia. They have a small ranch outside

Silver Springs. They're brothers and the only red-haired men in town. I find them a little rough around the edges, but aside from that, they're almost as good a catch as Emmett."

"Together? Or are you referring to them as individuals?

"Really, Mara, you're impossible. Of course, I meant that each man is a good catch. Nathaniel, over talking to Miss Amelia Carson, owns the newspaper. He's quiet and intellectual. That dark man with the lovely moustache is newly arrived in town. I don't know his name."

The unknown man appeared to be the best prospect for a woman in search of a husband. His expression was friendly and his bushy moustache gave him an air of distinction. At the moment he was standing alone, but I didn't think he would remain unclaimed for long.

The red-haired rancher brothers had finished their conversation with Reverend Winters. One of them, the taller of the two, turned and looked directly at us. He smiled. I couldn't tell whether Miss Eulalie or I had caught his attention. Probably, it was Miss Eulalie who had a special affinity for her countrymen.

"I'm happy that so many of us in Silver Springs are from the South," she said. "I could almost feel as if I'm back in Dixie again."

"Aren't you happy living in the West?" I asked.

"Of course. This is my home now. Would you like me to introduce you to Clay or Cade or maybe Nathaniel, if he can pry himself away from Miss Carson?"

"Not today."

"You haven't met very many people in Silver Springs," she said. "Only Emmett and the dubious Nicholas Breckinridge.

Oh, and Reverend Winters. Our Viola has already found herself a husband."

I felt as if Miss Eulalie knew well the reason for my apparent lack of interest in getting to know one of the eligible males in the Territory, but of course, she couldn't. The kisses Emmett and I had shared were a secret, one I would never reveal to another woman, no matter how close I was to her.

"Viola and I are different women," I said. "Maybe next Sunday, I'll let you introduce me to one of the Silver Springs' catches. You make them sound like trout, Miss Eulalie. Emmett didn't come to church."

"He attends sometimes. Whether he goes to church or not, he's a good man. There are plenty of men in Silver Springs, but you couldn't do any better for yourself than Emmett."

"Let's go along home now, Miss Eulalie," I said. "On the way, you can tell me why you're trying to steer me toward another man, since you like Emmett so well."

"That's not what I'm doing, Mara," she protested. As we walked away from the thinning crowd around the church, however, she deftly changed the subject to Eastern fashions and the new book of patterns she had ordered.

~ * ~

The next morning Viola appeared at breakfast wearing a dark red dress and a garnet ring.

"My, it's simply beautiful," Miss Eulalie said. "The stones are so perfect with your coloring."

"It belonged to Jeremiah's mother. We're going to get married sooner than we planned, Miss Eulalie, maybe late next week. Can we be ready by then?"

Miss Eulalie's gallant attempt to conceal her surprise failed. "Why the haste, Viola? We're only halfway to finishing your sewing."

"It won't matter if we don't complete everything," she said. "Jeremiah and I don't want to wait."

For a second I thought I detected a fleeting look of fear in Viola's eyes. Then it was gone. But that was absurd. She was smiling and admiring the way the sun made the garnets in her ring shine.

"Oh, Mara," Miss Eulalie said, "I picked up a letter for you. It came all the way from Michigan." She brought a small envelope out of her apron pocket and handed it to me across the table.

I recognized the neat, slanting handwriting. "It's from my friend, Eliza. Do you mind if I open it now?"

"Not at all. Read it out loud, if you will. Viola and I are curious."

I unfolded the letter and read:

> *Dear Mara,*
>
> *My father wants me to ask when you are going to come home. His main concern is that you may have fallen ill or met with some misfortune. We all miss you. I am writing to give you information I wrongly assumed you already possessed. You have expressed an interest in learning the identity of Jules Carron.*
>
> *I believe he was one of my mother's cousins. You will remember she deserted us and my father forbids her name to be spoken in our house. Our mothers were close friends who traveled to New*

Orleans one summer before we were born. Jules Carron lived there, and they must have seen him at that time. There is no way I can communicate with my mother's family. Please write to tell me about your adventures in the Wild West. I hope to see you at my wedding.

Your friend,
Eliza Cameron

Miss Eulalie dabbed at her eyes. "How very sad. They were in love, but fate tore them apart, never to reunite them on this earth."

"You've created a whole story after hearing one brief letter, Miss Eulalie," I said. "You should be a novelist. This does answer one of my questions, though. Jules Carron and my mother knew each other."

"For one short Louisiana summer. I wish we knew more. Are you planning to go back to Michigan for your friend's wedding?"

"No, my life is here now. I'll have to give Eliza my good wishes through the mail."

"I'm glad you've solved one of your mysteries, Mara," Viola said. "It's a pity you can't know all the details."

I set Eliza's letter on the table. As I did so, I wondered if my obsession with the past was finally over or only beginning.

I had been born in 1855. That suggested a remote possibility I didn't want to think about. If my mother had been in love with Jules Carron, how far had their relationship progressed? Could the mysterious Confederate soldier be my real father? If that were the case, it would explain the long silence that had surrounded their association.

This was a wildly improbable idea. I thought of the man who had raised me and taught me so many of life's lessons. I remembered nursing him through the years when he was ill and keeping a lonely vigil at his side during those sad last days. Adam Marsden was my father.

I still hoped to find another old letter, hidden in some secret place, this one addressed to me, that would show me how to connect all the pieces of the puzzle. Logically, that letter would be in my Pineville home, the one I had already searched thoroughly and in vain.

"Mara, honey, are you all right?" Miss Eulalie asked.

"I'm fine."

I folded Eliza's letter and set my thoughts aside until I could pursue them in some quiet, private place. "I'm more interested in the future now, but my new life is a direct result of previous connections and events."

"That's always true," Miss Eulalie said.

~ * ~

Finally Annabelle Westbrook returned to Silver Springs. She had been gone a week, but I was growing impatient. The mystery of Nicholas was not buried in the mists of the past. My questions could be simply answered, and Annabelle was the one who possessed the relevant information.

"I'm going over to Doctor Westbrook's house to talk to Annabelle about the new dress she wants, if you'd still like to come with me," Miss Eulalie said.

I set aside my journal. I had been writing for an hour, updating it with long paragraphs about my adventures with Emmett.

"I'll think of a subtle way to draw her out," I said. "I don't want her to think I'm an inquisitor."

"But that's what you are. I advise you to ask her outright."

"I only hope she'll talk to me. She gave me the impression that she didn't like me when we met at church."

"Annabelle wouldn't look favorably on any girl championed by Emmett Grandison."

"Is that what's he's doing with me?" I asked. "I hoped it was something more intimate."

"Well, you would know, dear. Not I."

Miss Eulalie was in a light-hearted, teasing mood, and we both enjoyed the short walk to Doctor Westbrook's house. We found Annabelle outside tending a small vegetable garden. Her fair hair was braided and pinned up, and she wore a large apron. She smiled at Miss Eulalie but seemed surprised that I had accompanied her.

"You remember Mara," Miss Eulalie said. "She wanted to talk to you, Annabelle. Is your grandfather out?"

"He always is. Someone is continually getting sick or hurting himself. No one watered my garden while I was gone. That was supposed to be Arabella's task, but Grandfather lets her run wild. Let's go inside."

She wiped her hands on her apron and removed it, as we followed her through the back door into the kitchen.

"Did you have a pleasant stay in Denver?" Miss Eulalie asked.

"It was entertaining, but I'm always happy to come home to Silver Springs. Before I tell you my ideas about the dress, what did you want to talk to me about, Miss Marsden?"

I felt uncomfortable with the direct approach Miss Eulalie had advocated, thinking it would sound rude, but, as I began speaking, I realized it was the best way to broach this delicate matter.

"You'll remember we saw each other on the night of July Fourth after the festival," I said."

"Yes?"

"I'm inquiring about the gentleman who escorted me home, Mr. Nicholas Breckinridge. Did you meet him before that evening?"

"Certainly," she said. "I wouldn't speak to a stranger."

"Can you tell me when you met him?"

"I can do that. Why do you want to know?"

Her tone had sharpened perceptibly. I wasn't fooled by Annabelle's willingness to cooperate with my inquiry. She didn't like me. She was being passably polite because I had come to her house with Miss Eulalie. I suspected that if I'd met her in town, she wouldn't have been so forthcoming. Probably she wouldn't even have spoken to me.

I said, "The gentleman told me that he didn't know you, that he had never been in Silver Springs before that night."

"For some reason, the gentleman isn't telling the truth," she said.

"Please tell me when you met him."

Annabelle said, "I don't remember the date. It was a few weeks before the Fourth. Around the middle of June."

That was when I thought I'd seen Nicholas in Silver Springs. When I *did* see him on the night of my accident. He was there.

"It isn't flattering that he would deny knowing me," Annabelle said. "Are you quite certain that's what he said?"

"I am. And how did you two meet?"

"I was coming out of the store and one of those wretched little boys who are always running in the street collided with me. He kept on going, but I dropped my purchases all over the sidewalk.

"As you can imagine, I was embarrassed and distressed, too, because a few items were ruined. I felt so clumsy, but Mr. Breckinridge stopped and helped me retrieve what we could. He said it wasn't my fault. Then he told me his name and said he was just passing through town.

"I saw him with you at the festival and hoped that he'd come back to town to stay. That's all. Now, Miss Eulalie, can we talk about my dress?"

That's all? It was enough to brand Nicholas Breckinridge a liar. He was always the gentleman. This time, his act of kindness had betrayed him. Now, I had to find out why he had deliberately misled me.

"Thank you, Annabelle," I said.

She smiled coolly, no doubt relieved to have the interview over.

While she and Miss Eulalie began a long discussion about materials, colors, and styles, I sat quietly, trying to decide the best way to use this new information. The next time Nicholas Breckinridge approached me, if indeed there was a next time, I was going to be ready for him.

Seventeen

Miss Eulalie rapped softly on my bedroom door. "You have a gentleman caller waiting for you in the parlor, Mara."

I closed my journal and set it aside. "Is it Nicholas?" I asked.

"No, dear, it's one of the Mallory brothers, Cade."

"But I don't know him."

"You soon will, when I introduce you. He's come to call on you."

As I followed Miss Eulalie downstairs, feeling unready for this surprise meeting, I recalled the red-haired man who had smiled at Miss Eulalie in church on Sunday. Why hadn't he approached us then?

"Cade is charming and gallant, like the dear, lost Southern boys of my girlhood days, and very, very handsome. But, you've seen him."

She had previously referred to the Mallory brothers as rough around the edges. Because we were at the foot of the stairs, so near the parlor that our guest could overhear our comments, I kept my observation to myself.

Cade Mallory rose when we entered the room. Amidst our familiar furnishings, he seemed taller than he'd been in the churchyard, and away from the sunlight, his hair was a darker shade of red. He wore a suit that looked new in spite of its old-fashioned cut. I suspected it was rarely worn. His eyes were dark brown, and I had to admit that he was attractive. Why, then, couldn't I summon any enthusiasm for this meeting?

"Miss Eulalie, ma'am," he drawled. "Thank you for allowing me the pleasure of meeting your charming houseguest."

He kissed Miss Eulalie's hand, as courtly a move as she could have wished. The smile he gave me was as bright as a Southern sun must be. It filled the parlor with heat and radiance. In a few more minutes, I would be longing for shade.

"Miss Mara, I've wanted to make your acquaintance since I saw y'all at church. It's my good fortune that you're a friend of our Miss Eulalie."

"I'll leave you two alone now," Miss Eulalie said. She didn't do that, however. She sat in her chair in a corner of the parlor, transferring yards of light green material from the table to her lap. She didn't even pretend to be sewing.

"I'm pleased to meet you, Mr. Mallory," I said. Desperately I searched for something else to say. With Nicholas on the train and with Emmett in any situation, I had always known how to converse intelligently. It had come as naturally to me as breathing. With Cade Mallory, I was floundering. Should I ask him if he had served in the Confederate army? That might not be a good idea. Certainly he must have done so, but he might find the topic too sensitive for casual discussion.

He didn't appear aware that I was uncomfortable or that anything was amiss.

"Please call me Cade, Miss Mara," he said. "I came to invite you to go riding with me after church next Sunday. If you're agreeable, we could go over to the Double C. That's our ranch. My brother and I run it together."

"Well," I said. "Next Sunday, Cade? Miss Eulalie and I may already have plans."

"No, we don't, Mara," Miss Eulalie said. "We're only going to church. After that, you're free."

"Well..."

He waited for my answer. I had to speak.

"There's some pretty country between here and the Double C, lots of nice flowers, and I'll take right good care of you, honey."

"I'm sure you will, Mr. Mallory," I said.

I couldn't think of an excuse that wouldn't offend this kind and earnest man, and time was passing. I could hear the ticking of the clock in the hall.

"All right, Cade, I'd like that very much."

"I'll meet you right after church," he said. "I've got to be on my way now. Miss Eulalie, thank you. Miss Mara, thank you too, in advance, for your company."

I walked with him to the door and bid him goodbye. When Miss Eulalie and I were alone, I said, "Why did I do that?"

"Why would you refuse? You have to find a husband, Mara. Cade is clearly interested. It's like I told you, honey, the Mallory boys are good catches."

"I didn't think my getting married was a life and death matter. I've been in Silver Springs since June. Why did Cade Mallory see me only last week?"

"You've only been to church twice. That's one of the places unattached people meet one another."

"That's not why I went."

"No, of course not, dear, but that doesn't alter the fact that church is a good place to find a husband. Now, next Sunday, you go along on your outing with Mr. Mallory. You might find him to your liking."

~ * ~

I waited for half an hour, plenty of time for Cade Mallory to have ridden out of Silver Springs. When I was fairly certain that I wouldn't encounter him outside the house, I left for a long walk. I was annoyed with myself for not having politely declined his invitation.

Emmett was a strong presence in my thoughts. I couldn't forget his kisses. In this state, I couldn't concentrate on the attentions of another man. The trouble was that I hadn't seen him since he'd brought me home from Trail's End, promising me that he'd be close by.

When I'd mentioned his absence to Miss Eulalie, she only said, "Sometimes Emmett gets busy on the X Bar G. Don't fret. He'll be around."

I hoped that was true, and I wished I knew what he was doing.

This was not a day to ponder the wayward ways of men. The sun was bright and warm, rather like Mr. Mallory's smile, and the world outside seemed to call to me. First I walked to the cemetery, where I said another prayer for the soul of Jules Carron and tried to turn my thoughts from the pleasures of this world to those of the next.

I was unsuccessful. Eventually I wandered back to the heart of town, where I felt immediately at home. At every step, I found something to catch my interest. I especially loved to walk down Main Street and mingle with the townspeople.

It was here that I saw a familiar face. The small woman who had been in the cemetery when I'd first found Jules Carron's grave was walking toward me. Her dark rose dress was too fancy for the noon hour, as was the elaborately trimmed hat that covered most of her golden curls. Her necklace was more appropriate for evening wear, and she wore a generous amount of face paint. I suspected that she was one of the saloon girls. Fancy ladies, Miss Eulalie had called them once.

She didn't notice my scrutiny, appearing to be unaware of anything except the wood plank sidewalk. When she reached the general store, she turned and went inside. That happened to be my destination, too.

Although I didn't need anything, I loved to browse among the vast array of merchandise, especially the ribbons and dime novels. I also wanted to know something more about the saloon girl, if that was what she was.

Of course she was a saloon girl, and she plied her trade at the Lost Duchess where Emmett was a frequent visitor. How well did he know her? I didn't like the direction my thoughts were taking. Surely there were other such establishments in town. It was possible that Emmett had never set eyes on her, but I didn't think it likely.

I opened the door and stepped over a small brown dog that lay asleep near a barrel of candy.

I headed for the aisle where I knew the books were kept. Several new titles had been added since my last visit. I had always been fond of reading, but access to books was limited on the frontier.

Eagerly I looked through the new arrivals, wondering which exciting tale would be the most likely to take my mind off my own tumultuous life. Finally I chose a book with a lurid cover depicting a sheriff drawing a gun on a female bandit with long red hair. I walked up to the counter with my purchase, only to discover that while I'd been looking at books, the golden-haired girl must have left the store.

I decided that I would never make a good sleuth, as I was too easily distracted. But in a way, I wasn't disappointed. I wasn't sure I wanted to know the girl who in all probability worked at the Lost Duchess, even though that wasn't the only saloon in town.

~ * ~

"Good day, Miss Mara."

Sitting tall on his horse, Emmett Grandison tipped his Stetson and brought his steed to a halt in my path. He seemed darker than when I'd last seen him and infinitely more powerful. And desirable.

All of the town and the passersby might have vanished around us, leaving us alone in some faraway place where a silver spring flowed and flowers grew wild.

"Good day to you, Mr. Grandison," I said.

"You're looking mighty pretty this mornin', Miss Mara. Has that haunt been stayin' away from you?"

"So far, yes. When will we see you?"

"Soon. Tomorrow maybe."

He tipped his hat again and rode on, leaving me to wonder if this was the man who had kissed me with such depth of feeling only a few days ago. Could his ardor have cooled overnight, or did I still have more to learn about the ways of men?

Most assuredly, yes, I did. Nothing in life was easy. Certainly nothing so eminently worth having as the love of Emmett Grandison.

Next Sunday, I was going riding with Cade Mallory. Maybe Miss Eulalie would tell Emmett, and he would be displeased. With that thought to cheer me, I headed back home with my new book. It was fortunate that we couldn't know the future. There was much to be said for anticipation.

~ * ~

Nicholas sat in the parlor, as elegant a figure as a hero from a romance novel, describing the sad events that led up to his return to Silver Springs.

"My sister's health took a turn for the worse, and she can't travel at this time. I've found a tenant for the house I purchased. I may go back to Boston and return with her in the fall, if she improves."

"I'm sorry about your sister, Nicholas. She's fortunate to have such a caring brother."

In the short, uncomfortable pause that followed, I wondered if the sole purpose of Nicholas' visit was to tell me about his travel plans. He hadn't said anything of a more personal nature, but I was glad of it. I was waiting for an opportunity to confront him with my new information.

"Will you have dinner with me again?" he asked.

I would have to say something soon. Now.

"Thank you for your invitation, Nicholas, but I don't think I should."

I could see that my response surprised him. Clearly, he was unused to rejection, but he recovered quickly.

"I see that I have lost you to that arrogant cowboy."

"If you're talking about Mr. Grandison, I'm not lost to any man."

"Then, have dinner with me tonight. You've dined with him at the Silver Palace. I can assure you I am much better company."

I didn't remember Nicholas having so exalted an opinion of himself, but of course I hadn't known him long or well. I felt uneasy. There was no clock in the parlor, for which I was grateful, or I would be stealing furtive glances at the time.

I found my solution in a simple statement of truth. "That may be, but I've learned that you weren't truthful about the date of your arrival in Silver Springs. I don't like being deceived."

"That you would doubt my word is very hurtful."

"Do you still claim that you first came to town on the Fourth of July?"

"I see that I can't, but I am going to have to ask you to trust me. I can't divulge the reason I was compelled to be less than truthful with you. It involves another."

So that was his explanation? More evasions? And he was asking me to accept it? With an effort, I kept my temper in check.

"I can't continue to trust you, Nicholas."

"I understand, but you can still have dinner with me."

"Even if I wished to, it would be impossible. We're having a wedding here next week. It's a busy time."

"You're not getting married, I hope?"

"No, Viola is marrying Jeremiah Brown."

"Our actress friend from the train? I thought she was going to stay in Denver."

"When she met Jeremiah, she changed her mind."

"Well, it's as I always believed. When you see a woman you want, you have to move fast before another man takes her."

Surely he wasn't referring to me? I chose to ignore the implication and take refuge in generality.

"This is especially true in a place where men outnumber women."

"Yes, in a frontier town like Silver Springs."

He rose and reached for my hands. "If you reconsider accepting my invitation, Mara, I'll be in town for a few more days. Your company would give me a great deal of pleasure."

"I'm sorry, Nicholas. I won't."

Now that I knew he was leaving, I felt more relaxed. Once the prospect of dining alone with Nicholas would have given me great pleasure, too. That was in another life. My thoughts kept straying to a silver stream and to another man whose kiss lived on in my memory.

Perhaps Nicholas was right, and I was lost to a man after all.

~ * ~

As the week wore on, the weather grew uncomfortably warm. Miss Eulalie was seldom seen without her fan, and the sewing piled up on the table beside her as she tried to create a cool oasis for herself. I often said that heat didn't bother me but found myself dabbing at my face with cold water several times a day.

One night the heat was so unbearable that I couldn't fall asleep. I kept turning on the bed, and even thoughts of Emmett and the stream didn't relax me. My thoughts turned to Trail's End and the night of the skinned-alive man's appearance.

I should have known better than to relive that experience. Before long I was asleep and trapped in a frightening dream about drums and hoof beats, Indians and a long, lethal knife. A sharp pain exploded in my head, and I looked down to see long strands of dark chestnut hair floating in a pool of blood on the rug. Somewhere, someone was laughing.

I woke up, and touched my head. I'd only suffered another nightmare and awakened with a headache. Still, I lay in bed for several minutes, breathing heavily and orienting myself to the waking world. Outside, the light was just beginning, and I could hear the murmur of voices downstairs in the kitchen.

As soon as I began the morning properly, I'd forget the nightmare. The pain was another matter.

I poured tepid water from the pitcher into the basin and bathed my face. Then I slipped into the green and white dress Emmett admired and touched my lips with a dab of the color Viola had given me. In spite of my efforts, Miss Eulalie surveyed me critically when I sat down at the breakfast table.

"You look unwell, Mara. Are you sickening for something?"

"I don't think so. I didn't sleep well and woke up with a headache."

"Oh, my dear, I know what you're feeling. If the pain doesn't go away, I'll give you some of my powder. Now, some good hot tea will set you right."

As she poured me a cup of the strong, steaming brew and handed me the plate of biscuits, she asked, "Shall I make you a special breakfast?"

"Thank you, but this is all I want."

"I'm fortunate," Viola said. "I've always been very healthy. Why don't you go back to bed, Mara?"

"I couldn't wait to get up. I was having a nightmare."

"About that horrible skinned-alive man?"

"No, I dreamed I was scalped."

"That's almost as bad," Miss Eulalie said. "It's that old house. If it had to be haunted, you'd think the ghost would be a more traditional one."

"It's a person, Miss Eulalie. It has to be."

Viola said, "I have a different explanation. While Mara is sleeping, her headache begins, and she dreams about a knife and cutting. Her mind is letting her know that something ails her body."

"That makes sense. Maybe I allowed myself to get too tired yesterday."

I helped myself to another biscuit. Miss Eulalie baked a fresh batch every morning. They were so delicious that I never grew tired of them. This morning I decided they also contained a healing agent as strong as her headache powder. I took one last swallow of tea and thought the pain was beginning to recede slightly.

"I'm going for a walk," I said. "I crave sunlight and fresh air. Would you like to come with me, Viola?"

"No, it's already too hot outside for me, but I need a few more yards of blue ribbon. Could I persuade you to go to the store for me?

"If you'll buy flour, I'll bake a cake for tonight," Miss Eulalie added.

"I want a few things too," I said. "Having a place to go is exactly what I need."

I left Miss Eulalie and Viola discussing the reception menu and went out of the door so quietly that Midnight didn't even wake up. Miss Eulalie once said that the best way to banish a headache was to keep busy, although often she chose to deal with one lying in bed.

By the time I reached Main Street, my pain and the remnants of my nightmare had slipped out of mind. Just when I thought all would be well, however, I was pulled back into the terrifying world that had disturbed my sleep.

In the heart of town, ahead of me, I saw the Indian.

Eighteen

He stood in front of the barbershop across from the livery stable as still and expressionless as a stone statue. There was nothing menacing in his appearance or stance. He wasn't watching me and didn't even appear to be aware of me.

After quickly committing a few of his distinctive features to memory, I walked briskly in the opposite direction toward the general store. Usually, this area was crowded with townsfolk coming or going, but today only a few people were in sight.

The dim, cool interior with its diverse attractions was a much better place to congregate and exchange gossip than the street. Tyler was inside talking to Arabella Westbrook, and Sheriff Bailey was looking over a small collection of pipes lately arrived from the East. Everything was ordinary and quiet, and, with a lawman so close, I had nothing to fear.

I bought Miss Eulalie's flour and the blue ribbon Viola requested, as well as a yellow one for myself. On the way up to the counter, I added a pound of hard candy.

When I left the store, I expected to see the Indian again, but he was gone. I had no reason to connect him with the haunting at Trail's End, and yet I did. I associated his appearance with my feeling that something unfortunate was going to happen to me.

The incident unnerved me. I was uneasy the rest of the afternoon. To add to my growing anxiety, I discovered that I was alone in the house. Miss Eulalie had gone out to take a basket of food to a bereaved family. Viola said she would be in the parlor sewing, but when I looked for her, she wasn't there.

Listless and having nothing I needed or wanted to do, I went up to my room and lay down. My thoughts turned to Emmett. I wondered if I would ever sew a gown for my own wedding. Was that what I truly wanted? And while I was thinking about marriage, why was Miss Eulalie nudging me gently in the direction of Cade Mallory? I couldn't see myself standing beside the red-haired Southern gentleman exchanging wedding vows. She must know that.

Soon I felt myself drifting gratefully into a light slumber. There were no dreams this time and not even the slightest sound in the room until someone's heavy breathing woke me. In the moment before I opened my eyes, I thought, *It's the Indian. He followed me home.*

The reality was much worse. The skinned-alive man was back.

Tottering in the doorway, illuminated in the glare of the late afternoon sun, he was a sight to chill a heart far braver than mine. He hadn't changed in appearance since our last encounter, but there were two gruesome additions. In the shapeless mass of red that served as his hand, he held a rusty, bloodstained knife, and his mouth was twisted into a hideous grimace.

While this was a terror-inspiring sight, it surpassed the limits of credibility. I didn't believe in the apparition, but certainly an unwelcome, living intruder had invaded my room. Without stopping to form a plan of action, I sprang out of bed and advanced on him.

Cowardly specter that he was, he backed away from me and made his way down the stairs in a remarkably agile manner for one supposedly suspended between life and death. I followed and would have caught him, if Midnight hadn't tripped me in her run to join the fray. Frantically I grabbed for the banister, caught it, and saved myself from a fall.

From the kitchen I heard a terrible din: The crashing of glass on the floor, a splattering, and a pain-filled yelp, followed by the most unghostly curse imaginable. I resumed my pursuit, but I was too late. The door leading to the garden was open. The spectral man had escaped, leaving a trail of spilled berries in his wake.

Midnight was under the table licking her chops. Her fur was splattered with red juice, and Miss Eulalie's neat kitchen was a wreck.

"Good girl," I said. "Why didn't you bite him?"

She followed me into the garden. There was no sign of the invader, and apparently no one had noticed the disturbance. I saw only a small boy tossing sticks for his dog to catch, a horse waiting for its owner to complete a visit, and Arabella Westbrook walking alone down the street.

Then the Indian moved slowly into the light. He had been standing behind a wide tree that hid him from the view of the casual passerby. It was likely that Arabella had passed by without noticing him.

From a relatively safe distance, I looked directly at him. Cold, stony eyes stared back at me.

"Go away! I said and closed the door.

I set about cleaning the kitchen and salvaging what I could of the spilled berries. I wished for Viola's return, as she was a more accomplished housekeeper than I was. But I managed well enough and was pleased with myself that I had confronted my worst fear. The skinned-alive man had run away from me, and I suspected that if I looked out of the window, the Indian would be gone.

As soon as I'd restored Miss Eulalie's kitchen to its former pristine state, I tested my theory. There was nobody in the street at all.

~ * ~

"The skinned-alive man is a fraud," I said, later that evening. "He ran from me. He can't be as dangerous as we thought."

We sat in the parlor. Emmett frowned as Miss Eulalie passed around cups of coffee and slices of her berry cake.

"We salvaged something from the afternoon's fracas, but be wary of bits of broken glass in the batter," I added.

Miss Eulalie said, "Really, Mara. There's no such thing. To think of that ghost man in my kitchen! It fairly makes me shudder."

Viola's contribution to the discussion was more perceptive. "He followed you here from Trail's End, Mara. How else could he know where you are?"

"You're not helpin', Miss Viola," Emmett said. "I been askin' around all over. Nobody in town admits to seein' these two gentlemen. They just up and vanished."

"That's impossible. With their distinctive appearances, someone should have noticed them."

"Not if they came from the world beyond," Miss Eulalie said. "This whole business frightens me, Emmett."

"I don't like it either, Miss Lallie. Can't you ladies stay together till we find out what's goin' on? I'll be around when I can. If you need to leave the house, don't go alone."

"We might as well be in prison," I said.

Because the skinned-alive man had fled from me, I regarded him as a perplexing curiosity rather than a threat. As for the Indian, he had simply come and gone. Still, it was obvious that someone wanted to harm me, or at least frighten me. That person was the one to beware of, but I didn't intend to allow him to curtail my activities.

I said, "If my enemy wants me, he'll find me in spite of our precautions, and it will be when I least expect it."

Miss Eulalie shuddered. "Mara, you're saying the most outrageous things tonight."

From across the room, Emmett's smile reached me, and I felt a familiar warmth wrapping around me again.

"I wish I could stay by your side day and night, Miss Mara," he said.

I could think of no reply to make to this unexpected utterance, particularly when I realized that the others had fallen silent.

"We could set a trap for him," Viola said. "Let it be known all over town that Mara and I are going to spend the night alone at Trail's End. Emmett and Jeremiah can come along later in secret, and we'll all wait for him to appear."

"I won't sit around in the dark waitin' for somebody to drop in. Don't even think about goin' to that house again." Emmett's answer was for Viola, but he looked at me.

Although I bristled at his authoritarian manner, I said, "I won't have to go to the ranch, Emmett. The skinned-alive man knows where I live."

Emmett didn't have an answer for that. None of them did.

~ * ~

Still later, when we were alone and preparing for bed, I visited Viola in her room. Since her engagement, she was usually with Jeremiah, and I had missed our conversations. Soon she would be gone.

I sat down on her bed. "Won't you regret not pursuing your acting career, Viola?"

"We don't know what the future holds, but marrying Jeremiah is what I want."

She looked up at my reflection behind her in the mirror. Her black hair had a blue sheen in the lamplight, and she brushed it with slow, lazy strokes.

"As I told you, the life of an actress isn't as glamorous as you might think, although once that was all I wanted. Now I shall marry Jeremiah and be a lawyer's wife in a frontier town. My marriage will take precedent over all other interests."

She laid down the brush and turned around to face me. "Your secret wish could come true, Mara. Nicholas would be very attentive to you, I think."

"As far as I am concerned, Nicholas has lost much of his luster. Since Annabelle's account of their meeting, well before the Fourth of July, I no longer trust him. He passes through Silver Springs as if it were a station on the railroad line. I suspect he is involved in something illegal."

"I see. I didn't know that your feelings had changed."

Strangely she seemed disappointed.

Emmett was watching Nicholas. He'd told me so this evening when we were alone for a short time in the kitchen. "He comes and goes, mysterious like, and keeps that suite of his ready whether he's usin' it or not. I aim to find out what he's doin' in our town."

I was about to tell this to Viola when she said, "In spite of yourself, you're thinking about Nicholas now. Admit it."

"I wasn't. Not exactly."

"That's fortunate then. I'm glad. Nicholas was seen with Annabelle Westbook last night."

"Seen by whom?"

"Jeremiah. He told me about it."

"She must have forgiven him for pretending not to know her. Miss Eulalie hasn't been able to remember where she saw him. She says he looked different then."

"I can't imagine Nicholas Breckinridge looking any other way. That's enough talk about the man. I am so looking forward to my marriage. I want to be happy."

"You will be, Viola," I said. "Very soon now."

~ * ~

When Sunday dawned, I remembered that I had agreed to go driving with Cade Mallory after services. I hadn't really forgotten, but I had been thinking of the excursion as an event in the distant future. I wished the invitation had come from Emmett, but I was determined not to let Mr. Mallory suspect that I would prefer the company of another man.

While I was dressing, Miss Eulalie knocked on the door of my bedroom. She carried a lovely dress in a color that combined green and blue in an extremely pleasing way. She cast a disparaging look at my gray shirtwast that lay on the bed.

"I finished your new dress just in time," she said. "You're going to be the prettiest girl Cade Mallory ever took out driving."

I ran my hand over the fabric. It was crisp and silky at the same time and trimmed with fine lace edging.

"I'll help you with the buttons," she said.

"It's beautiful, Miss Eulalie, but too fancy for church."

"Nonsense. It's plain enough; only the rich turquoise color and the lace make it seem elaborate."

She stepped back to survey her work, with pleasure and pride.

"In that dress, you look just like your mother in the painting. This vibrant shade makes your eyes greener and is a perfect contrast for your pretty dark hair. Cade Mallory will surely think he's snared a prize."

"Please, Miss Eulalie," I said. "I'm not a possession to be acquired."

"No, dear, of course not. That isn't what I meant."

But I felt like a prize when Cade came to claim me after the services.

"Lord, Miss Mara, you sure are a pretty sight," he said. "I'll take good care of her, ma'am, and get her home all safe and sound."

"See that you do, Mr. Mallory," Miss Eulalie said.

Cade took my arm, and led me to an old buggy that reminded me of the one Miss Eulalie rarely used. It looked as new as if he had just purchased it.

He helped me into the high seat, asking me twice if I was comfortable. Then, with a wave and smile for Miss Eulalie, he drove us away from the church. Because we were traveling in a different direction from the way to Trail's End and Emmett's ranch, the scenery was new to me.

On the way, Cade entertained me with tales of his plantation home in Georgia before the War, where life was slower and easier.

"On Sundays, our whole family and our friends would have dinner together. My brothers and I would take the dogs out and go riding. Afterwards, we'd all gather in the library to talk about hunting or politics. Likely there'd be a barbecue and cake with cold drinks in the shade. Plenty to eat and good company. We thought it would go on forever."

"That sounds lovely, Cade," I said. "Very different from the way I used to live when I was growing up."

"That world is gone now, but we have the Double C. It's not the same, but it's ours."

When Cade wasn't reliving the glory days of his Georgia home, he concerned himself with my comfort. I felt as if I were adrift in a sea of Southern charm and courtesy. Since I'd come to the Colorado Territory, I'd been enjoying an independence that is not always available to women. Cade regarded females as beings to be cherished and protected from all harm, and possibly even from the heat of the sun or a sudden breeze.

I considered this an outdated notion, one that made me uncomfortable. Still, Cade Mallory was an attractive and affable companion, and if we stayed on the subjects of Georgia before the War and the Double C, he was a man with whom I could easily converse.

When we reached his ranch, he brought the buggy to a stop and turned to me. "This is a right fine piece of land and a good, sturdy house. Nothing like what we had back home before the War, but it'll do."

"I'll have to agree with you, Cade. It's very impressive."

I spoke the truth, for everything in my view was well appointed and tidy, even though the Double C couldn't compare in grandeur to Emmett's ranch.

"All the house needs is a mistress. A woman is the heart of a home."

"I suppose that's true. Does your brother live here, too?"

"Yes, and also our foreman. Clay's gone up to Wyoming Territory for a spell. A woman in the house makes all the difference," he added.

He jumped down from the buggy and reached up for me, keeping his hands around my waist longer than necessary.

"Let's get on in out of the sun, Miss Mara. Old Jarrod's promised to cook us up some refreshments."

In the buggy, I'd felt more comfortable with Cade than I did now, but there was no reason to feel uneasy, even if he was rather outspoken about his underlying reason for inviting me on this ride today.

He wanted a wife. That wasn't so unusual. Wasn't it true that a man needs a woman alongside him in the West? No, it was just the opposite, and Emmett had said this to me on the night of our first dinner.

I wouldn't deny that men and women needed each other and eligible females were in much demand in the Colorado Territory, but this was a conversation I didn't want to pursue with Cade Mallory at this time.

"Do you have only one brother?" I asked.

"There were five of us once," he said. "Three of my brothers were killed in the War. Now, Miss Mara, let me show you what a fine new house we have. It's a place any woman would be proud to call home."

~ * ~

When Cade Mallory brought me home, Miss Eulalie was waiting for us, sitting in the parlor and not doing anything in particular that I could see. All of her sewing materials had vanished, and she was in an extremely talkative mood.

She insisted on serving Cade a cup of Louisiana coffee, straight from the sunny old South, and then she wanted to hear all about our afternoon. Cade was more than willing to indulge her. With some amusement, I listened to him describe our afternoon's activities. I hadn't thought I was so entertaining.

"May I call on you again, Miss Mara?" he asked. "Next Sunday, maybe?"

Since, according to him, we'd had such a good time together, I didn't see how I could refuse graciously, but I deferred to Miss Eulalie.

"Yes, Cade, unless Miss Eulalie has made other plans for us. We're having a wedding soon."

"There's nothing to keep you in the house, Mara," Miss Eulalie said. "Viola and I are taking care of everything."

"Then, I suppose the answer is yes, but perhaps next week is too soon."

"Whatever you say, honey," he said. "I'll see you in church."

"Yes. Next Sunday."

I showed him the door and watched him drive away, the horses' hooves the only sound on the silent street.

"He is such a charming man," Miss Eulalie said, when I rejoined her, "such a genuine gentleman, but of course he would be, and so very attractive. That red shade of hair is unusual in a man and rather nice, don't you think?"

"I think I'm waiting to see those rough edges you mentioned."

"What? Oh, yes. Well I may have been mistaken about that. Cade Mallory has remained true to his Southern heritage. Even in the West, he is as he always was."

"You sound as if you knew him before you came to Silver Springs," I said.

"No, dear, I didn't. It's only that the true Southern gentleman never changes. Now, as soon as Viola comes home, I can relax. You two are like my daughters. I want only the best for you."

I rose dutifully and began to clear away the coffee cups. Because Miss Eulalie hadn't mentioned Emmett, I asked her why she had appeared to switch her alliance.

"I've done no such thing," she protested. "I can't imagine why you'd think that. Emmett will always be my favorite."

~ * ~

On the day before her wedding, I looked in on Viola. She was attaching a row of lace to a nightgown and humming softly to herself. I recognized the melody of *Come Where My Love Lies Dreaming*.

I didn't interrupt her but watched for a moment as her hands moved slowly and lovingly across the material, pushing the needle in and through the lacy edging. The garnets in her ring sparkled in the lamplight.

I remember every detail about the scene because that was the last time I saw her.

Later, neither Miss Eulalie nor I could say when she had ceased to be in the house. Young Matt Martin, who lived nearby, had been building a fort of logs all afternoon. He swore that no one had left the house all day.

When the hours passed and Viola remained away, Miss Eulalie dissolved into tears.

"We must notify Jeremiah and Emmett. We have to get word to Emmett. Do you suppose your ghost carried her away, Mara?"

"I told you, Miss Eulalie, there is no such thing. I don't think anyone kidnapped Viola."

"She wouldn't have just left. Look, she was still working on her nightgown."

We were in Viola's bedroom, where the unfinished garment was our only clue. Neither Miss Eulalie nor I could understand the story it told.

"She wouldn't have gone away without telling us, would she?" Miss Eulalie asked. "And surely she's coming back. She wouldn't be late to her own wedding."

She repeated these sentiments to Jeremiah when Emmett arrived on the scene. Powerful, able, and ready to take charge, he asked us to tell him the plain facts.

I said, "The last time I saw Viola, she was in her room sewing, but we didn't speak. I was in the parlor all afternoon reading and writing in my journal. I didn't see her go out through the front door."

Miss Eulalie added, "She would have to come through the kitchen to leave by the back way. I was baking layers for the wedding cake."

"Have you searched the house thoroughly, every room?" Jeremiah asked.

"We have," I said. "Viola must have gone out. Matt Martin couldn't have been watching our house continuously."

"Maybe she was abducted by this intruder Mara keeps seeing," Jeremiah said.

Being a man of action and not given to theorizing, Emmett walked briskly to the door.

"We're wastin' time. Let's organize a search party. Do you still keep a list of mysteries, Miss Mara? Don't forget to add this one."

"But where will you look?" Miss Eulalie asked.

Neither man answered her, for they were already out of the door and on their way to the rescue. Defeated, she sank into her chair, all but disappearing into it. I went to her and hushed a whining Midnight. The house hadn't been so quiet since the night of my arrival.

Lowering her voice, she said, "Jeremiah thinks Viola left because she decided not to marry him after all."

"It may look that way, but he's wrong. Viola wanted the marriage very much."

"Then where is she? We can't have the wedding without the bride."

I walked over to the window and stared out into the fading light, wondering if Viola's disappearance could be part of the same mystery that surrounded me. That was a frightening theory, but I couldn't push it away, as much as I wished to do so.

Viola had been with me on the train when Mrs. Haskins had told us about the man who had been skinned alive by Indians in forty-nine. She'd accompanied me to Trail's End, helped me sweep the house clean and, except for her fall from the buckboard, she would have been there on the night of the apparition's first visit. When it had followed me to Miss Eulalie's house, however, she'd been away.

Mrs. Haskins' stories had never affected Viola as they had me, and she didn't seem unduly afraid of the skinned-alive man, but then he appeared to be mainly interested in me.

Why was that? Still, even though it was Viola to whom some dreadful thing might have happened, I could well be the next victim. For this and many other reasons, we had to find out what had happened to Viola. And we had to bring her home.

"Do you think we'll ever see Viola again?" Miss Eulalie asked.

I had almost forgotten that she was present, still sitting in the chair, holding Midnight and looking bewildered.

"I surely hope so," I said. "Let's wait up for Emmett."

Nineteen

Emmett returned at ten to tell us that the men would resume their search in the morning.

"They'll find her, if she hasn't run clear out of the Territory. A fancy actress like that, she probably decided she didn't want to live in a frontier town."

"That's unfair, Emmett. Have you forgotten about the skinned-alive man and the Indian? Maybe one of them took Viola instead of me. If I were the one out there in the night, I hope you wouldn't think I ran away to Wyoming Territory in search of greener pastures."

"You're not the disappearin' kind, Miss Mara."

"That's no answer."

"Mara and Emmett, quarreling won't bring Viola back," said Miss Eulalie.

"You knew your Boston friend left town again, didn't you?" Emmett asked.

"What does that have to do with Viola? And of course I did."

"Maybe nothin', Miss Mara. Could be they left together."

"That isn't likely. We three met on the train, but Nicholas and Viola never seemed overly fond of each other. She loved Jeremiah."

"Yes, but tomorrow's the day she was goin' to marry him. Where is she?"

"Viola's lost," I said. "I hope the search party will find her."

But when twenty-four hours passed, and Viola remained missing, I found it difficult to hold on to hope.

"Nobody saw her leave town," Jeremiah said. "She wasn't on the train, she didn't hire a buckboard, she hasn't been seen on foot or horseback. She's not here."

"She has to be somewhere," I said.

"I only know she's gone. I loved her so much. Now it's over."

"Don't give up so easily, Jeremiah."

I tried to sympathize with him, but while I understood his disappointment, I was impatient with his lack of spirit. He had ridden with the search party, but that was the extent of his endeavors. He wasn't a man of action like Emmett. In this case, however, what could he do?

Viola was my friend, and I couldn't think of a way to help her. In a sense, it seemed as if she had never left the house. That was because all her possessions were still here. There weren't many, but each one reminded me of her.

Her dresses, the hairbrush she'd been using the last time I'd talked to her, *The Tempest,* and the sketches, souvenirs of our trip to Carron Creek—every object held a memory of our friendship. There were more pictures of Emmett on her dresser. All of them were wonderful but none captured the essence of Emmett as completely as the one she had given me. Finally, folded neatly in a rocking chair was a white nightgown with half of its lace edging attached.

It was as if a giant hand had descended and gathered up Viola, leaving everything else untouched. I was thinking like Miss Eulalie now.

If Viola had gone away of her own accord, she would never have left her prized possessions behind. Miss Eulalie said that we were to leave her belongings undisturbed so that when she returned, she would find everything where she left it. She refused to believe that this might not happen.

With a sigh, I closed the door to her room and started to turn around. I gasped as Emmett came up behind me so quietly that I didn't hear him until he was there. I hadn't realized he was in the house. He circled my waist with his arms, and I leaned back against his chest, grateful for his presence.

"Mara," he said. "If it'd been you, I don't know what I'd do."

He kissed me again then, a much gentler kiss this time, and held me, as I'd dreamed he would. A feeling of incredible joy settled snugly around me. It surpassed any emotion I could ever have imagined. And yet even Emmett couldn't drive away the realization that had just come to me.

In some way that I didn't yet understand, Viola's fate was inextricably bound with mine. I couldn't escape it.

~ * ~

"From now on, I'm going to be on my guard," I said. "I won't be taken unaware, and I'm not going to let that gruesome pair spoil one more minute of this happy summer."

I sat in the living room of Emmett's ranch house. It was roomy and comfortable, a man's residence, and, best of all, a place that felt like home to me.

How could any evil thing follow me here, especially when Mac, Tyler and all the other men who worked at the X Bar G were around? I felt safe now, and I was happy.

Amidst our speculation about the fate of Viola, Emmett said, "I heard you went out driving with Cade Mallory last Sunday. You got to be careful around those Southern gentlemen Miss Eulalie dredges up."

"Who told you?" I asked.

"Miss Lallie."

"I'm always careful, Emmett, and I assure you I was in safe hands the entire time."

"Until you know who's tryin to scare you or worse, you should stay with the folks you know."

"Like you?" I asked.

"Like me. Sure."

He held his cup of coffee in midair, not drinking, absorbed in his own thoughts. Between sips of my own drink, I studied his face. The lines around his eyes gave him a dark, brooding look; but even when he was frowning, he was a fine, handsome man. No change of mood could alter that fact.

Emmett wasn't pleased about my afternoon with Cade Mallory. I was sure of it.

He set the cup down on the table in front of him with a resolute bang.

"How do you keep your dishes intact if you handle them so roughly?" I asked.

"I don't use 'em much. There's one thing you don't know, Mara. At the Lost Duchess there was a gambler, name of Bret. He's gone now, went off the same day as Viola did."

I waited for him to go on, although I knew what he was going to say.

"Sally fancied him. She thought he found a new lady."

Instead of seizing on this information as a clue to Viola's whereabouts, I asked, "Who is Sally?"

"She's one of the saloon girls."

In my mind a glittering image of a woman bedecked in sparkling jewelry flickered and went out. Then she moved closer, and I could see her face and the golden color of her hair. I felt certain that she was the person I'd seen in the cemetery and later observed on Main Street.

I had no doubt that Sally was one of the reasons Emmett patronized the Lost Duchess. Now that I thought of it, Miss Eulalie had practically said so. Rather, she had blushed and been evasive, which amounted to the same thing.

If that were the case, I wouldn't like it. Although this passing reference to Sally came as an unpleasant surprise to me, I decided to dismiss her for the moment.

"Are you suggesting that Viola and this gambler, Bret, ran away together?"

"Could be."

"I don't know how Viola would have met a gambler from the Lost Duchess. She's been spending all of her time with Jeremiah." I placed my empty cup on the table alongside his. "The other day you said there were no more places to look. Did you remember to search Trail's End?"

"That was one of the first places we went. The place is as empty as a graveyard, the way it should be. One day you might get a letter from Miss Viola, postmarked San Francisco."

"I don't agree with you, Emmett, but as Miss Eulalie says, time will tell. Do you know Sally well?"

"Sure," he said. "She's a friendly little thing. Pretty, too."

He had answered my question briefly but more thoroughly than I would have liked, leaving me in an unhappy mood.

"I think I should go home now."

"I'll come around tonight and take you to dinner," he said, making it sound more like a command than an invitation.

I was about to decline when his kisses began to replay themselves in my mind. Also, I didn't want Emmett to seek out this saloon girl, Sally, after he escorted me home. What I'd really like was to know something about her, the kind of information a man wouldn't be likely to divulge. Perhaps Miss Eulalie could enlighten me.

"I'll be pleased to dine with you," I said. "Will you take me home now? I need time to get dressed."

"You look mighty fine now."

As do you, I thought, *but I'm going to look better than fine for tonight.*

"Thank you for the compliment, Emmet, but I still have to go back to Miss Eulalie's."

"All right," he said, "we'll go now."

I planned to take special care with my appearance. With a combination of skill and luck, perhaps I could make Emmett forget the girl from the Lost Duchess.

~ * ~

I peered into the cheval mirror and surveyed my reflection unhappily. I was wearing one of the new dresses Miss Eulalie had made for me. It was a flattering shade of deep blue with ecru lace at the collar and cuffs. We were both pleased with it, and yet now I found it inadequate for my purpose.

In a frontier schoolroom, I'd look crisp and efficient. If I were to step inside the Lost Duchess, I'd be invisible. Were Emmett to see me this very instant, he wouldn't notice any change.

I touched my lips with a dab of the color Viola had given me and coaxed my hair into curls to frame my face. That was some slight improvement.

If Emmett thought I'd looked mighty fine three hours ago, perhaps he'd be pleased with me after all. I might as well stop combing curls into a fringe, go downstairs, and wait for him to arrive.

When she saw me, Miss Eulalie smiled in approval. "You look very pretty tonight, Mara, a little rosier than usual, but nice. Ah! That must be Emmett. It's his special knock. Will you let him in, dear?"

I reached for my shawl and hurried to open the front door, expecting to see Emmett. Instead a fair-haired young man stood on the porch. He was dressed as a wrangler. As he looked beyond me into the hall, he turned his Stetson hat around and around in his hands. He seemed ill at ease and unsure of his surroundings, like one who is unused to being in town.

"Yes?" I said. "Did you want to see Miss Langlinais?"

I had never set eyes on the man before, but he was looking directly at me.

I heard Miss Eulalie's footsteps in the hall. She was behind me, her voice sharp with curiosity.

"To whom are you speaking Mara?"

"I'm Lance, ma'am, from out at the X Bar G," the young man said. "If you're Miss Marsden, I came to fetch you. Mr. Grandison sends his regrets. There was an accident..."

"Oh, my dear." Miss Eulalie stepped back in search of a piece of furniture to hold.

"I'm Miss Marsden," I said. "Did something happen to Emmet?"

"He had a mishap with a new horse. Leg's broke, I think."

"The horse's leg or Mr. Grandison's?"

"It was the boss that got hurt. He sent me to find you, ma'am, and take you out to the ranch."

"Oh, my poor Emmett," Miss Eulalie said. "How could this happen?"

It took a few minutes for me to realize exactly what I'd heard. I couldn't imagine the mighty Emmett Grandison of the X Bar G felled by a horse or any other living creature on four legs or two.

When had I first begun to think of him as a giant? To me he was simply Emmett, sometimes infuriating but, in my view, invincible and irreplaceable.

This preemptory summary, so in character for him, must be obeyed. In spite of a nagging doubt, I never considered doing otherwise. But why hadn't Emmett sent Mac or Tyler, a man I knew, to escort me back to the ranch? Probably if he was badly wounded and in pain, he wouldn't have thought of it.

"Of course I'll go," I said.

"Wait!"

Miss Eulalie stood at my side, clutching at my arm. "It's late, Mara. It might be better to go to Emmett in the morning. I'll accompany you then, and we can bring Doctor Westbrook along. Besides, you can't possibly stay at the X Bar G overnight."

Usually when Miss Eulalie called on propriety, there was no way to sway her. With Emmett lying helpless at the ranch, however, I didn't intend to be kept from his side for any reason.

"I want to be with him, and it's still early."

To my astonishment, she capitulated without further argument. "Then go, dear. Tell him I'll be along early tomorrow morning."

Lance, who had stood silently by during our conversation, seemed relieved. "The boss said to hurry, Miss Marsden, and not to ride in the dark."

Hastily I went back upstairs, threw my hairbrush into a carpetbag, and gathered a few other articles that I deemed necessary, items I knew wouldn't be found at the X Bar G. After a moment's consideration, I added a nightgown. Then, with a final farewell and words of assurance to Miss Eulalie, I was ready.

"Are you absolutely certain you should do this, Mara?" she asked. "I've been thinking..."

I didn't want her to finish that sentence. "Don't worry, Miss Eulalie. It's going to be all right."

"You ready, ma'am?" Lance asked.

"Yes, let's get started."

He took the carpetbag from me, and Miss Eulalie accompanied us out to the street where a buckboard waited to transport us to the X Bar G.

"Be careful, Mara," she said. "Tell Emmett I love him."

"I will."

Lance helped me up onto the seat and handed me my bag. "We're off," he said, as he took the reins and set the horses in motion, all efficiently and with great speed.

I gathered my shawl tightly around my shoulders. In spite of the heat of the afternoon, I felt a chill.

How strangely things worked out sometimes. We'd assumed I would be the target of misfortune, but Emmett had been the one struck down. As we drove away from Silver Springs, I had time to wonder if somehow, in some mad plan I couldn't fathom, he was taking my place.

Twenty

I soon discovered that Lance wasn't fond of talking. We must have covered several miles before he spoke. When he did, he made a terse observation about the weather.

"Should be enough daylight left to get us to the X Bar G, but those look like storm clouds up ahead. The boss showed me a short cut to the ranch. We'd best take it."

I scanned the sky with apprehension. It was beautiful and in no way threatening. Grayish-white clouds moved slowly across the blue expanse, constantly changing shape, losing pieces of themselves and reforming. I could watch them for hours.

"I don't think we're in danger of being caught in the rain any time soon," I said. "I've never seen you at the X Bar G, Lance. Have you been working for Mr. Grandison long?"

"I came to Colorado Territory at the beginning of summer," he said.

"So did I. Where was your home before?"

"I'm from Texas, ma'am, near Fort Worth. Emmett's my cousin," he added. "I aim to learn the cattle trade from him. Someday I'm goin' to be the boss on a spread of my own."

I looked more closely at him, trying to see if I could detect a family resemblance. There was none, except for his hair. The color was a few shades lighter than Emmett's and appeared to have a similar texture.

"Since you're Emmett's relative, I'm surprised he didn't introduce us," I said.

"I'm not near the bunkhouse much, ma'am," he said. "Like as not, he'll tell you all about me when we get there."

With this comment, Lance lapsed into silence. Perhaps he was worried that the storm would overtake us, in which case Emmett wouldn't be pleased.

We were passing through a scenic but wild part of the Territory. The terrain grew progressively rougher and more desolate. This was indeed a lonesome trail and one best traversed with a more talkative companion, but Lance refused to be drawn into further conversation.

I could only admire the sky and scenery for a while. Besides, something felt wrong. Faint alarm bells began to ring in my mind.

"If this is a short cut, it seems longer than the usual way. We're not lost, are we, Lance?"

I had visions of rain or night, perhaps both, overtaking us while we were still on the trail. Lance was an apprentice cowboy only recently arrived in the Territory, and I was even less familiar with directions and routes. Miss Eulalie's warning to be careful took on an ominous new significance.

"No, ma'am," Lance said. "I know exactly where we are."

"As do I. In the middle of nowhere."

Ahead of us rose four giant boulders that appeared to have been set down in an artistically arranged pattern, almost as if they were intended to form the backdrop of a play set in the West. We'd been moving slowly and now came to a complete stop.

"What's wrong?" I asked.

"The horses need to rest."

I stared at him in disbelief. The alarm bells were clanging now.

"But you yourself said we had to hurry. We can't be that far from the X Bar G. Let's go on."

As Lance didn't reply, I was about to rephrase my speech in clearer terms when I heard distant hoof beats behind us. I turned around to see who was sharing these godforsaken acres with us. All I could make out was the shape of a horseman. He was still some distance away from us, riding through a cloud of dust, gaining on us.

"Someone's coming," I said. "I hope he's friendly."

"I'm right sorry, Miss Marsden." At that moment something heavy that smelled of the damp earth and some other vile substance was dropped over my head and pulled so tightly about my neck that I thought I would choke. Someone who could only be Lance began to bind my ankles and wrists with what felt like leather strips. Then he flung me against the side of the buckboard, and we were again in motion.

In less time than it would take to tell my story, I'd been subdued and abducted. Had it been like this for Viola? I would never know now. As for Lance, he couldn't possibly be Emmett's kin. Why hadn't I realized this before walking willingly into his trap?

I hoped the rider would come to my aid but soon realized that this was unlikely. He must have witnessed Lance's actions but hadn't interfered with them. He was, therefore, involved in the plot to take me captive. Realizing that struggling would be futile, I leaned back and centered my thoughts on Emmett.

Maybe he'll come riding to your rescue.

I reconstructed the previous scene. In my mind, Emmett rode up to the buckboard, dispatched Lance and the shadowy horseman, took me up on his horse, and transported me to the X Bar G.

I imagined myself sitting with him on the porch of his ranch house at some happy future time. It would still be summer and very warm. We'd eat slices of cold chicken and freshly baked bread and sip lemonade chilled with ice. And it would be forever.

I couldn't have remained long in this state. Soon I felt excessively drowsy. My porch vision began to fade, its colors running together in a watery haze.

Keep thinking about Emmett, I commanded myself, and it was his face that accompanied me down to the darkness.

~ * ~

When I returned to consciousness, I was lying on the floor in an enclosure with one small window above me. Moonlight pouring through the glass indicated that several hours had passed.

I turned painfully on the hard surface where I'd been tossed like a sack of flour. The head covering was gone, and my wrists and ankles were free; but they throbbed painfully where the bonds had been. I swallowed. That hurt, too. My mouth tasted of leather. I would give anything for a drink of cold water or even hot tea and one of Miss Eulalie's morning biscuits, but at least I was alive.

Don't think about food or drink.

You'll pay for this, Lance, I vowed. Emmett will avenge me.

This was a comforting thought, but I had no real hope of being saved. Instead of thinking about revenge, I needed to find a way out of my prison.

Taking deep breaths of dry, musty air, I rose and walked over to the window, wondering if I could crawl through it and make my escape. I moved my hands along the walls and across the dust-coated glass and concluded that I must be in a cabin. Gingerly I continued my exploration until I came to a corner.

A single trip around the structure gave me further details. The building had a door, but it was locked. The place was extremely small and consisted of this one room only. Since I was able to walk back and forth without tripping over any object, it must be unfurnished.

I returned to the window and tentatively sent my fist into the glass, which remained intact. I needed a hard object to hurl through it, but that would be certain to attract the attention of my captor, assuming he was stationed nearby and hadn't left me here to die.

Don't think about that either.

If only I could think of a quieter way to break out of my cell...

My thoughts came to a standstill. I didn't know where I was. My abductor might have taken me out of the Territory. Once I climbed through the window or discovered another exit, what could I do?

The answer was obvious: Choose a direction and start walking. The darkness would hide my movements, along with the snakes and whatever wild beasts inhabited the region. I would deal with one adversity at a time.

First, I had to find the way out.

I sat down on the floor and leaned against the log wall. Somebody had brought me here for a reason, and I couldn't have made it easier for him.

You were a gullible fool, Mara. Try to redeem yourself now.

~ * ~

I made a gallant attempt to do so, examining one unfeasible plan after another. Finally I occupied myself with attempts to identify my enemy. I could think of only two people who might wish to harm me. They were my old nemesis, the skinned-alive man, whom I had recently labeled as a fraud, and the Indian.

I didn't consider Lance because obviously he had been hired for the purpose of luring me into this trap. Someone must have told him about my attachment to Emmett. Lance knew the exact words that would make me leave the safety of Miss Eulalie's house and place myself in a vulnerable position.

Would Emmett think I had followed Viola's example and left Silver Springs for some unknown destination? This was unlikely, for Miss Eulalie had been present when Lance had spun his tale. She'd believed him, too.

Emmett wouldn't know where I'd been taken, though, so I could stop hoping for him to come galloping to my rescue. That only happened in novels.

You're wandering away, Mara. Concentrate.

Again I tried to open the door. It was an impossible task, but that was to be expected, as it served to keep unwelcome guests away. Suddenly aware of a different kind of brightness mixing with the moonlight, I hurried to the window.

A figure crouched over the fire about ten yards from the cabin. The man was an Indian, although I couldn't be certain he was the man I'd seen in the streets of Silver Springs. While I watched him in the circle of light cast by the flames, he glanced quickly toward the cabin and away again.

Was he the one who had brought me to this place?

He appeared to be roasting a small animal or bird, and I fervently hoped the meal wasn't intended for me. I craved water, not unidentifiable meat served to me by a man I might have reason to fear.

I didn't allow myself to think about rusty bloodstained knives and Indian atrocities, the stuff of horror stories and nightmares. Soon it became apparent that the man was preparing his dinner, nothing more elaborate or threatening. After a short while, he ate, smothered the flames, and left the clearing.

Once again I was alone and likely to remain so until my abductor decided to make an appearance. Resigned to additional hours of uncertainty, I sat down and leaned back against the wall of the cabin, as I had earlier in the buckboard. I suspected this was going to be the longest night I'd ever experienced. Nevertheless, I closed my eyes and tried to rest.

~ * ~

The door was open. Bright morning light poured into my prison, along with an abundance of air and a cooling breeze. Beyond the cabin, an enticing glimpse of green forest and freedom beckoned to me.

Here was my chance to escape, and I didn't hesitate. I pushed my hair out of my face, rubbed my eyes, and smoothed down the folds of my dress. How limp and worn it was after I'd slept in it.

Remembering how carefully I had prepared for my dinner date with Emmett, I rolled up my sleeves and examined my damaged wrists. For the first time I became aware of all the other parts of my body that were hurting.

Ignore the pain. Start walking in the blessed light and warmth of the sun.

I stepped outside into an extravagance of brightness and breathed in the fresh air. Ahead of me I spied the remnants of the Indian's fire and a path of sorts. Where it led hardly mattered, as I was lost. But if I followed it, I might meet a fellow traveler, a man who bore me no ill will and would help me reach my home.

I met him sooner than I could have imagined. He stepped out of the woods as quickly as if he had been waiting for me to emerge. Suddenly the whole strange affair made sense, in a mad sort of way.

The man was Silver Jake, resplendent in his Confederate uniform, not en route to the South to rejoin his regiment, but keeping a lonely vigil outside the cabin door. He was the one responsible for my dilemma after all.

I had an uncanny feeling that I had stepped onto a stage where some lunatic melodrama was being played out. Now that I had found my kidnapper, how should I talk to him? I decided to proceed as if he were sane.

"Good morning, Major. What are you doing here?"

"Been waiting for you to wake up. I saw him bring you here. I come to take you home."

"Then you weren't the man who had me abducted?"

The look of deep shock that crossed his face convinced me of his sincerity. "No, ma'am, I'd never do that."

"Did you open the door?"

"That I did, Miss Margaret."

If I continued asking him questions, I might be able to understand what had happened to me.

"Did a cowboy bring me here?"

He looked away from me toward the blackened remains of the Indian's fire. "Mr. Grandison, you mean?"

"No, a younger man with light hair."

I thought he wasn't going to answer me. He stared at the path as if the answer lay there. Perhaps he hadn't seen anything that was real at all. Still, I persisted.

"Or was he an Indian?"

Finally he said, "There wasn't any such man here."

"Did you build the fire?"

"He was a white man dressed like a Cheyenne, not a true Indian. Might be the shack belongs to him."

At this point I was certain that Silver Jake possessed some significant information, but his answers confused me. The man who had built the fire wasn't a genuine Indian, but whoever he was, I had seen him leave last night. He might return any time. Getting away from this place before he came back was more important than an authentic account of what Silver Jake had witnessed.

"You said you were going to take me home, Silver Jake. Will you do that?"

"Sure thing. I'll take you straight back to the portrait. Was it that Indian who let you out?"

I willed myself to be patient, to speak softly. "You're confusing me with my mother. The picture is of her. I'm Mara, her daughter. Don't you remember? Mr. Grandison and I came to visit you at your cabin."

"Mara. Not Margaret? Are you sure?"

"I'm positive. Mr. Grandison will be grateful to you for taking me home."

"I'll take you to Trail's End, but you'll have to ride with me. I have only one horse."

I spoke more sharply than I'd intended. "No, I don't want to go there."

"Where then?"

I longed for the sight of Emmett and almost said, "The X Bar G, Emmett Grandison's ranch," but stopped myself in time. I knew how bedraggled I must look. Now that my survival was more or less assured, I could spare a thought for vanity. What I wanted at that moment was warm water in Miss Eulalie's tub and clean clothing.

"I took the portrait to my friend's house in Silver Springs," I said. "Will you take me there instead?"

"So you can go back to the portrait?"

"Yes, but I'd much rather stay outside with the sky and grass and air."

"I like to eat and sleep out in the open too," he said. "Can't stand being shut up in a house for long. If you're hungry, there's a stream up a ways where I left Charger. You could use some water. Maybe we'll catch some fish."

"That's a wonderful idea, Silver Jake. Everything is going to be all right."

~ * ~

Soon after we left the stream, we met Emmett on the trail. He was unshaven, and his eyes were tired. Even from a distance I could see that they were furious. We might be heading into the eye of a hurricane. I had never seen him so angry and had to remind myself that he was my deliverer.

"Let go of her, you madman!" he roared.

He grabbed Charger's reins, almost throwing me backward to the ground. The horse came to a stop. A cloud of dust rose up, choking me. Emmett drew out his gun and aimed it at Silver Jake. With his left hand, he lifted me out of the saddle and dismounted.

"Get down, Jake, now!"

Silver Jake obeyed the command. As he stood in front of Emmett, he appeared to shrink to a small size. He needed my help now.

"Emmett, wait! Don't shoot him. He never hurt me."

Emmett looked uncertain but shoved the gun back into its holster. "Don't move, Silver Jake. Not an inch. Mara, what happened?"

I told him about my capture and incarceration, ending with my encounter with Silver Jake outside the cabin. "I'm sure he wasn't involved, Emmett."

Emmett frowned, looked at Silver Jake thoughtfully and came to a decision.

"Get back on your horse and ride on, Jake. Don't come near this lady again, unless you want to deal with me."

Without a word of protest or farewell, Silver Jake did as he was told. Emmett held me with both hands now, but his fury hadn't subsided. It was trapped in his storm-cloud eyes and the set of his mouth

"Silver Jake helped me get this far, Emmett," I said.

"All right. If that's true, I'll make it up to him, but maybe he should be locked up in one of those lunatic houses."

"Oh, no. He likes to be outside. He can't lose his freedom."

"Leave Silver Jake to me. Hold on tight, Mara. We're ridin' home."

He mounted his horse and lifted me up onto the saddle in front of him.

"I thought you were hurt," I said. "I only wanted to go to you."

"So Miss Lallie said. Honey, Lance is no kin of mine. I been searchin' for you most of the night. I agree with you. I don't think Silver Jake was behind this kidnapping. He's a simple kind of man."

"He has me confused with my mother. He said something about putting me back in the portrait. Maybe I should take it back to Trail's End where I found it."

"You're not goin' back there to do anythin', Mara, and I don't want you near Silver Jake, sane or crazy."

"Lance came to Miss Eulalie's house," I reminded him.

"That's one more enemy to find before somethin' else happens."

I didn't want to think about any future catastrophes at the moment. I'd put myself in danger to go to Emmett, and he had been looking for me. Miss Eulalie would say it was destined to be. I thought so, too.

"I wonder if Viola was abducted," I said.

"Could be, but I think this is somethin' different. You're sure you're not hurt, Mara?"

"I'm only tired. Silver Jake found water and food for me."

Emmett didn't say anything more about Silver Jake or my ordeal. We rode on, and I leaned against him, thankful that I'd been delivered from captivity, death or whatever gruesome fate my captor planned for me. This was a far happier state.

At last Emmett said, "There's Silver Springs up ahead."

We dismounted in front of the general store, and Emmett led me to a bench at the edge of town. We sat down in clear view of the townspeople who happened to be on Main Street at this time. I can't remember when I was so happy to have a crowd around me.

Emmett was suddenly very quiet. It was as if he were seeing me for the first time.

"I'm goin' to find out who hurt you," he said.

"But I'm all right." I raised my hand to my face. The only looking glass I'd had was the stream, and I hadn't noticed any bruises.

He took my arm, frowning angrily as he pushed my sleeve higher. "What's this then?" he demanded.

I couldn't keep from flinching, although his touch was gentle.

"Looks like someone tied a rope around your neck, too."

"It was something like that."

Incredibly, Emmett seemed to be angry with me. With his attention fixed on my many wounds, I felt that I was in worse shape than I had supposed.

"The marks are from the bonds. They'll soon fade."

He brushed a strand of my hair aside and caressed my face.

"I'll take you home. After what happened with Viola, Miss Eulalie thought she'd never see you again. Mara, honey, you can brush your hair and wash your face if you want to, but you look pretty enough to me just like you are."

He pulled me up from the bench, as he had from Charger, and held me, unmindful of the three little boys who had stopped to stare at us and laugh.

"I can't believe I was so easily fooled," I said. "It won't happen again."

"You're damn right it won't."

As we walked to Miss Eulalie's house, hand in hand, I believed that with Emmett at my side, I would be safe forever.

Twenty-one

"Your dress is ruined, Mara, but we'll make you another one," Miss Eulalie said. "After breakfast, we'll go up to the sewing room and look at my supply of material."

"I'd like one that's a little fancier and in a brighter color."

"You'll need a new shawl and a nightgown. I wonder where the carpetbag is now."

"Still on the buckboard, I suppose, or destroyed," I said. "I'll have to buy another hairbrush."

I had a thick slice of ham and a warm biscuit on my plate, with a cup of hot tea to drink. Miss Eulalie was showering me with attention, Midnight sat at my feet watching me eat and begging for crumbs, and the sun was shining. What more could I want? I sighed. Only Emmett.

After he'd gone home last night, I lay in bed and thought about him. How could I doubt the extent of his affection for me after his loving words? Although he had offered no formal proposal, I'd given my heart to him freely. Our futures would be entwined, and he would be my husband. I didn't doubt it.

I was forgetting Cade Mallory, to whom I had promised another Sunday afternoon. I'd have to tell him that I couldn't see him again because of my affection for another man.

"Once again Emmett saved your life," Miss Eulalie said. "It's destiny, Mara."

"Actually, Silver Jake did that, but I agree with you. I think fate wants Emmett and me to be together. I don't know that my kidnapper was going to kill me, though. I'm not sure what his plan was."

"Even now, I shudder to think of it. You were so brave." She glanced through the kitchen window in the garden. "I don't think I'll ever feel safe again. Emmett gave me a gun and taught me to shoot it, but the thought of killing someone frightens me."

She had been voicing similar sentiments ever since Emmett had brought me home. At her insistence, I told the story of my experience over and over again. Together we sought a motive for the abduction, but it remained a mystery.

She said, "If it wasn't Silver Jake, then it had to be the ghost or the Indian. But why?"

"I thought it was better to escape while I could and investigate later."

"Yes, that was a wise decision. If ever I see that Lance in Silver Springs, I'll have some answers out of him."

I helped myself to another biscuit. "I don't think you will, Miss Eulalie. He's most likely a drifter."

As I finished my breakfast, I found myself looking through the window as Miss Eulalie had done. The skinned-alive man had come through this very room a few days ago, making his escape into the garden. Later I'd stood in the doorway and seen the Indian emerge from behind the tree.

I was safely returned to the sanctuary of Miss Eulalie's home, rested, well fed, and showered with attention. But I knew that another man with a different lure could snatch me away at any time.

Yesterday I'd assured Emmett that I wouldn't allow myself to be fooled again, but how could I know what would happen in the future? Like a feral creature that had followed me home from my wilderness prison, fear insinuated itself into my life. The new development was unforeseen and unwelcome.

~ * ~

On the surface, everything was the same as before. Viola was still missing, but nobody was searching for her. Once on a visit to Jeremiah's office, I found him reading a San Francisco newspaper.

I worked alongside Miss Eulalie in her garden, and she taught me to bake Emmett's favorite cake. My new dress, with its pattern of tiny daisies against a background of soft peach, replaced the blue one that had been laundered and cut into rags. By the end of the week, the physical evidence of my rough handling faded, and I was again preoccupied with curls and lip color.

At times, however, there came over me a strong sense of foreboding. Sometimes in the middle of the night for no apparent reason, I awoke with my heart pounding and my neck and chest drenched with sweat.

I relived my hours in captivity, dwelling on what might have happened. Whenever I stepped outside, I had a feeling that somebody was watching me. No one was ever there. Gradually, a deep malaise settled around me.

I thought no one knew what I felt, but I was mistaken. One day Miss Eulalie and I were in the garden, pulling the weeds that threatened to choke her cherished plants. I mounded a bit of dirt around a fragile flower, and began to cry.

"Helping flowers to grow should be a happy and relaxing activity, Mara," Miss Eulalie said. "Don't you find it so?"

I brushed away my tears. "Ever since I escaped from the cabin, I've been waiting for something else to happen. I know it's foolish, but I can't help it."

"The answer to your problem is time. You have things out of order. You weren't afraid when you were held captive, and it's caught up to you now. Don't you fret. A few more summer days and sunrises, and one morning you'll wake up and feel like your old self again."

"During that time I was very frightened," I said.

"Yes, but you dealt with your fear."

"You may be right. I'll be patient and think about those sunrises."

Emmett had another solution. We were sitting in the parlor that evening at a later hour than would be considered proper, but Miss Eulalie appeared to have abandoned her adherence to propriety.

An oil lamp burned on a three-footed table, and a candle flickered on the hearth. It was an enchantingly romantic setting, if ever there was one.

"You could marry me, Mara," Emmett said. "You'll be safer out at the ranch than here. No one and nothin' can get to you at the X Bar G."

It was uncanny how Emmett managed to turn a proposal of marriage into a near command. Had I missed the part where he declared his undying love for me? No, he hadn't said anything about his affections at all.

His offer lingered in the air, a tangible thing. I had only to grasp it. A few days ago, I had imagined us bound together by destiny. Now, however, something felt wrong.

I wanted my union with Emmett to be a joyous affair, but someone had unfinished business with me that I had to settle before I agreed to become his wife. It was about time and order again.

I hesitated too long. In the end what I said didn't convey my true feelings. "Thank you, Emmett, but I can't marry you for protection." The words sounded stilted and inadequate.

"I want to marry you, Mara," he said. "Protectin' is only part of it."

"I know, but there are matters I need to settle first. It's too soon to talk about marriage."

He didn't press the matter, which was unlike him. All he said was, "Goodnight, Miss Mara."

I could almost see the icicles forming around his words, and I felt colder than I had in the bitterest of Michigan winters. He rose to take his leave. We might have been strangers, parting at the end of a social affair.

I thought, *Now you have lost him*; and there was nobody to contradict me.

I sank into a chair and listened to the sound of his horse's hoof beats fading away. The deep night silence closed in on me.

What had I done?

~ * ~

After that, I didn't see Emmett for several days. Without him, my world turned from bright to bleak, but still he kept his distance. It was as if he had dropped off the face of the earth.

"This is a busy time at the X Bar G," Miss Eulalie said. "Emmett has to take care of his ranch."

"He asked me to marry him, and I turned him down."

"I know."

"I had a notion that I should tie together the strands of my old life before I begin a new one."

"You could still say yes," she said.

"He was so angry with me. I can't see myself saying, 'I've changed my mind, Emmett; I will marry you.' He'll probably tell me that now he's reconsidered. I'd rather confront the skinned-alive man again."

"Sometimes I don't think you understand yourself, Mara."

"I know that I've lost him. I wish Viola were here to advise me."

"Since she isn't, listen to me. Tell Emmett you love him. That'll be all you have to say."

"I don't think I can," I said. "I'm so unhappy."

"What foolishness! You're on the wrong trail, child. You need to turn yourself around and get going in the right direction."

I agreed with her picturesque assessment of the situation but could find no practical way to apply it, and Emmett continued to stay away from me.

One afternoon, Cade Mallory called on me and said that he understood my previous attachment to Mr. Grandison but would be honored if I would consider him a friend.

I said, "You're very thoughtful, Cade. Of course we are friends."

"You'd think the men of Silver Springs would be up in arms after that scoundrel, Lance, snatched you away from your own home."

I glanced at Miss Eulalie, wondering what she had said to him. Her expression told me nothing. She was completely absorbed in the apron she was making. She might as well have been a hundred miles away.

"It's over, and in the end, I was unharmed," I said.

"Come out with me today, honey. I brought the buggy. It's a little cooler, but you can take your shawl."

Miss Eulalie looked up from the apron. "A nice drive in the country would do you good, Mara."

"You *did* say you would see me again," Cade reminded me.

In truth, I couldn't understand myself. Here was a kind, congenial Southern gentleman, as attractive a man as Emmett or Nicholas, asking politely for a few hours of my time. All I wanted to do was stay inside the house.

"If you were mine, I'd see that you were never in danger," he said.

"I'm sure you're able to care of your own—possessions, Cade."

"I don't see that Mr. Grandison is doing anything to keep you safe."

"Emmett is busy at the X Bar G, and I don't think I'm in any imminent danger."

"Then you'll come out with me," he said.

"Didn't you say it was cool outside?"

"Goodness sakes, Mara! It's summertime," Miss Eulalie said.

I rose, took my shawl from the back of the chair, and said, "All right, Cade, but only for a little while."

As he escorted me out to the buggy, I wondered why I'd agreed to this excursion. As gallant as Cade Mallory was, I wasn't entirely comfortable with him. He wanted something more from me than friendship. Whatever I had to give belonged to Emmett Grandison, whether he chose to take it or not.

This would be the last time I'd succumb to Southern charm and allow Cade to persuade me to join him for any purpose.

~ * ~

I believed in the healing power of time, but, growing impatient with its painfully slow passage, decided to take charge of my destiny once again. When had I become a helpless female wandering from one calamity to another, waiting for a knight to come riding to my rescue? Certainly I could manage my affairs more capably.

Selling Trail's End would be a good beginning. The place had long since lost its fascination for me. Now I thought of it in terms of financial security.

One afternoon I sought out Jeremiah in his law office. "You look in better spirits today. Have you had a message from Viola?"

"No, and I don't expect one."

"I'll never believe that she disappeared of her own free will. She was truly looking forward to marrying you. There was something strange, though. Every now and then she seemed to be afraid of something."

"Of being tied to me, no doubt. It's in the past, Mara. I've forgotten it."

So he said, but once again I saw a San Francisco paper lying amidst his correspondence.

"Do you hope to read a news story about her?" I asked.

"I feel certain she went to California. If I'm ever to know anything about her, I think this is where I'll find it."

"What if she didn't go to San Francisco?"

"Then I don't know where she is. All along, I've been looking for her quietly, but my inquiries have been in vain."

"Perhaps one day, it will be different. I hope so. Now, I want you to handle the sale of Trail's End for me, if you will."

"You're going to sell to Emmett then? I thought you were going to marry him."

"I'm not. If Emmett wants to buy my property, he's welcome to it. I'll trust you to obtain a fair price for it. I'm longing for a change of scenery."

"If you're certain that's what you want me to do, I'll take care of it," Jeremiah said. "Where will you go?"

"Not far. I'd like to see more of the Territory. I thought I'd take a little trip to Denver before the summer ends."

~ * ~

"I have a good friend in Denver," Miss Eulalie said. "Her name is Mrs. Edgar Barron. We came West together as young women the way you and Viola did. Unfortunately, we can't see each other often now."

"I'll call on her, but I think I'd like to explore Denver on my own," I said.

"Haven't you learned how dangerous a solitary excursion can be?"

"Nobody will know me there. These creatures who have been shadowing me won't follow me to the Territorial capital."

"You don't know that, and strangers can be trouble, too. I'll give you a letter of introduction to Mrs. Barron. It'll be lonely here without you, but Midnight will keep me company."

The small dog sat on her lap. Hearing her name, she lifted her head and stared adoringly at Miss Eulalie.

"Midnight has become more your dog than mine," I said.

"It's because I feed her. You're always away having adventures. When are you leaving?"

"In a few days. Maybe a week."

"We'll have to sew a new wardrobe. Denver isn't Silver Springs. You'll need more sophisticated clothing."

"I'm going there to see the sights," I said.

"Still, you'll have to have proper dresses. Let's start planning."

~ * ~

The sun was warm, oppressively so, but the general store was cool and inviting although crowded. As I gathered thread and sugar for Miss Eulalie and whatever little items I thought might prove useful on my trip to Denver, I became aware of the girl with the golden hair at the counter.

She was buying lengths of old rose satin and white lace, as well as ribbons in rainbow hues. Today her dress was similar in color to the material, and her blonde hair, an impossible shade of golden yellow, cascaded in soft curls over a ruffled collar of pristine white. She reminded me of a doll, a fragile, expensive toy dressed to attend an elegant tea party.

She was conversing familiarly with the proprietor, Mr. Greer, who appeared to be oblivious of his other customers.

I was about to set my own purchases on the counter and begin a conversation with her when I heard her say in a deeply accented voice that suggested a Southern heritage, "Please charge these items to Mr. Grandison of the X Bar G. Oh, and this as well." She laid a long, snowy undergarment on top of the rose material.

"Sure thing, Miss Sally."

Rarely in my life have things become so clear so quickly. Pieces of a puzzle I wasn't sure existed came crashing together with such speed that they seemed to hit me in a thousand places.

I was right about Emmett and the girl, Sally, but it gave me no pleasure. I wondered if Emmett had been courting her all along. Or had he turned to her when I refused him? If I had accepted his proposal of marriage, would there still be a Sally?

To my dismay, I was close to tears. That would never do. When one is the cause of her own undoing, it is futile to dwell on what might have been. I resolved never to let Emmett or anyone else know that I cared. Abandoning my purchases and the sugar and thread as well, I slipped out of the store as unobtrusively as possible.

My Denver trip was going to happen at the right time.

~ * ~

"Did Emmett ever mention someone named Sally to you?" I asked Miss Eulalie that evening, as we sat together in the parlor enjoying one last cup of tea before bed.

"The girl at the Lost Duchess? Yes, he has, many times. She comes from North Carolina. Why do you ask?"

I told her, but then had to add that I'd left her sugar and thread behind. I suspected she knew why I'd done this.

"I'll go back to the store tomorrow," I said.

"There's no need, dear. I'll do it myself. I've gotten right lazy having you to run my errands."

"About Sally, do you think Emmett is fond of her?"

"I'm sure he is. I've never met her, but he's told me about her. The poor little thing doesn't have any family, but apparently she's very popular at the saloon."

"And do you think he's befriended her out of the kindness of his heart? I don't."

"You're probably right, Mara."

I could tell by a slightly perceptible heightening of color in her face that Miss Eulalie was uncomfortable with the conversation, but I persisted.

"Do you think I should consider her a rival?"

"It all depends," she said. "A rival in what way?"

"For Emmett."

"I think only Emmett can answer that, Mara, but you can hardly ask him now with matters stalled between the two of you."

Miss Eulalie busied herself pouring more tea for both of us. Idly she lifted the top of the teapot and said, "Maybe I should make some more."

"I think I must ask him, or I'll never know."

"But first you'll have to mend this rift. As for Sally, not that I'd ever have followed the profession she chose, but I suppose she's doing what she feels she must. I think she's like Viola when she first came to Silver Springs, making the most of her talents in order to survive."

I was surprised that Miss Eulalie felt this way about Sally and wished she would say more, but she began to talk about

Denver again and Mrs. Barron who had four sons, all of them grown men.

"Perhaps one of them will escort you around Denver," she said. "The attention of a gentleman always adds an extra flourish to a trip."

~ * ~

I saw Sally on one other occasion. She stood in front of the livery stable in full daylight, laughing up at Emmett. Their air of familiarity with each other battered my heart.

Once again, I retreated. Had Miss Eulalie once called me brave? She didn't know me well at all. As far as I knew, Sally hadn't seen me since the day she had walked past me in the cemetery, and then she hadn't really looked at me. I hoped she didn't know of my existence. If Emmett had found a new ladylove, he would have no reason to tell her about me.

Don't be naïve, Mara, I told myself. *Sally isn't Emmett's ladylove. She's a saloon girl who entertains him and gives him a brief time of pleasure for a price*. Or was I wrong about the nature of their relationship? Perhaps she was more to Emmett than an hour's enjoyment.

I continued to torment myself with visions of the two of them together and to speculate about the depth of their relationship. In any version of my imaginings, I saw myself alone and unhappy.

So Emmett was the last person I expected to see at Miss Eulalie's front door on the morning of my departure.

"I've come to take you to the train, Miss Mara," he said in his usual authoritative manner.

This was my chance to say something to change our situation, but I allowed the thought of Sally to come between us and kept silent. Let the creature console him in my absence. Hadn't she been doing so in my presence?

"Well, then, thank you," I said.

We didn't speak as we walked the short distance to the station. Just before I was to board, he said, "I watched you when you first got off the train from Denver, Miss Mara."

"I know you did. I noticed you, too, at the hotel."

"I thought you were the prettiest lady I ever saw. I'm goin' to miss you. I know it's only for a few days. I made you a respectable offer. Think on it while you're in Denver."

"I will," I promised.

While I was on the train, I would have a long time to think about Emmett's proposal and figure out where Sally fit into the picture.

Once he would have taken me into his arms and held me close. Now he only said, "I'll be waitin'."

I stepped up to board the train and followed the conductor down the aisle to my seat, seeing only Emmett's face, still hearing his voice. I realized I was more affected by his reappearance than I would have thought possible.

He waited on the platform as the train pulled out, with all of Main Street as a backdrop. I didn't see Sally. Maybe I could take her out of the scene after all. But how?

A tall figure passed in front of me, and a familiar voice said, "Well, Mara, we'll be traveling companions again. This is a lucky day for me."

There was Nicholas, smiling down at me.

Twenty-two

"You're the last person I expected to see, Nicholas," I said. "I thought you went back to Boston days ago."

He sat down across from me, as he had on our trip out West. This time we shared the compartment with a family group, a father, mother and two daughters, along with a gentleman who bore a slight resemblance to Silver Jake. Only Nicholas and I were conversing.

I studied his face, marveling that I had ever thought him magnificent. As always, he was handsome, courtly, and as elegantly dressed as any visiting gentleman from Boston might be, but now I sensed a certain roughness mixed in with his charm, perhaps acquired from living these past weeks on the frontier.

"I didn't stay long. I won't return until the end of the summer. I've been traveling around the Territory. In my opinion, Silver Springs is the friendliest and fastest growing town in the West. I assume you're going to Denver?"

"Yes, I never really saw the capital."

"Are you settled in at your ranch now? Trail's End, was it?"

"At present, I'm still staying with Miss Langlinais."

"Well. You surprise me, too, Mara. I thought you would be married to the hotheaded Mr. Grandison by now."

"Emmett had nothing to do with my decision to go to Denver," I said.

Nicholas reached over and held my hand in a tight grip. "I must talk to you, Mara, privately and now. We don't have the luxury of time."

How appropriate could this compartment be for a confidential conversation with our traveling companions listening to every word we said? I glanced at them and discovered that the father had gone to sleep, his wife was gazing out the window, and both girls were reading books. Only the second gentleman might be interested in what we were saying, but he was seated the farthest from us.

"After we arrive in Denver," I said. "Perhaps then but not here."

He lowered his voice. "It must be now. I have to be certain that you aren't serious about this cattleman."

"If you're referring to Mr. Grandison, there is no connection between us, but that can't possibly concern you."

"It does, Mara. Believe me. I hoped never to have to tell you this. If you'd married Grandison, I would have found another way, but now you have set me free to do what I came to the Territory for."

"That's the strangest speech I ever heard. I don't understand."

"I haven't always been honest with you, Mara. That has been for your safety. Does this mean anything to you?"

Out of his pocket he drew a tin star and held it up to the light. He'd done something similar with a pocket watch on the night of the Centennial celebration before he kissed me and hung an emerald pendant around my neck.

Without waiting for a reply, he returned the badge to his pocket.

"Of course it does," I said. "Where did you get it?"

"It's mine. I'm a company detective, Mara. My business is with Grandison."

"I still don't understand."

"Have you ever heard of the Swinging Lady Gang? They're a band of desperadoes."

"I've heard them mentioned. Why?"

"Your fine Emmett Grandison is their leader. No, Mara, don't hasten to his defense. I have proof and enough evidence to arrest him."

Inside the moving train, time stopped. Somewhere a cold wind began to blow and found its way into the compartment, chilling my hands. I clasped them together so that Nicholas wouldn't see that they were shaking.

"I don't believe a word of this," I said. "It's a fantastic story only. You're as good at telling tales as that horrible Mrs. Haskins."

"I've told you the truth, Mara. I wouldn't lie about a man who was once important to you."

"You're saying that Emmett is an outlaw? It isn't possible."

"Oh, but it is, and he's the most dangerous of his kind because he masquerades as a rancher and pretends to interest himself in civic affairs. The people respect him, and all the while he uses your own property as a robbers' roost."

I recalled that Nicholas had reacted strangely when I'd first mentioned Trail's End, but I didn't think it significant at the time.

"I'll begin again," Nicholas said. "I'm a detective, but my interest in Grandison is more personal. He killed my brother, Micah Breckinridge. I intend to see him hang. That is the fate reserved for men who live outside the law."

"That man isn't Emmett."

"You are loyal, Mara. I admire that quality in a woman. I have a story to tell, and you must listen. When you hear it, you'll change your mind.

"My brother came West in fifty-nine. He had a partner, your friend, Mr. Grandison. Micah trusted him and was swindled out of a fortune in silver. Soon afterward, he died under mysterious circumstances.

"Grandison acquired two partners, Jules Carron and his cousin, Jacques, the man you know as Silver Jake. They were common outlaws, robbers of stages, trains, and banks. Trail's End was an ideal place for them to hide their stolen wealth. Then Jules died and Jacques went mad. Emmett Grandison had it all. Did you ever wonder how he became so prosperous?"

"He started with two acres and a few cows, and he worked hard."

"Add to that whatever he could steal along the way. He wanted to buy Trail's End and make it part of the X Bar G, but that was impossible because it was willed to your mother."

"You have quite an imagination, Nicholas," I said. "Are you a writer of dime novels?"

"I'm only halfway through my story, Mara. When you came to Silver Springs, Grandison seized his chance. He began to court you."

"You can't possibly believe that was the reason for his attentions," I said. "I've never been so insulted. I don't want to hear anymore."

We'd kept our voices low, but now I was beyond caring what our fellow passengers might think. I started to rise, but Nicholas stopped me with a strong hand on my arm.

"Be honest, Mara, if only with yourself. Haven't you been often frightened lately, deliberately and in a particularly gruesome way? I know about it. At first, your coming out West was an unforeseen obstacle for Grandison. He either wanted you to leave the Territory or to marry him, in which case your property and you yourself would be under his control."

"Again, you are not flattering me."

"From the first moment he met you, Grandison took command of your life. He offered to buy your land. When you refused to sell, he managed to install you in the household of a woman who would do anything for him. Then he initiated a series of terrifying sightings to keep you away from the ranch."

Nicholas had found the way to break through my defenses, and he was battering me relentlessly, even though I didn't believe in the authenticity of the badge that had so quickly disappeared into his pocket. The idea of Emmett as the leader of a band of outlaws was ludicrous.

I knew that he was in real danger, though. For some reason, Nicholas meant to destroy him. Since he had confided in me, I was in a position to protect Emmett.

Nicholas had reached the end of his tale, and he sat quietly, watching me. At last he said, "I see that Grandison has everything, even the affection of the woman I could have loved."

He reached over to caress my cheek, and I drew back. What a masterly touch! Did I look like the kind of fool who would believe this nonsense?

"What are you going to do?" I asked.

"Now that you will be safe in Denver, I'm going back to apprehend Grandison. You may have wondered why I have often been away from Silver Springs and on occasion found it necessary to mislead you. All this time I've been gathering evidence. The last proof I need is concealed at Trail's End."

"Then why are you on a train bound for Denver?"

"I saw you at the station and followed you on board. It's the first chance I've had to confide in you."

"We were recently alone in Miss Eulalie's parlor," I reminded him.

"I thought you were in love with Grandison then."

He always had answers, but the more plausible they were, the less inclined I was to believe him.

"The ranch is mine, Nicholas," I said. "I give you no permission to trespass."

"You don't believe in badges and authority, do you, Mara? I don't need your leave to search Trail's End, but I will ask for it. You can even accompany me. If you want to be present when I take Grandison, I'll see that you come to no harm."

"That's where I want to be. Right beside you."

I had to find a way to warn Emmett about the plot about to be set into motion. I resolved that he would have my continued loyalty and help in this affair. If there were even a strand of truth in Nicholas' wild story, then I would stand by him still. So intent was I on finding a way to protect Emmett that I realized I'd erased Sally, if not from the scene, then from my thoughts.

"When will there be a train going back to Silver Springs?" I asked.

"Later this morning. You'll be safe with me, Mara, I promise it; and when this unpleasantness is over, we can begin again."

He reached out to touch me once more, and this time I allowed the caress. I had to convince him of my sincerity and cooperation.

"I'm glad things have worked out this way," he said. "If you'd become seriously involved with Grandison, you would soon have come to grief."

That would still happen if I allowed Nicholas to harm Emmett. I didn't believe the story of the murdered brother, but of the ill will Nicholas bore Emmett I had no doubt. Of one thing I was certain. I must never let Nicholas catch me off guard again. Inadvertently, my hand strayed to my neck, and I shuddered.

The train came to a stop. As Nicholas assisted me to my feet, my hand accidentally brushed against his coat, and I felt the unmistakable outline of a gun.

"I am a law enforcer," he said. "Now let's wile away the hours until we can board the next train back to Silver Springs."

Twenty-three

Once again I stepped down from a train in Silver Springs. This time Nicholas walked close behind me. Unfortunately I was still without a plan to protect Emmett, other than to stay near to Nicholas and see what he intended to do.

This would involve visiting my least favorite place in the Colorado Territory. Once I thought a herd of wild horses couldn't drag me back to Trail's End, but here I was, practically on the way there.

Although it was around noon, Main Street was almost deserted. The clouds were gray and low, almost pressing on the buildings, and a smell of rain scented the air. Remembering the wild storm that swirled around Silver Springs on the night of the skinned-alive man's first appearance, I hoped the unsettled weather wasn't a portent of disaster.

"Wait here while I hire the buckboard," Nicholas said. "We have no time to lose."

I did as he said, still trying to think of a way to alert Emmett to the danger. From where I stood, I couldn't see Miss Eulalie's house. There was a chance that Emmett was visiting her, and I wished I were there with them. If I succeeded in derailing Nicholas, perhaps tomorrow I would be.

When Nicholas came around with the buckboard, lifted my valise, and helped me climb up beside him. I had a feeling that I had lived through a similar experience with Lance. Could I be walking into another abduction?

For a moment I considered jumping down to the ground and running back to the sanctuary of Miss Eulalie's house. If Nicholas intended to kidnap me, he would hardly pursue me through the town. Then I thought of his vendetta. Somebody had to help Emmett. Possibly I was the only one who could do it.

"What do you expect to find at Trail's End?" I asked. "When we cleaned the house, we searched it well."

He took up the reins. "A last piece of evidence certain to seal Grandison's fate. Are you ready?"

"Yes, but it looks like rain. Maybe we should wait in the hotel lobby until the storm passes by."

"We don't want to be seen. If we went to the Palace, Grandison would know about it in a matter of minutes. It's my duty to keep you away from all danger."

I looked away. Nicholas held the reins in one hand. With the other, he turned my face around.

"I hope you won't want to be present when they hang him."

"What a cruel thing to say!"

"I'm sorry, Mara. I forgot you were once fond of the man."

We were rapidly leaving Silver Springs behind, but I couldn't resist taking one last look at the town I had come to love. I wished I could have found a way to warn Emmett before setting out for Trail's End, but I didn't see how I could have done so, while maintaining my pretense and keeping Nicholas in my view.

"I think you're right about the rain," he said. "Hold on. I'll get us to Trail's End before it starts."

At a speed that I considered dangerous, he set the buckboard racing toward our destination, while the countryside blurred and clouds moved ahead of us, threatening to burst and drench us at any minute.

The storm was foretelling disaster for someone. I fervently hoped it wasn't for Emmett or me.

~ * ~

The downpour began as we reached the first of the outlying buildings. We scrambled out of the buckboard and rushed to the door. The battering of the rain on my body was almost painful. Soon I was thoroughly soaked, with my hair hanging down in long wet strands. Nicholas fared no better.

I had given Jeremiah the key to the house, but we didn't need one. Nicholas gave the door a mighty shove, and it swung open onto darkness. I stood still inside, shivering. My dress clung to me, and falling water formed a pool at my feet.

"Is there a lamp here?" he asked.

"Take a few steps to the right. There should be one on the table. The candles are in the kitchen."

"Ah, here it is. Mara, you're drenched. You should get out of that wet dress before you take a chill."

"I left the valise in the buckboard."

"Didn't you leave any clothing here?" he asked.

"No. Why would I?"

"I'll get it when the rain lets up. In the meantime..." He set the lamp on the table, where its light created a soft, eerie circle around us. "Let's get a fire started. I hope you left some provisions here. I'm thinking about coffee, preserves, something more substantial. I'll look around while you change clothes."

"My dresses are in my valise," I reminded him. "On the buckboard."

"You may find something to wear here. Did the late Mr. Carron leave any clothing that would fit me?"

There was only the Confederate uniform, still hanging in the armoire. I wouldn't tell Nicholas about that.

"Most of his possessions went into a bonfire. If you don't want to go outside again, I'll get the valise." I moved toward the door, but he was there ahead of me.

"No, you stay inside where it's dry."

He disappeared into the thick wall of rain, only to return seconds later in a worse state. As he carried the valise into the room, he left a trail of water on the floor.

"Thank you, Nicholas. I'll change, and you can dry off by the fire when you build it," I said.

"Where are you going?"

"To a small bedroom at the end of the hall."

Before he could say anything more, I picked up the valise and fled.

~ * ~

When I rejoined Nicholas a little later, he was sitting on the floor beside the fire holding his coat up to the flames to dry. He smiled at me, and I saw a strange look cross his face. It was a mixture of approval, appreciation, and something sinister. Once again, alarm bells were sounding. This time I listened to them.

All I'd done was dry my hair and don a plain brown dress with a modicum of trim, but he couldn't stop looking at me.

"You are suddenly different, Mara. More alluring. Are you a temptress, come to lead me from my duty? I might allow it. Come, sit here beside me, and we'll get warm together."

"That's an odd way of talking, Nicholas," I said. "You also are unlike your usual self tonight."

His loud merry laughter sounded wrong in the silent house.

I chose a chair on the opposite side of the room. Too late I realized that this was where I had found the loathsome skin. That was irrelevant now.

I realized that I had done a foolish thing in accompanying Nicholas to Trail's End. I imagined myself telling Emmett, "I only did this to help you." I could hear his angry voice demanding, "Help me? How?"

Nicholas said, "While you were changing into that enchanting dress, I discovered all sorts of food. Let's pretend we've moved our picnic indoors because of the rain."

"I'm sure I only left preserves here and coffee."

"There's a jar of canned meat, Miss Langlinais' contribution, I don't doubt, and even a bottle of brandy."

I hadn't seen the dusty bottle until he held it up to the firelight.

"I can't imagine how this food found its way to Trail's End. Maybe somebody has been camping out in the house."

"It's possible," Nicholas said. "If that's the case, I'm glad they left some supplies here for us. While the storm lasts, we're fairly isolated. I think I can postpone my business with Grandison for pleasure."

"Once again, I don't understand you."

"Are you sure? I'll tend the fire while you get together a light supper. First, let's have some brandy."

While he was talking, he filled two glasses and handed me one. I accepted it but set it aside.

"You have never looked lovelier, Mara," he said.

"I'm unchanged. The firelight gives people and their surroundings a softer appearance."

"You're far too modest. I never told you this, but there's something about you that caught my imagination from the beginning. Finally we have an opportunity to explore it."

Feeling in need of some kind of fortification, I reached for the glass.

~ * ~

As we ate, in a roundabout way Nicholas began to talk about the fortune in silver reputed to be hidden somewhere on the ranch.

"I heard a song called *The Treasure of Trail's End* when I was in Denver. One night at the Lost Duchess, a pretty young lady told me the story. I assume you're aware of it."

At last we were on safer ground.

"I think it's a tale made up by Silver Jake. No one believes it."

"These old legends are often based on fact. When you cleaned the house, did you find anything unusual?"

"Are you talking about the treasure now?"

"Yes. I'm thinking about a map or written directions to a hiding place."

"We were thorough. Nothing could have remained hidden from us. I'm certain it's only a story."

"Did you find anything at all that might be construed as a clue?"

Without pausing to think, I said, "Only a letter from Jules Carron to my mother with the word 'treasure' in it."

Nicholas leaned forward, all thoughts of food and brandy forgotten. The lascivious look in his eyes was replaced by one of pure avarice.

"That's exactly what I'm looking for. Do you still have it?"

How I wished I'd never mentioned the letter. "Yes, but not with me."

"Where is it?" he demanded.

"With my other belongings, at Miss Eulalie's house."

"Think, Mara," he said. "Remember. What did he write?"

Nicholas' interest was disturbing, and I didn't care for the fanatical gleam in his eyes. I decided to give him only the merest sliver of information in the hope that he would be satisfied.

"I don't remember much because it was in French, and I didn't actually read it. Miss Eulalie translated it for me. He referred to a treasure once. There was nothing more."

"Jules Carron would have had to tell your mother what the treasure was and where to find it. Otherwise, what would be the point of mentioning it at all? I am convinced there is another letter or a map."

I looked at him, alarmed by the threatening tone that had crept into his voice. "Why, no, there can't be."

"You're very sure of that?"

"If another letter existed, one he didn't post, I would have found it. Besides, the one we found sounded like a farewell."

In his feverish enthusiasm, Nicholas grabbed my wrist. I struggled to free myself from his grasp with no success.

"Please don't keep talking about this, Nicholas. Emmett says..."

Emmett! Why hadn't I realized it sooner? Nicholas was more interested in the treasure of Trail's End than in apprehending Emmett. He wasn't talking like a lawman now.

At last I had the good sense to be afraid. What did I know of Nicholas after all? When I looked at him, I saw a man with a strikingly handsome face, considerable charm, and a seductive way with words. About the real Nicholas I knew nothing at all, except that on one occasion he had lied to me.

"We'll search every inch of the house," he said. "A letter or a map, something. It has to be here."

"You can do so. I'm not interested in mythical gold and silver." I walked over to the window, trying to appear casual. "I think the rain is stopping. It's lighter out, too. We should go back to Silver Springs."

"Not empty handed."

"Feel free to look around, Nicholas. I'm sure you won't find anything."

I pretended an interest in the scenery while, behind me, I heard Nicholas moving noisily through the house, tossing articles roughly to the floor and even tapping on walls. Once I thought I heard him laughing toward the back of the house.

I wished myself a hundred miles away. I wondered if I could make a successful dash for the buckboard while Nicholas was absorbed in his search. Could I move fast enough? Yes. Unfortunately, I'd delayed too long. I heard the sound of his footsteps approaching. Then he was in the room with me.

"I believe I'll have some more brandy, Mara. This treasure hunting is dusty work. I insist that you help me."

"Very well. I'll start at the back of the house."

Leaving Nicholas at the fireside, I wandered back to the small room where I'd changed into my dry dress. I thought I might be able to make my escape through the window and walk around to the buckboard while he was drinking his brandy.

I opened the door and stifled a cry as I found myself staring into the artfully drawn face of a younger Nicholas.

I was looking at a cardboard poster, the kind in popular use to advertise plays. It had been placed against the bed so that I would be certain to see it as soon as I entered the room.

The man in the poster wore black and held a gun in each hand. Behind him, the artist had drawn scenery in muted colors of the earth, subtly suggesting any Territorial locale.

Nicholas Breckinridge
Famous European Actor
Appearing
At the Silver Nugget Theater as

Outlaw Jim
In
The Revenge of Outlaw Jim
Saturday, October Twenty-third

So Miss Eulalie had seen Nicholas after all. He had never been a Boston gentleman, but, being an actor, had easily masqueraded as one. Suddenly everything was as clear as the mountain air.

On the night of the Centennial fireworks, Nicholas held a pocket watch up to the sky and made his appearance, that very dramatic entrance. All of his fine words were dialogue. He'd listened to Mrs. Haskins' story of the man who had been skinned alive and no doubt created a costume realistic down to the last grisly detail.

Only a short time ago, there was no poster in the room. He must have just placed it here, intending me to learn of his real identity in this manner. Remembering his laughter, I was sure this was what had happened. But what reason could he have for revealing his identity in this melodramatic fashion?

My question was answered almost immediately. Nicholas stood in the doorway, blocking my means of exit. He was in no way menacing. On the contrary, he appeared to be inordinately pleased with my discovery.

"I knew you'd find the poster sooner or later. You are so predictable and easy to deceive. You've given me many hours of entertainment, my dear Mara."

"I'm glad you enjoyed your little game," I said. "Surely you are the grand deceiver. You've shattered all my illusions, but I never believed what you said about Emmett."

"I'm a master at my craft, though, don't you agree?"

"Oh, you've done very well, but why did you go to such lengths? I don't believe you were looking for a diversion."

His answer was simple and chilling. "Why, to frighten you. I wanted you away from Trail's End. I knew about the treasure long before you did. It was mine to find, and you were in the way.

"When I first met you, you were afraid of your own shadow, reduced to a quivering state because of a foolish woman's story. I knew I'd be able to deceive you. At first you cooperated. I couldn't have asked for a better response. But you refused to stay frightened, and you kept running back to your rancher lover. He was another matter."

"So you were the skinned-alive man, Nicholas. Did you pretend to be an Indian, too?"

"No, he's an actor, but not a very clever man. He allowed that lunatic to rescue you before I could implement the second part of my plan."

"Did it involve another appearance by that grisly creature?" I asked.

"Yes, and I had disguises even more revolting and innovative props. Alas, I'll never have a chance to use the rest of them now. I'll wager one day you thought you found a piece of human skin."

I didn't give him the satisfaction of reacting to that. "So you were my abductor. I never suspected you, Nicholas. I can't believe I was such a fool."

"I watched you for a long time," he said. "I saw you with Grandison and knew what lure would work best."

"You used it twice now. To say that I was easy to deceive is a kindness. Who was Emmett's so-called cousin, Lance?"

"A young man who needed money for an immediate departure out of the Territory."

"And the man on horseback?"

Nicholas laughed.

"You ask a great many questions, my dear. You didn't recognize me, did you? That was not the time to unmask, but I wanted to make sure Lance followed my instructions."

"You were less frightening in your disguise, Nicholas," I said. "I didn't know you were capable of such evil."

"I'm sorry if you think so. For me, this has been a delightful interlude, but we're at the end of our little drama. You're going to give me the other letter or map and tell me whatever you know. This will happen today before Grandison can interfere again."

I was relieved that all pretense between us had dissolved. It would be easier to fight an adversary who was direct, even a diabolical one. I could lose nothing by standing up to him.

"I'm not afraid of an actor. A man who dresses in outrageous costumes and lurks in the dark has no power over me. You're living a play instead of life. Now, get out of my house, Nicholas!"

This was an unwise thing to say. I'd forgotten that Nicholas had a gun. In an instant, he drew it and pointed at me.

"Not that I will need this, for you will come with me. You can do nothing else."

"You may be right."

Nicholas laughed once again. I would hear the terrible sound of it in my dreams until the day I died.

"I never took you on that sightseeing tour of Denver," he said. "That was remiss of me, but I'm going to take you to see my sister tonight. Her name is Viola."

Twenty-four

I never expected that Nicholas could further shock and wound me.

"Viola is your sister, Nicholas? Why did you pretend you were strangers? And you know where she is? Does your deception have no limits?"

"Four questions! Be patient, Mara. Soon you'll have all your answers. Now, move."

"Where are we going?"

"I already told you. To visit my sister, Viola."

His tone was congenial, but he still held the gun. He nudged me in the ribs with it, and I feared the worst was yet to come. As much as I had dreaded returning to Trail's End, now I was loath to leave it.

"I can't possibly keep up with your constant changes," I said. "First you say you're looking for evidence to arrest Emmett. Then you tell me it's really the treasure you want. You admit you tried to frighten me away from Trail's End, but today you ordered me to help you search. Now you're taking me away. If you're going to kill me, wouldn't it make more sense to do it on my own land? You could bury me here, and nobody would ever know."

Abruptly I ended my speech. I didn't need to give Nicholas any additional ideas.

"I don't intend to harm you, unless you continue to annoy me with these incessant questions. We have a long ride ahead of us. Let's get started."

Shoving the gun into its holster, he took my arm, not gently, almost dragging me outside. I expected that we would use the buckboard again, but to my surprise, he led me into the old barn where I saw two horses saddled and waiting for us.

"Where did they come from?" I demanded.

"They've been here all along. Your stable is in deplorable condition, but it was sufficient for my purposes."

"How long have you been helping yourself to my property?"

"Whenever it was necessary. Why, do you mind? You weren't interested in it. Now, up on the horse and follow me."

As we rode away from Trail's End, he added, "I suspect you know very well where the treasure is hidden. Tonight you'll have sufficient time to ponder the consequences of withholding this information from me."

Although this was a threat, it was also a reprieve. Secure in the knowledge that I wasn't about to be killed, I turned my thoughts to Viola. If what Nicholas said was true, and I didn't doubt it, she was a deceiver as well. I had accepted the actor brother in San Francisco and the ailing sister in Boston with never a doubt.

On reflection, I decided not to berate myself. I had been trusting, but why would I have reason to think that Nicholas and Viola were dishonest? Now, every unusual comment Viola ever made took on a new significance, and the mysteries surrounding Nicholas became clear. What didn't fit was Viola's engagement to Jeremiah. He had been similarly duped.

"Viola's betrayal is more difficult to accept than yours, Nicholas," I said. "I thought she was my friend."

"She is my sister first. No more questions until we arrive. We aren't going to stop for even a short rest. We still have a way to go, and I want to get there before dark."

The light was beginning to fade, and the clouds were low when we reached a house with an inviting façade. Wildflowers bloomed around the entrance, and to the right was a patch of land, originally cultivated for a garden but now choked with weeds. On the wide front porch two rocking chairs faced each other, one at each end.

This was an oasis of civilization in the wilderness. Surely no bad thing would happen to me here.

Viola came out to meet us. She seemed the same as always, although more subdued in appearance in a simple dark dress. She still wore her garnet engagement ring.

With a semblance of his former gallantry, Nicholas assisted me down from the horse, and we climbed the steps to the porch.

"I've brought you some company, Viola," Nicholas said. "As we left in haste, I hope you can lend Mara some necessities for the night. As for myself, I can't stay."

He didn't offer an explanation, and she didn't ask for one. With no farewell, he took the reins of the horse I'd ridden, mounted his own again and left, taking his gun and his threats with him, along with my only means of transportation out of this place. Viola and I were alone, and it was as if we were strangers.

She pulled the chairs close together. "Let's sit outside for a while, shall we, Mara? It's still light and cool."

Remembering a time when we shared a home, confidences, and adventures, all of them an act, I made an attempt to salvage our relationship.

"I'm glad to see you alive and well, Viola. Did Nicholas bring you here by force?"

"In a way," she said.

"Can you leave, if you wish?"

"Yes and no. Both answers are true. There are no bars to hold me. Still I can't leave. There's nothing but grass and space around us. I don't have a horse, and there isn't a wagon, but I'm comfortable enough. It won't be for long."

"Do you know why Nicholas brought me here?"

Viola looked away from me, suddenly interested in the overgrown garden.

"I suppose he wanted to move you away from Emmett. Nicholas thinks you know where the treasure is. He plans to force you to tell him."

She spoke of his intentions as if she condoned them.

Be careful, I thought. *You may not be safe with Viola either*.

"I can't tell Nicholas how to find something that doesn't exist," I said.

"He believes in the treasure, and he can be excessive. My brother creates grand schemes and gets swept up in them. The idea of searching for hidden riches excites him, but even more important to him is setting a scene in motion and playing a part in it."

She added, "I don't think you're in any real danger. Nicholas has grown fond of you, and his attention is already turning to San Francisco, where we will go in September for a new business venture."

"He forced me to come here at gunpoint," I said.

"Yes, but to my knowledge, Nicholas has never killed anyone."

"That's some comfort, but the idea of attempted force is unsettling, and I can't believe that I'm not in danger. Was anything you told me true, or were you a part of this chicanery from the beginning? Are you even an actress?"

Viola paused, as if she were weighing her words carefully. "Much of what I told you was the truth. At times, however, I've strayed from the facts and perhaps embroidered them a little. Some information I've kept back, with good reason."

"In other words, you lied to us."

"You could say that. Has Nicholas hurt you in any way, Mara?"

I didn't answer at once as I recalled words of admiration and courtship, sentiments dripping like honey, a kiss, and a pendant hung around my neck. Nicholas had done me no physical harm.

In the end, I said, "No, but like you, he deceived me."

"I did try to warn you," she reminded me.

"Yes, with your talk of tarnished silver and fools' gold, but I never made the connection. At one time I thought you wanted Nicholas for yourself."

The awkwardness that had sprung up between us was slowly beginning to break, but a discernible chill remained in the air. The day was winding down, and we needed to say more to each other.

I noticed that Viola frequently touched her engagement ring and turned it around on her finger so that the stones faced inward.

"When you disappeared on the day before your wedding, didn't you spare a thought for Jeremiah?" I asked.

"He's one of the reasons I'm here. It's getting late, Mara. Let's share a pot of tea, and I'll fix us something to eat. We can make ourselves comfortable the way we used to. My story is long and not easily told, but I find that I want you to know who I really am."

~ * ~

The parlor was comfortably furnished with chairs and a small oval table covered with a lace cloth. Viola poured the tea and cut small slices of a cake. It was almost as if she'd been expecting us, but that wasn't possible.

"Is this Nicholas' house?" I asked.

"It belongs to one of his friends who lives in San Francisco for most of the year. Nicholas and I often stay here. As you know, he's my older brother and the only family I have. When I was a child, he was always traveling, but we kept in touch. My life really began when he invited me to join him in New York. At the time I was alone and without resources."

"You said your father was the famous Richard Courtenay."

"That was one of my half truths. He never actually appeared on the stage. He's been away for several years, in England, I think. Now, I can truthfully describe myself as an aspiring actress with very little experience. Did Nicholas tell you that he's an actor, too?"

"He arranged for me to find out."

She didn't ask me to explain. Now that she'd begun to talk, she didn't seem to want to stop.

"When I came to live with Nicholas, he was appearing in a play. I soon learned that he liked money well enough, but didn't care to work. He had some success on the stage, but he was restless, always looking for the winning hand, the willing heiress, some dubious venture or other. At first, he did this between roles, but eventually there were only schemes.

"We were constantly traveling. We made our way down to New Orleans and on to San Francisco with so many stops in little towns on the way that I lost count."

"That sounds like an exciting way to live."

"I thought so as well. Soon I discovered that I could be a help to Nicholas in his enterprises. I did it gladly, and I was good at it. People came into our lives and went. Nothing was permanent. Every morning provided fresh excitement.

"I thought our way of life would go on forever. One day I knew I didn't want to be always on the move. I wanted a quieter kind of life. That was the day you introduced me to Jeremiah. I desperately wanted to have a happy future with him, but there were complications."

"Was Nicholas opposed to your engagement?"

"At first he didn't know about it. He was too busy following you. Whichever way I looked, I saw problems and no way out. Nicholas and I have operated outside the law. I couldn't let Jeremiah know that.

"At times I thought I would withhold my past indiscretions until we were married, but I realized I had to tell him before the ceremony. If he knew the truth, I would lose him. Then there was Nicholas."

"Were you afraid he'd tell Jeremiah about your past?"

"Not exactly. Nicholas learned about my engagement from you, Mara. He persuaded me to come away with him and think about it. He spirited me out of the house, and no one ever saw us. I was sorry to leave that way, but it was best for everyone."

"For you and Nicholas, you mean. Jeremiah thinks you didn't want to marry a frontier town lawyer."

"Jeremiah will be happier without me. In time, he'll forget we ever met. He's probably already done so."

"I don't think that's true, but he doesn't believe he'll see you again."

Once again, she turned her ring around on her finger.

"You've left some parts out of your narrative, Viola," I said. "Tell me how I came to play a role in your scheme."

"Nicholas and I always pretended to be strangers when we traveled. When you mentioned Trail's End, Nicholas remembered a story he'd once heard. Do you remember the night when we three parted in Denver? Nicholas and I met later to put the finishing touches on our plan. I was to befriend you, while he arranged a series of harmless pranks to keep you away from the ranch so he could look for the treasure in private."

I almost slammed the teacup down into the saucer, as Emmett would have done. "That's the most ridiculous thing I've ever heard. There's nothing remotely normal about Nicholas' behavior, and yet you present it in a matter-of-fact way. His actions lead me to believe that his mind is affected. You were supposed to be my friend. How could you have gone along with him?"

"I always did what Nicholas wanted. I'm his partner as well as his sister. Besides, I thought you were too intelligent to be taken in by costumes and counterfeit blood, even if you *did* succumb to his charms at first."

"That's what I most regret," I said.

"To be charming and seductive is simply Nicholas' way. You weren't the first woman to fall under his spell. Besides, you have Emmett."

"I hope I do. I'm no longer sure."

"You'll have to tell me the newest developments in your romance," Viola said. "While we've been talking, it's grown dark. I'll light some candles."

All of a sudden, I was afraid again. I now knew where Viola's allegiance lay. Nicholas was a wild card, and Emmett thought I was in Denver. At best, my future looked uncertain.

"If Nicholas doesn't find the treasure that doesn't exist, will he take me home?" I asked.

"I don't know, Mara. You look so tired. Maybe we'd better go to bed now. We can talk again in the morning."

She showed me to a bedroom at the back of the house where I took off my dress, washed away the dust of the trail, and lay down on the bed. Although I was tired, I stayed awake late thinking. Most of my questions had been answered, except for the most important one of all. What was going to happen to me was still a mystery.

My life was in the hands of a determined rogue who had a light grip on reality, but I should be able to find a way out of this dilemma. Before I fell asleep, I posed a final question to myself.

What if the legend were true? Everything would change then.

Twenty-five

The sun had scarcely risen in the sky when Nicholas returned the next morning. He arrived in a wagon, looking disheveled and dusty. The feverish look in his eyes and a new energy didn't bode well for me.

Viola and I were sitting on the porch drinking tea and discussing her doomed romance and my ailing one.

"I assume Nicholas didn't find the treasure," I said. "I wonder what he'll do next."

He advanced and stood towering over me in a manner obviously intended to intimidate me.

"My patience is at an end, Mara. It's time to stop stalling and tell me what I want to know."

His voice was as sharp and smooth as a blade. While not making a specific threat, his tone conveyed that he had ample means of persuasion at his disposal.

I reminded myself that Nicholas was an actor playing the part of a villain. He was all words and tone and dramatic stance rather than a source of danger. I could be a pretender, too.

"For a time Jules Carron lived in a mining town that no longer exists except in ruins," I said. "It's the perfect place to hide a treasure."

I was gratified to see the spark of interest in his eyes.

"You should know the way," I added. "You met us there by chance one day, and we all rode back to town together."

I reasoned that once we were in Carron Creek, we'd be closer to Silver Springs. In the meantime, I'd have more time to plan my escape.

Nicholas neatly fell into my trap.

"I remember the area well. We'll leave right away. You come with us, Viola. I think we're finally going in the right direction.

~ * ~

Throughout the ride, I told Nicholas a long, rambling narrative about Jules Carron and his attachment to his silver mine, hoping he wouldn't realize that it was wholly fictitious.

The nearer we drew to our destination, however, the more apprehensive I became. My mind had shut down several miles ago, yielding only the most implausible ideas. The best plan involved overpowering Nicholas in some as yet unspecified way, after which I would take the wagon and put as much space between us as possible. Without a horse, he'd be unable to follow me. Of course, I couldn't count on Viola's help in the matter.

I feared I might have once again made my situation worse, but at least every mile brought me closer to Emmett.

My luck took a sudden upward turn when Viola announced that she was hungry.

"I must get down from this wagon. We didn't eat breakfast, and I'm growing ill. Can't we stop, Nicholas, please? You can build a fire, catch a fish if there's a lake nearby or perhaps a fowl, and we'll cook."

"If we rest and have something to eat, we'll be more alert," I added.

To my surprise, Nicholas agreed. "I'll do it."

The reprieve gave me an opportunity to work on my list of ideas. I'd seen a shovel in the wagon that would prove helpful if I could lure Nicholas into a tunnel or call his attention to a piece of land under which the treasure was likely to be buried. Then, while he was distracted, I would strike him unconscious.

This was as mad a scenario as any Nicholas might devise. He wouldn't be likely to take his eyes off me while he considered me an asset. I had a half dozen more plans, but every one of them fell to pieces as I played it out in my mind. My contrivances came to an abrupt end when Nicholas smothered the fire and turned to me.

"Now that we're fed and rested, let's talk about the treasure."

"I may be mistaken, Nicholas. If we don't find it—"

Losing all control, he wrenched me up by the arm. "Tell me what you know. Now!"

I cried out in pain, wondering if my bones could withstand his grasp. At my side, I heard Viola gasp. My imaginative powers collapsed. All I could manage was a plea. "I can't tell you anything more. Let me go."

"Not until you talk."

Through my pain, I heard a new, familiar voice enter the dispute.

"Why are you hurting her?"

With my wrist still trapped in Nicholas' hand, I whirled around to behold Silver Jake walking slowly up the trail. Clad in his Confederate uniform, he looked formidable, although he didn't have his sword. I hoped he was lucid today.

Nicholas stared at Silver Jake in disbelief, but he recovered quickly, saying in a sharp, threatening tone of voice, "This is sane people's business. It doesn't concern you. Go back to your mountain hideaway."

With dismay, I saw Silver Jake crumble. He backed away as if he'd been physically assaulted.

"That's no way to talk to him, Nicholas. He may be of help to us. Major, have you returned from the fighting?"

"I ran away after the battle, Miss Margaret. I wish I could go back and undo what I did."

"You were brave to go at all. You could have stayed in the Territory and remained out of the fray. I heard the War is already lost."

Nicholas, apparently preferring his own delusions to those of another, grew angrier with every word I spoke, but he finally released my wrist.

"You have a strange circle of friends, Mara. Or should I call you Margaret? We're here for a reason. Stop talking to that madman and concentrate on our project."

"Don't hurt Miss Margaret," Silver Jake said.

"I told you to go away, soldier," Nicholas said. "This is our property, and you're trespassing. You should be locked up. I'm going to see to it that you are."

Instead of taking flight or cowering away, Silver Jake moved closer to me and said in a soft voice, "If you're sure about the War, there's something I have to do. The money won't be needed now. He meant you to have it."

Nicholas pounced on the magic word. "What's this you're talking about?"

"The treasure," he said. "I've guarded it once for the South and now for you, Miss Margaret."

Nicholas grabbed Silver Jake with both hands and shook him violently. "You *do* know where it is, old man. Tell me."

"Don't do it, Silver Jake," I said.

"Jules took a portion, and I kept the rest. When he died, I guarded it all these years, first in his house, then in my cabin."

"Ah! At last! I knew it. Take me there now. Did you come on horseback?"

Silver Jake gestured vaguely down the trail and said, "I have my horse, Charger."

Nicholas was exultant, but I knew how easily Silver Jake could drift away. I still wasn't certain there was a treasure, but now I had a champion and therefore my situation was greatly improved. For that I was grateful.

~ * ~

As we approached Silver Jake's cabin, silver nuggets danced through my head, along with golden coins and precious stones added by my imagination. All I wanted, though, was a glimpse of the treasure. I had lived without it until now and would continue to do so, as riches couldn't buy my heart's desire.

I would let Nicholas take it, whereupon he would free me and leave for San Francisco and his next venture. Then I would find Emmett.

Viola's scream shattered my rosy vision of the future.

Around the south side of the cabin bounded Silver Jake's dog, Wolf. He lunged toward us with bared fangs.

"He's rabid," she cried.

"That's only Wolf," Silver Jake said. "He's harmless, but I'll tie him to the tree."

While he set about restraining his pet, Nicholas seized the opportunity to rush into the cabin ahead of us. I was about to follow him when I heard the hoof beats.

"That's two horses coming," Silver Jake said. "I don't like all these people on my land."

I knew that riders in this isolated area could be a fresh source of danger for us, and not one of us, except perhaps Wolf, was capable of mounting a defense.

"What now?" Viola asked, glancing toward the cabin. "Let's go inside, Mara. Quickly! Nicholas!"

She dashed through the door, but I remained where I was, my eyes fixed on the trail, so I was the first to see Emmett and Tyler ride into the clearing. Emmett's gun was drawn, and he looked angrier and more dangerous than Wolf. He dismounted and took a few steps toward me.

"Emmett," I said. "I'm so glad to see you."

Nicholas appeared at the door, with his own gun in his hand. In a second, he was down the steps, on the ground, and reaching for me, no doubt intending to use me as a hostage. Emmett intercepted him with a mighty blow that sent him flying several feet through the air. He came to rest in the dust in a shower of blood, where he lay very still.

With a cry, Viola rushed to kneel at her brother's side, while I looked at Emmett, willing him to say something to me. His gray eyes were dark with some powerful emotion.

"Tyler was in town yesterday," he said. "He saw you get off the train with this polecat. I didn't believe him at first. Why, Mara?"

I couldn't bear to know that Emmett's trust in me had been shaken. Nor did I want to admit what a fool I'd been in the presence of an audience.

I lowered my voice so that only he could hear. "I'll tell you when we're alone, Emmett. But please, not here."

He nodded his head.

With her white handkerchief, Viola gently dabbed at the blood trickling down onto Nicholas' shirt. She helped him to rise.

Nicholas appeared to be oblivious of Emmett and his loaded gun. As if he'd forgotten that Emmett had just knocked him to the ground, he grabbed his arm. "The treasure, Grandison. The lunatic had it in his cabin all along."

I looked for Silver Jake, but he must have gone inside.

"You're a fool, Breckinridge, and I should shoot you dead now," Emmett said.

"Emmett, you can't mean that."

"Stay out of this, Mara."

Emmett aimed the gun, but again it was Silver Jake who shattered a tense moment. He came out of his cabin, taking no notice of the confrontation.

"Come along inside, Miss Margaret," he said. "It's all yours now."

Emmett returned his gun to his holster. Nicholas, who hadn't paid much attention to Emmett anyway, was the first one in the cabin, knocking Viola off balance in his haste to enter. Tyler helped her to her feet. From the tree to which he was tied, Wolf barked and strained at his rope.

Silver Jake held out his hand to assist me into the cabin. He might be a lunatic, but he was still a Southern gentleman. I looked behind me, and saw Emmett following us, the last one to enter the cabin. I still couldn't tell what he was thinking.

Twenty-six

A large wooden trunk occupied the center of the sparsely furnished room. Pushing open its lid, Silver Jake said, "Look, Miss Margaret! Twenty thousand dollars and much more for you. Jules feared you might be in want some day."

As he reached for a handful of bills and offered it to me, his eyes glowed with pleasure and excitement. There were hundreds of stacks of similar bills, a fortune in Confederate money, and not one of them held any value in our year of 1876.

"You damned, demented old fool!" Nicholas snarled. "You madman."

In a fury, he knocked the bills I held in my hand to the floor. Then, like a child in the grip of a tantrum, he set about hurling stacks of money in every direction.

"Seems to me you're the damn' fool, Breckinridge," said Emmett. "Getting' all worked up over money you can't spend. Take your treasure. Enjoy yourself. Buy yourself the city of Atlanta."

Viola said, "Stop, Nicholas, please. This is pointless."

For a short time no one spoke. We all looked at the mess Nicholas had made, but he was quick to rebound. He stamped on a pool of bills and kicked them out of his way.

"So let the curtain fall on our little melodrama," he said. "I've devoted weeks to this treasure hunt, but my time hasn't been entirely wasted."

He glanced at me in a way that made me feel uncomfortable. Emmett's hand moved slowly to his gun.

"You've played your part well, Nicholas," I said, "but now hadn't you better return to your other profession in the Swinging Lady Gang?"

He laughed, the last trace of his rancor gone.

"What a truly marvelous antagonist you've been, Mara, my dear. Our play has been more fun than the treasure hunt, but you're right. It's time for us to leave."

"Hold on, Breckinridge," Emmett said. "You're not goin' anywhere. You're guilty of abducting two ladies. You're goin' to swing from a rope."

"For kidnapping? You'll have to shoot me first."

I said, "Emmett, I came away with Nicholas of my own free will, and he never harmed me. Viola will tell you the same thing. Nicholas is her brother. You must let him go."

Slowly, Emmett replaced his gun in its holster, and we all breathed more easily. I didn't think he would have pulled the trigger, but I wasn't certain.

Silver Jake gathered up his scattered money, bill by bill. There were tears in his eyes. I wondered what had upset him, but Nicholas had my attention again.

"I'm leaving for San Francisco," he said. "I won't return to the Colorado Territory. People here aren't as friendly as I thought. Are you ready, Viola?"

"Not this time, Nicholas," she said. "First I must talk to Jeremiah. I may join you later."

"As you wish. Mara, will you come? You would make an admirable consort for Outlaw Jim. There's more to the West than Silver Springs and this blustery cowboy."

He held out his hand to me. I couldn't believe his audacity. Unmindful of Emmett's growing anger, he blundered on. "A kiss, then, to cheer me on the trail."

Emmett struck him across the temple with the handle of the gun. The blow sounded like gunfire, and Nicholas staggered back.

"Get out of the Colorado Territory, Breckinridge. Don't let me see your face in these parts again."

Holding his hand to his head, Nicholas backed out of the cabin without delay. For a consummate villain, it was an ignoble exit.

"I hope you won't dispose of all my gentlemen admirers in so uncivil a way, Emmett," I said.

"This is the last one, Mara."

I wanted to go to him, but I was unsure of his reaction, even now, so I walked over to help Silver Jake instead. He was still collecting the scattered Confederate bills.

"They'll be ruined, Miss Margaret. The roof leaks in the rain. They got to be put back in the trunk, and Emmett will take it home for you."

I glanced at Emmett. He'd found a chair to sit in and was watching us, but not interfering. I didn't see Viola. She must have wandered outside for a private farewell with Nicholas.

"Let me help you, Silver Jake," I said.

I began stacking the money in neat rows, but for some reason, this agitated him.

"No, Miss Margaret. That's not the way you do it. Make the stacks high and have seven in a row. You got to be careful to hide the silver."

"There's only Confederate money here."

"No, look!"

He scooped the remaining bills up, set them on the floor, and lifted the trunk's false bottom. The flash of silver coins and nuggets blinded me.

"It's the treasure!" I cried.

I picked up a nugget and held it in my hand. It was smooth and hard and, best of all, real.

"That's what I've been telling you."

"Now this you can spend no matter who won the War, honey," Emmett said.

Viola, who had rejoined us after her farewell with Nicholas, had a new lightness of spirit about her. Although her eyes were wet, she said, "My brother has ridden off into the sunset too soon."

I said, "That's fortunate. If he hadn't left before we learned the true nature of the treasure, he would have attempted to take it."

Viola glanced at Emmett surreptitiously and added in a soft voice, "And probably be dead."

"You're a rich woman, Mara," Emmett said. "Reckon you can go wherever you want now."

As Silver Jake trailed his hand through the silver, he said, "I've kept my promise and guarded this for many a year for you, Miss Margaret, but I'm as glad to turn it over now. He wanted you to come to Trail's End someday, but not while he was still alive. He didn't want you to see him. You wouldn't think he was so handsome after that shell caught him in the nose.

"I killed him. When he was dead, I knew it was wrong, but he didn't suffer anymore. The last thing I told him was I'd give the treasure to you. Now I've seen what a fine lady you are, I know you'd have looked at him, even though he had a damaged face."

I had one of the answers to my mystery now, but it didn't bring me happiness. Jules Carron's story was sadder than I'd ever imagined. I had a fervent wish to see this entire affair end.

"It wouldn't have mattered to me," I said. "I hope he knew that."

Emmett was quiet now. Beside him, Viola touched her white handkerchief to her eyes.

"The treasure will be safer with you," I said. "Your dog will guard the trunk, and we're the only ones who know of its existence. Will you keep watching over it for me until it is truly needed, perhaps at some future time?"

The change that came over Silver Jake's face was my reward. I was returning his life's task to him, giving him something to focus on besides the past.

"I hope you know what you're sayin', Mara," Emmett said.

"I do. For now, I'll say goodbye, Silver Jake. We'll come to see you soon."

Viola said, "I'm going to go straight to Miss Eulalie to explain my deception to her. Tyler says he'll accompany me. Perhaps she'll forgive me."

"I know she will, Viola."

"Then I'll see Jeremiah."

"Go on," Emmett said, "we'll follow."

I took a deep breath. I still couldn't determine Emmett's feelings for me. In spite of the one endearment he'd used a few minutes ago, I thought he was still angry.

Without a word, he took my hand, and we walked together a little ways apart into the woods that grew almost to the side of the cabin. I could hear birds and insects and the pounding of my own heart.

"My offer still stands, Mara," he said.

"To buy Trail's End?"

"No, to marry me. I want you. I know you were in love with Breckinridge, but you've seen what kind of man he is. You wouldn't have believed me if I told you."

"I was never in love with him, only infatuated for a short time. That was long ago."

"Why were you with him then?"

"Nicholas was on the train to Denver that morning. He claimed to be a detective and said you were an outlaw who had killed his brother. He was going to see you hang, but he was an actor.

"He disguised himself as the skinned-alive man and hired Lance and the Indian to help him. It was part of his plan to keep me away from Trail's End so that he could steal the treasure. I just wanted to help you."

As I spoke, I thought, *This is all so fantastic. How can I expect Emmett to believe it?*

"You believed him? Mara, that's how he fooled you before."

It was true, but I didn't like to hear it, so I said, "For that matter, Emmett, why were you with Sally? And why were you buying her clothes?"

He frowned. "Sally?"

"You do remember her?"

"Sure I know Miss Sally," he said. "So did your actor friend and most everyone. I see her in town sometime."

"Isn't she a special friend of yours?"

"She is, but you don't need to know about me and Sally, Mara. Tell me what you meant about me buyin' her clothes."

"It was something I saw. It isn't important."

In the matter of the undergarment Sally had asked to be placed on Emmett's account, I didn't doubt his sincerity. If Sally knew Nicholas, she might simply be another one of his pawns. I would seek her out someday and talk to her.

"Why are we talkin' about Sally and Nicholas?" Emmett demanded. "*Will* you marry me? We got rid of that actor who was hauntin' Trail's End, so you don't need to look on it as protectin'."

"I will. I accept your offer, but why haven't you said that you love me?"

Again, he frowned. "I thought I was tellin' you all along, Mara. Do you want fancy speeches like you got from the actin' man?"

Before I could answer, he took me in his arms and told me what I wanted to know in a way that had no need of words. As he kissed me with a new urgency and moved his hands slowly over my body, I felt a crush of desire so intense that it almost left me breathless.

When he finally released me, I made an attempt to regain my composure but gave it up and threw my arms around him instead.

"We can be married by the end of the year," I said. "Around Christmastime maybe? I think Miss Eulalie and I can be ready by then."

"You'll marry me by the end of the week," Emmett said. "Not tomorrow, though. That's the day they're havin' the celebration of the century in Silver Springs."

"Another one? Have a hundred year passed while I've been away?"

"While you all were chasin' after that treasure, a big change happened. It's a new month today, August first, and we've been admitted to the United States of America. We're a genuine state."

"You once said that I came to Colorado at exactly the right time," I said. "It's true for so many reasons."

"If you're talkin' about you and me, Miss Eulalie keeps sayin' it's destiny."

He took my hand, and we walked to the tree where he had tethered his horse. Everybody had left except for Silver Jake, who was watching us from the window.

"Is there room in the ranch house for some of my family's furniture and a few mementos I had to leave behind?" I asked.

"Sure, anythin' you want. We'll burn the house at Trail's End to the ground. Next year it'll be pasture for Star, and we'll start buildin' new memories in the state of Colorado."

"We'll be happy, and it'll be forever. Emmett, Jules Carron willed me more than he could possibly have known."

"That he did, honey," he said. "There's the real treasure." He lifted me off the ground and kissed me again; then he set me up on his horse. "Let's get along home now. We got a wedding to plan."

Meet Dorothy Bodoin

Dorothy Bodoin lives in Michigan with her black collie, Holly, near the fictional setting of the Foxglove Corners series. She has a Master's Degree in English from Oakland University in Rochester, Michigan, and taught secondary English for several years. Now she writes full-time, alternating between cozy mysteries and novels of romantic suspense with gothic elements. Her first published novel was *Darkness at Foxglove Corners*.

Dorothy is a member of Sisters in Crime and Romance Writers of America. At present she is working on another Jennet Greenway mystery, *The Witches of Foxglove Corners*.

VISIT OUR WEBSITE
FOR THE FULL INVENTORY
OF QUALITY BOOKS:

http://www.wings-press.com

Quality trade paperbacks and downloads
in multiple formats,
in genres ranging from light romantic comedy to general fiction and horror. Wings has something for every reader's taste.
Visit the website, then bookmark it.
We add new titles each month!